Ruth Dudley Edwards

Ruth Dudley Edwards was born and brought up in Dublin. Since she graduated she has lived in England, where she has been a teacher, a Cambridge postgraduate student, a marketing executive, a civil servant and finally, a freelance writer and journalist.

A historian and prize-winning biographer, her most recent non-fiction includes the authorized history of *The Economist, True Brits: Inside the Foreign Office*, and *The Faithful Tribe: An Intimate Portrait of the Loyal Institutions*.

She feels intellectually English and temperamentally Irish. *Publish and Be Murdered* is the eighth crime novel in her hilarious and uncompromising series poking fun at the British Establishment.

RUTH DUDLEY EDWARDS

PUBLISH AND BE MURDERED

HarperCollins*Publishers*

HarperCollins*Publishers*
77–85 Fulham Palace Road,
Hammersmith, London W6 8JB

This paperback edition 1999

1 3 5 7 9 8 6 4 2

First published in Great Britain by
HarperCollins*Publishers* 1998

ISBN 0 00 649863 9

Set in Meridien and Bodoni

Printed and bound in Great Britain by
Caledonian International Book Manufacturing Ltd, Glasgow

To Paul, friend and pedant, and, of course,
as usual, to John.

My friends were as wonderful as ever, but I must single
out for special thanks for encouragement, help or
inspiration on this book, Andrew Boyd, Máirín Carter,
Betsy Crabtree, Sylvia Kalisch, Kathryn Kennison, Paul
Le Druillenec (to whom it is dedicated), Gordon and Ken
Lee, James McGuire, Sean O'Callaghan, Carol Scott, my
publisher, Julia Wisdom, who showed enough patience for
someone twice her size, and my gentle, literate and sane
copy-editor, Karen Godfrey.

Yes, I did write a history of *The Economist*. And, yes, I drew some inspiration from its past for this book. But in all essentials – including the ethics and habits of its editors – the modern *Economist* bears no resemblance whatsoever to *The Wrangler*.

1

'Bertie Ormerod says you're a tactful sort of fellow. Won't frighten the horses or get the dowagers all of a twitter.'

Lord Papworth's rheumy eyes fixed themselves upon Amiss. 'Smart too. Said you were as sharp as a whippet. So the upshot – the nub and gist as it were – is . . . can you help?'

'I hope so,' said Amiss hesitantly. 'If I'm what you want, that is. Though I'm not really sure I'm what you need.'

Papworth grunted. 'Want and need's two different things, I grant you. You sound just like my old nanny.' He brooded for a moment. 'Well, I think I need what I want on this occasion and vice versa. And that's you.'

'If you say so, Lord Papworth. I've always enjoyed *The Wrangler* and I'd be honoured to be its manager. But I must warn you that while I'm OK at administration, I haven't much to offer in the way of advanced computer skills or knowledge of company law or accountancy.'

Papworth emitted a cackle so loud and derisive as to cause several of the other denizens of the Pugin Room to peer at him covertly. 'I don't think you quite understand. I'm not attempting to have my journal dragged into the twenty-first century: I merely have a modest aspiration that it should be assisted into the second half of the twentieth. And that that be achieved with the minimum of disruption to a largely loyal – if eccentric – workforce.' He drained his glass, placed it firmly on the table, leaned forward and tapped Amiss on the knee. 'What I neither need nor want is a sharp-suited young man who puts machines before people. It's got to be someone with common sense and humanity who can

1

staunch the haemorrhage cascading from the Papworth coffers. Drink?'

'Thank you. Another gin and tonic would be very nice.'

Papworth flapped an arm towards the bar and pointed at their glasses.

'Is this a new problem?' asked Amiss, when his host had focused on him once more. 'I mean, has there been some kind of management hiatus recently?'

'No, no.' Papworth cackled again. 'It's a very old problem that's been neglected for years. I suppose I simply wasn't prepared to face up to it until my son gave me a talking-to recently. Said it was all very well and grand to do one's bit *pro bono publico*, but that the losses had got beyond a joke and I might bloody well remember that it was his patrimony I was playing silly buggers with.

'"What's more", he added, "you're getting on and won't be around much longer."' Papworth smiled proudly. 'Callous devil, isn't he? But it's a fair point nonetheless. The old *Wrangler*'s a heavy burden on the estate. I can see why Piers doesn't take kindly to seeing me losing the best part of a quarter of a million a year when it probably isn't necessary. Or most of it isn't.'

'You're not tempted to sell?'

Papworth looked horrified. 'Family's owned *The Wrangler* for close on two hundred years. Not going to part with it now. *Noblesse oblige* and all that.'

He turned to greet the waitress as she put the drinks on the table. 'Thank you, my dear. And how's the arthritis?' He counted out coins on to her tray.

'No better, my lord. I'm thinking of packing the job in.'

'My goodness, Rose, you must never do that.' He waved towards the stately Thames as it passed serenely by the terraces of the Houses of Parliament. 'Like Ol' Man River, my dear Rose, you must go on and on and on.'

'That's what Lady Thatcher said she was going to do,' said Rose sharply. 'And look what happened to her.' She grinned sardonically and left.

'Serves me right for producing clichés,' said Papworth.

'Now where was I? Ah, yes. Where my son is right, Mr Amiss, is in saying that while I have properly treated *The Wrangler* with the respect due to a family treasure, I have – like my old father before me – been guilty of gross financial irresponsibility.' He took a thoughtful sip of whisky. 'Not all my fault, mind you. There's a tendency for the buggers who run the paper to carry on as if I should be down on my knees thanking them brokenly for the opportunity to subsidise them lavishly.'

He put his glass down, and for the first time, indicated resentment. 'I mean, dammit, I had Willie Lambie Crump . . . d'you know who I mean?'

'The *Wrangler* editor. Yes. I've seen him on TV a couple of times.'

'Well, there he was at dinner the other week complaining that not enough was spent on maintaining the building, while still absolutely refusing to consider moving to cheaper premises.'

'Where's the office?'

'Mayfair.'

'Seems a strange place for a poor magazine.'

'Journal,' said Papworth automatically.

'Is there a difference?'

'Not really, now that you mention it. It's just that we started out as a journal, and *Wrangler* editors thought the word "magazine" was vulgar.'

'Fair enough. Mayfair seems a strange place for a poor journal.'

Papworth looked at Amiss ruefully. 'The building's worth a packet but the trust doesn't allow its sale without the agreement of the editor and the editor insists the paper would not flourish anywhere else. Bloody convenient principle on which to stick, especially since he's got a flat at the top. But when I reminded him what supporting *The Wrangler* was costing me, he said loftily that privilege had its penalties and that he couldn't see that my wealth could be put to any better use than keeping *The Wrangler*'s standard fluttering nobly in the intellectual breeze.'

He fell silent for a moment, took another sip and put his glass down with what was close to being a thump. 'That's the trouble with institutions: they tend to take themselves seriously. Doesn't matter if it's parliament or the Jockey Club or Oxbridge colleges or gentlemen's clubs: they're all prone to be pompous and given to flummery. But mostly that's harmless enough. If you ask me, the worst offenders are their greatest critics – the bloody press.'

'Take the monarchy, for instance. Fat chance the poor old royals have to be complacent these days, what with journalists pointing out their shortcomings from dawn to dusk, doing shock exposés, invading their private lives and crying "scandal" and condemning them for being out of date and wasteful of taxpayers' money. And we're the same in the Lords, with all the abuse thrown at us and no recognition of what we do that's good.'

He thrust out his lip pugnaciously. 'But of course it's all different when the institution in question is a newspaper, magazine, journal, call it what you will. You don't get any of that. Oh no. Journalists are beyond criticism. Dog doesn't eat dog. Hack doesn't eat hack. They hardly ever attack each other because they never know who they'll be working with next week or begging a job from.'

He snorted. 'Find me any shock-horror analysis of the dreadful management of *The Wrangler*, and I'll give you a thousand quid. But don't waste too much time looking. Because no journalist or editor will have taken the risk.' He snorted again. 'Hacks look after hacks and hunt in packs.'

His head fell on his chest: the diatribe appeared to be over.

'So you're not very keen on the profession which you so generously endow?' proffered Amiss.

Papworth sat up straight. 'I'm keen on *The Wrangler* for reasons of sentiment and habit and because I genuinely approve of its ideals. Like the paper, I believe that tradition's good, change for change's sake is bad and I applaud honourable intellectual enquiry with a big dash of humour. We've got to have a journal that'll stand up to those puritan lefties who

4

infest the chattering classes of every generation. God, how I hate liberals!'

Amiss wriggled uncomfortably. 'Lord Papworth, I have to tell you that fundamentally I'm a liberal.'

Papworth shook his head. 'Bertie put me right on that. Said you were sound through and through, just sometimes had to recite mantras about your liberal instincts to reassure yourself that you hadn't sold out to the forces of reaction.' He patted Amiss's knee consolingly. 'Don't worry about that, dear boy. Shan't hold it against you. Whatever you call yourself, you've obviously got the right stuff in you. Bertie told me of the great work you and that splendid Troutbeck battleaxe did to scupper that anti-hunting bill. Don't you worry about that liberal nonsense. You'll slough it all off soon enough.'

The words, 'That's what I'm afraid of,' rose to Amiss's lips, but remained unsaid. He needed a job, so he swallowed his scruples along with some more gin.

Papworth ruminated some more. 'Mind you, *The Wrangler* trust hasn't exactly been a spur to modernization.'

'I hadn't realized there was a trust. I thought you owned it outright.'

'Oh, I own it. But I can't meddle with it without the approval of the trustees.'

'So you've got the worst of both worlds. How did that happen?'

'Sometime in the late 'twenties, some ghastly jumped-up merchant was showing an interest in buying it and there was a mass outbreak of panic among the journalists: cries of doom and disaster and the death of editorial freedom and all that.

'Of course, Papa reassured them that he wouldn't dream of selling, but then they pointed out that he could die tomorrow and there was absolutely nothing to stop me selling up the day after. And despite Papa's protestations and my reassurances the outcry continued.'

He laughed. 'Mind you, in fairness, they had some justification for being worried about me. I was only ten and there was no knowing how I was going to turn out; indeed, I'd been heard to express a few bolshie opinions. The upshot was that Papa set up a trust to guard the soul of the paper. Very high-minded, my old father.'

'What is the role of the trust?'

'Protects the editor against the proprietor essentially. I can neither hire nor fire an editor without the trustees' approval. And if I behave towards the editor in any way that he regards as interfering with the ethos of the paper, he goes off whingeing to the trustees and they rebuke and overrule me. They've got total editorial control, which in practice they cede to the editor.'

'Does the system work?'

'Oh yes. It works. For the editor, anyway. The proprietor is impotent. D'you know, thoughtlessly I once asked a *Wrangler* editor if he wouldn't mind being kind to a book by my mate Freddie Dalrymple and he promptly gave the book for review to Freddie's greatest enemy.'

Papworth chuckled genially. 'I didn't mind really. Should have known better. Still, sometimes it's hard not to feel a bit fed up at the high-handed way some of these buggers treat me. In the view of *Wrangler* staff, the proprietor's only role is to pick up the bill. Oh, yes, and to host the annual party and give the odd dinner for the trustees, the staff and various notables they'd like to meet. And they'll give me an affectionate obituary when I turn up my toes.

'However, bearing in mind what my son said so trenchantly, I have to accept that I'm being a touch profligate in paying over two hundred thousand pounds a year for the few privileges I've just outlined. I'd be glad if you'll do what you can.'

'Am I replacing anyone?'

'No, you're a new appointment.'

'But that means that in hiring me you're adding another thirty thou to your outgoings.'

'My dear boy, from what Bertie tells me of your resourcefulness and from what I know of the staff's inefficiency, you'll have no difficulty whatsoever in rapidly making savings that will more than compensate for that. Just remember I want no blood on the carpet.'

He rose. 'Now come along and let us dine and I'll tell you a bit more about my tribulations with the inhabitants of Number ten, Percy Square.'

2

Wrangler HQ was a shabby five-storey house in a Georgian terrace. When Amiss pulled the bell, the door was opened immediately by a small teenager in livery, who ushered him into a splendid panelled hall chock-a-block with Georgian and Victorian artifacts. The effect was somewhat marred by mid-twentieth-century office interpolations.

There were, for instance, several nineteenth-century portraits, a heavy Victorian glass-fronted bookcase, two elegant chairs that Amiss tentatively identified as Chippendale and a fine Victorian desk incongruously topped by a 1950s switchboard, whose operator who looked as if she had been delivered with the equipment in a package marked 'Dragon'.

The youthful flunkey took Amiss over to the desk, nodded at the dragon, who was talking briskly into a receiver, and said, 'Miss Mercatroid will sort you out.' She did not look up. The lad abandoned his charge and returned to his lair – a large Victorian carver, in which he curled up cosily with what looked like a football fanzine.

Amiss stood in front of Miss Mercatroid trying to look nonchalant and after a couple of minutes she ceased doing things with plugs, looked up and barked, 'Yes?'

He simpered ingratiatingly and received in exchange a withering glance.

'Robert Amiss. I'm here to see Mr Crump.'

She looked at him in shock and distaste. 'You mean Mr Lambie Crump. He is never, but never, referred to as Mr Crump.'

She pointed to a fragile gilt chair, on which Amiss seated

himself gingerly. 'Ay will see if he is at home.' Her vowels were so fluted as to give her accent a quality of ultra-refinement not heard in England in forty years outside Buckingham Palace.

Switchboard activities prohibited Miss Mercatroid for more than ten minutes from getting through to William Lambie Crump, during which time Amiss contented himself with dipping into parts of *Challenging Change: The Wrangler, 1805–1955*, which lay on the Sheraton table beside him.

He had just learned of the duel between the co-editors in 1829 over Catholic Emancipation (the duelling pistols were still among the treasures of the journal) when Miss Mercatroid looked at him frostily and told him to go upstairs where someone 'will attend to you'.

The someone turned out to be a woman in her mid-seventies, wearing a high-necked white lace blouse, a dirndl skirt of mauve gingham and a crocheted cardigan. The enamelled brooch at her throat featured a ferocious-looking bulldog – designed, presumably, to ward off unacceptable advances.

'I will take you to wait in the editor's anteroom,' she said. Her voice took on a note of awe: 'Mr Lambie Crump is writing, so he cannot be interrupted.' She turned and led Amiss into a magnificently proportioned room disfigured by a partition which cut in half a magnificent bay window. It was occupied by five elderly women who sat in rows in front of stout manual typewriters: the clatter was overwhelming.

Facing them sat a large woman in battleship-grey – clearly the supervisor. She was jabbing her finger at a page of typescript annotated in red ink. 'Are you going quite blind, Mavis?' she asked the crone standing before her. 'Redo.' Shaking visibly, and looking on the edge of tears, her victim tottered away.

Amiss was led through the door in the partition and placed in a Victorian button-back armchair beside another Sheraton table bearing a copy of *The Wrangler*'s history. 'Would you care for afternoon tea?' she asked.

'How delightful. Yes, please.'

She vanished and reappeared fifteen minutes later with a tray bearing a teapot, water jug, strainer, milk jug and sugar

9

basin complete with tongs: all looked Georgian and silver. There were also doilied china plates of cucumber sandwiches and what in Amiss's youth had been called fancy cakes.

By the time Lambie Crump deigned to emerge from his office and shake hands with his guest, Amiss was replete and had progressed in his studies to the great scandal of the 1840s when the editor put the journal's spare cash into railway shares: in the resulting crash the Papworths had to stump up a vast sum of money to keep the journal afloat.

'Just a moment.' Lambie Crump darted through the partition and came back divested of the several sheets of handwritten paper he'd been carrying. 'Sorry about that. One had to finish a rather tricky analysis of the latest New Labour proposals for creating constitutional mayhem. Pray, come in.'

Amiss followed him into a room far too grand to be described as an office. Had the effect not been slightly spoiled by the shabbiness of the paintwork, its spaciousness, ornate gilt decoration, fine furniture and splendid fireplace dominated by a magnificent gilt-framed rural landscape, would have been appropriate to a foreign secretary.

Lambie Crump suited his surroundings, being the epitome of those known popularly as Young Fogeys, although he was taller and skinnier than the norm and being by now in his forties was perilously close to graduating to full-blown fogeyhood. His blond hair flopped Byronically over his brow, slightly obscuring the right side of his pince-nez; across his three-piece, hairy, yellowish suit and check shirt was strung a heavy gold watch chain; his tie was that of a gentleman's club known to Amiss as the Highest of all High Tory fortresses; and his brogues looked both handmade and ancient.

On the coatstand was a brown trilby hat, a long cashmere coat and a black umbrella, and nestling beside Lambie Crump's desk was a Gladstone bag of considerable age. The glass-fronted bookcase contained hundreds of leather-bound volumes.

Lambie Crump fussed around Amiss as he seated him and then threw himself into the vast chair behind his desk, which looked to be the twin of the doorkeeper's. 'It is good of you to call, Mr Amiss. Good of you to call.'

'Not at all, Mr Lambie Crump. A pleasure.'

Lambie Crump placed the tips of his fingers together and looked portentous. 'One is reluctant to begin crassly, but it is proper to mention that one has a veto over your appointment. While one's freedom of action is confined to matters editorial, in practice it is so closely combined with the managerial side of the paper that the trustees would not countenance having imposed upon one anyone with whom one could not work.' He leaned his chin on the tips of his steepled fingers and peered at Amiss over the top of his glasses. 'For some reason that eludes one, the trustees appear to think one's welfare is their concern.'

He threw back his head and emitted a sound which Amiss thought was intended to express amusement, but which more resembled the distress call of an anxious horse. When the sound had faded away, he balanced his head again on his fingers and looked solemn. 'You will understand, therefore, that while one was happy to leave it to Charlie Papworth to suggest the name of someone who might assist, one could accept no one who fails to understand that one can accomplish nothing without tranquillity. A manager will have to understand that editorial takes precedence over managerial at all times.'

'Of course, Mr Lambie Crump. I should wish it to be no other way. My concern is to make your life easier, not add to its vexations.'

That circumlocution went down noticeably well with Lambie Crump, who now went to the trouble of looking at Amiss appraisingly. Having taken in the inoffensive tweed and the check shirt, his gaze lighted on Amiss's tie. 'Ah, how interesting. You are a member of ffeatherstonehaugh's. That is a club one has occasionally been tempted to join. Wonderful cellar, one is told, though, forgive me, do its members not have a somewhat licentious reputation?'

'Less so, these days, I think. I joined simply to oblige an old friend.'

11

'Would this be a friend one might know?'

Amiss resisted the temptation to explain brightly that his friend had been head waiter at ffeatherstonehaugh's when he had been a gallery steward; he chose instead to lie.

'Baroness Troutbeck.'

'Really!' Lambie Crump almost squeaked. 'Goodness gracious. Our paths have never crossed, but one cannot but respect the lady. Perhaps you might bring her to luncheon someday.' He recollected that he was conducting an interview. 'If you join us, that is, of course.'

His gaze swept again over Amiss, who sat there trying to look like the persona he was now adopting: amiable, unthreatening, conservative, intelligent but not too intelligent and an efficient but not too efficient mopper-up-of-messes, while not too innovative. In other words, someone who would serve Lambie Crump, make his life easier and make painless savings on the cost front sufficient to shut up the proprietor without threatening any aspect of the cushy life enjoyed by the *Wrangler* editor.

'It would be wrong to pretend,' said Lambie Crump sententiously, 'that this place is not in need of a measure of administrative attention. When one is as busy as one is, one must eschew the minutiae of office routines.' He steepled his fingers again and gazed down them at Amiss.

'One must, however, be frank. One is so antipathetic to dreary technical matters that one has, perhaps, occasionally been a trifle remiss. It is true, for instance, that some innovations are overdue. The telephones, for instance, are not all they might be. Yet it cannot be stressed too strongly that the place must not be plunged into disharmony by any threats to the happiness and livelihood of *Wrangler* staff.' He paused for a moment. 'Editorial staff, anyway.'

Amiss smiled seraphically. 'I think if you ask the Duke of Ormerod, whom I once had the honour of serving as a private secretary, he will reassure you that I have no aspirations to be the efficient Baxter.'

This was a double whammy. Lambie Crump was a notorious snob as well as an avowed admirer of P. G. Wodehouse, whose memorable secretary, Rupert Baxter, had so terror-ized Lord Emsworth with his remorseless efficiency. Lambie Crump's expression was so ecstatic that Amiss hugged himself mentally for his brilliance in agreeing that lie with Ormerod.

'Since you lack the horn-rimmed spectacles, Mr Amiss, it is obvious that you are no Baxter.' Lambie Crump neighed. 'Any more than Bertie Ormerod is a Lord Emsworth. How long were you with him?'

'Just for a few months when he needed a stand-in. Later, I performed the same function for the Bishop of Westonbury, before he headed back to academia.'

'My dear chap.' Lambie Crump's suspicions were wholly allayed. 'We have the same kind of friends, I see.' A thought struck him. 'One takes it you know about running offices and directing underlings and all that kind of tiresome business?'

Amiss laughed carelessly. 'Oh that? 'Fraid so. Used to be a civil servant, I'm sorry to say. Couldn't stand the bureaucracy though. Had to get out. And then of course the people were rather . . .' He wrinkled his nose.

'All is clear,' said Lambie Crump. 'How terrible for you.' He launched into an assault on the wicked dirigisme of the home civil service and the scandalous iniquity of the Foreign Office, whose sole *raison d'être* was apparently to sell Britain out to the enemy. Amiss felt it prudent not to mention that he lived with a diplomat and instead let the flow of anathematizing continue unchallenged, nodding and smiling mendaciously at appropriate times to indicate agreement. He endeavoured too to look impressed every time Lambie Crump mentioned yet another foreign secretary, senior functionary or government adviser who had demonstrated in conver-sation with him their intellectual puerility or absence of gung ho patriotism.

An hour and a half had passed amicably when there was a tap on the door. The supervisor came in, laid some papers reverentially on the desk and left. Lambie Crump picked then up. 'This is regrettable, Robert – if one may make so bold as thus to address you, and you will, perhaps, be so kind as to call me Willie – but, alas, one has to get on. Delighted,

delighted to make your acquaintance. It will be a pleasure to have you here. When will you come?'

'Whenever suits you. Perhaps on a day you might have time to introduce me to the staff?'

'Friday then,' said Lambie Crump cheerily. 'Come here to luncheon at one o'clock. Even with the lamentable condition of the roads, one should by then have returned from All Souls. Afterwards, we might pay a visit below stairs.' He neighed and stood up. 'There can be little doubt that you will fit in well. Just do remember how important it is that no one is upset. It is not easy to write limpidly when people are being emotional.' He ushered Amiss out swiftly, led him through the anteroom and the typing pool, shook hands at the top of the staircase, bowed and bade him farewell.

As he walked down to the hall, Amiss heard from down the other corridor a sudden outbreak of angry voices – one high-pitched and female; the other deep and male. He tried to look unconscious of the noise while straining to hear what the row was about. The only word he picked up was 'Aristotle'. Miss Mercatroid, who appeared completely unaware of the din, nodded a chilly goodbye. Slightly disconcerted, he smiled at her sweetly, and passing by the liveried lad, who had fallen asleep over his rag, he let himself out quietly.

3

'It's Robert, Jack. I've got a proper job at last.'

'Hah!' shouted Baroness Troutbeck down the line. 'And about bloody time too. What is it?'

'It's with *The Wrangler*.'

'Doing what?'

'Managing it.'

'Why aren't you editing it?' she demanded. 'You don't aspire high enough, my lad. Anyone would be better than that little Crump twerp. Should have been drowned at birth.'

'Odd. I thought you'd share *The Wrangler*'s prejudices.'

'There's more to life than prejudices. I grant you little Crump is ideologically sound, but he's not a man to go into the jungle – or even into a restaurant – with. Heard him give an after-dinner speech recently. Christ, he's so precious he should be deposited in a Knightsbridge bank vault. Preferably with no air supply.'

'On the evidence so far, I can't fault your analysis.'

'Did he name-drop at you?'

'Incessantly.'

'I'm surprised he took you, considering you're halfway to being a human being.'

'You're being less than encouraging, Jack. This is a real job. I haven't had one of those for two years.'

'I found you dozens.'

'Three, to be precise: all temporary and leading nowhere and just a cover for being your fixer. This has the potential to be permanent, substantial and lead to greater things.'

'It won't be half as much fun as what I got you into.'

15

'Thank God for that. I could do with a long respite from any collaboration with mad baronesses.'

She chortled. 'Don't get complacent: fate may yet throw us together.'

'Not if I've got anything to do with it,' said Amiss firmly.

'Just us for luncheon today. Would not normally be able to entertain you here – or anywhere else for that matter. One is rarely free. But the Chancellor had to cancel because of the emergency summit, so it was possible to accommodate you. Thought of rounding up a few colleagues to meet you, but a tête-à-tête is preferable in the circumstances.'

Lambie Crump opened a door at the back of his office and ushered Amiss into a tiny mahogany-panelled, mirrored lift. 'We'll have a spot of luncheon and a chat, so we can be sure we're both seeing things the same way. Too bad about the Chancellor, but I'm sure you'll be better company. He's so drearily Calvinist, don't you think?'

He neighed. 'One longs for some of these people to commit a few colourful sins.' He pressed a button. 'Anyway, after we've eaten, we'll go and inspect the natives.'

They ascended at a stately pace to the sixth floor and disembarked into a large, L-shaped dining room. 'It might have been pleasanter to eat in my rooms, but I thought you might as well have the benefit of the full *Wrangler* hospitality.'

On cue, a frock-coated butler hove into view bearing a silver salver. He inclined his head. 'Good afternoon, sir.'

'Ah, thank you, Tozer. This is Mr Amiss. He is joining us here to help run things more smoothly, so you will, no doubt, be seeing something of him. Robert, please to help yourself to champagne.'

As they each took a glass, Lambie Crump lowered his voice confidingly. 'One finds it wise to drink little at luncheon, but a pick-me-up does not go amiss in the middle of a taxing day. Now let me take you on a perambulation around our rogues' gallery.'

This tour of the portraits on the dining room walls was clearly one that delighted Lambie Crump, for it enabled him to scatter into his speeches aphorisms, quotations and bon mots, the apparent spontaneity of which he had burnished to perfection. 'Ah, me. My predecessors. How their intellectual distinction weighs upon me!' He delivered himself of a particularly happy neigh. 'Here we have Seymour Spragge, our founder. Not perhaps, exceptionally gifted intellectually, but one cannot fault what vulgarians would nowadays no doubt deem his "marketing skills". It was Spragge, after all, who persuaded the third Earl of Papworth in 1805 that he should provide all the capital to set up *The Wrangler*, leave Spragge to run it as he thought fit and pay him fifty per cent of the gross income.'

'I've heard of blank cheques,' said Amiss, 'but that's pretty spectacular. Unless, of course, Papworth had some control over the outgoings.'

'Nothing so coarse,' said Lambie Crump. 'Papworth was uninterested in commerce and was also in thrall to Spragge, whom he regarded as the greatest mind of his age.' He neighed again. 'Sadly, one must challenge that assessment, for, alas, Spragge's was not an original mind.'

He took a sip of champagne and smiled in a superior manner. 'One must hope standards have risen a touch since then. Still, one should not disparage one's predecessors. Spragge did put *The Wrangler* on the map. At the very least, even though his mind was superficial, he had a feel for the fashion of the times. One cannot go far wrong being an intellectual slave of Edmund Burke and a hero-worshipper of the Duke of Wellington. And I grant you, he had an eye for talent.' Lambie Crump raised his glass patronizingly to his founder's portrait. 'So all in all, not a bad editor.' He smiled at Amiss. 'As they went.'

Amiss quickly learned that there had never been an editor on an intellectual par with Lambie Crump. This one was pedestrian, that one a crook and though these two had enlivened things by shooting each other in the head, their heads hadn't been worth much anyway.

About the inadequates, Lambie Crump was relatively benign: the heretics earned only excoriation. There was the one who

17

went all the way with Disraeli on extending the franchise, the reprehensible flirter with Gladstone over Irish Home Rule and – above all – the apostate who failed to admit that the only respectable intellectual position on the American Civil War was to back the South.

When it came to America – which to Amiss's surprise loomed large in the paper's concerns – all popular heroes were villains and villains were heroes. Abraham Lincoln was a counter-jumper and militarist bully, Franklin Roosevelt a fiscal nihilist and John F. Kennedy a priapic and unprincipled plastic-Irish scoundrel. Inevitably, therefore, the heroes were Lyndon Johnson, Richard Nixon and Ronald Reagan, the success of the century: Barry Goldwater was the best president America had never had.

'President Clinton, Willie?' Amiss said mischievously. 'Any virtues?'

'Please, Robert. Not before lunch. The very thought of the fellow makes one quite faint. Tozer, some more medicinal champagne, if you will be so kind.'

Revived by several more sips, he looked seriously at Amiss. 'You must forgive one's emotion at the very mention of that' – he paused – 'that hobbledehoy. But America matters to us on this journal. We care about it and take seriously our role in guiding it on a wiser path.

'The Empire is dead, the Commonwealth beyond rescuing and Europe doesn't speak English. But though we don't have a big sale in America, we have an influential circulation among colonial brethren who draw from us intellectual and moral succour. It is our duty to continue to give them a lead in standing up against the barbarians, who have breached the walls of Washington.'

Lunch was light but expensive. The overheads, thought Amiss, must be horrendous, for there was a cook as well as a butler. They started with a spinach soufflé, accompanied by what Lambie Crump described as 'a rather decent little Montrachet'. Dover sole, asparagus and tiny new potatoes followed, and although Lambie Crump and Amiss both refused the Stilton, in aroma and texture it was of a quality that would have made the baroness swoon lustfully. When they had finished their coffee – served in tiny and exquisite china – Lambie Crump looked at his watch and crumpled up his linen napkin. 'Let us inspect the minions.'

Amiss – who was by now very tired of listening to Lambie Crump disparaging the intellect and the principles of apparently every politician and editor in London – jumped to his feet eagerly.

'We'll start with the playroom.' Lambie Crump threw open the door leading off the dining room. A missile flew through the open door and hit Amiss painfully on the side of the head. He stumbled and fell, bleeding copiously.

'Tozer, quick. Move him. He's ruining the rug.'

'If you'll excuse me, sir, I think this might be more efficacious.' Combining humanity with practicality, Tozer lifted Amiss's head gently, turned his wounded side uppermost and placed on it a capacious napkin. 'Just stay there for a moment, sir, and try to hold this to your ear. I'll go and fetch the first-aid kit.'

Obediently Amiss clasped the napkin to his throbbing ear and lay supine. Above him he could hear a distressed elderly voice squeaking: 'It was Lloyd George I was aiming at, sir. Lloyd George. I do beg the gentleman's pardon, sir. My aim went completely.'

'Don't vex yourself, Ricketts,' said Lambie Crump. 'You must not fret over this slight mishap. I'm sure Mr Amiss will recover swiftly. Go now, and perhaps we may pay you a visit later on.'

The quavering voice faded into the distance as Tozer re-appeared, put his arm under Amiss's shoulders, gently and efficiently mopped his ear with a damp cloth and then firmly affixed sticking plaster. 'All right now, sir?'

'Thank you,' said Amiss faintly.

As Lambie Crump gazed on with little sign of concern, Tozer helped Amiss to his feet. Amiss staggered for the first few paces and then steadied himself. 'Thank you very much indeed, Mr Tozer. I feel fine now.'

Lambie Crump looked him up and down. 'Your shirt is

'soiled,' he said with distaste. 'And your coat, too, it would seem. Tozer?'

'Allow me, sir.' Tozer rubbed Amiss's front diligently for a minute or two. 'Sorry, sir. That is the best I can do while you are actually wearing the garments.'

'Oh, it will have to do,' said Lambie Crump impatiently. 'Can you continue now? Have you pulled yourself together?'

'Yes, I'm OK now. Sorry for collapsing like that, Willie. It was a bit of a shock.'

'Well, as long as you've stopped bleeding, we can recommence.'

'Yes, I think it's stopped. It was just a nick.'

'Good, good. Let's get on now.'

'Just before we do, Willie. What exactly happened?'

'Oh, didn't you pick that up? Ricketts was throwing a dart at Lloyd George just as the door opened, and unfortunately he missed the old reprobate completely and hit you instead.' He neighed. 'An amusing instance of mistaken identity, *n'est pas*?'

Amiss, who was feeling slightly queasy, tried not to sound querulous. 'Still not with you, I'm afraid. Firing a dart at Lloyd George?'

Lambie Crump sighed. 'Ah, me. Of course, I haven't yet explained the playroom to you. Come along and see it now.' He neighed. 'It's safe now, I think, but just in case, I'll go ahead of you.'

'Excuse me, sir. You might wish to replace the dart.' Tozer presented Lambie Crump with the offending article, now wiped clean of Amiss's blood, and bowed as they left the dining room and moved into a room of modest size, wall-papered with portraits and photographs. Most were riddled with holes.

'We puncture our enemies here,' explained his host. 'Our founder thought it a valuable form of catharsis.'

Amiss easily identified Napoleon, Gladstone and – just beside the door – Lloyd George. 'Willie, why is Lloyd George the largest target? Because of what he did to the House of Lords?'

'And death duties. Worst damage ever done to the landed interest.'

As Amiss tried to place a balding man with a large double chin, Lambie Crump explained: 'Charles James Fox. One of our chief villains.'

'Because he was in favour of the French Revolution and fell out with Edmund Burke?'

Lambie Crump nodded approvingly. 'Precisely. Among other offences. Such as believing the people were right.'

'And is that Bismarck?' asked Amiss hesitantly.

'Correct. Up there beside the Kaiser, Hitler and Chancellor Kohl. We're not too keen here on imperialistic Germans. Or imperialist anyone else for that matter.'

'Except us, I presume,' offered Amiss.

'Well, yes. Obviously of course except us. And the United States, if they'd do it properly. But they're simply not up to it. Look at Vietnam. No idea how to run that war.'

Amiss, who had little time for armchair generals, moved to another wall. 'Not much here from the early part of the century, is there? I see Attlee, Harold Wilson and Tony Blair along with a couple of Liberals, but I can't see anyone from the first half of the century except Lloyd George.'

'We've replaced them,' said Lambie Crump. 'We keep the nineteenth-century portraits for reasons of tradition, but you don't get people wishing to vent their feelings on Asquith these days. You'll find several pockmarked portraits in the attic which have been replaced by these blown-up photographs of our more recent enemies.' He neighed. 'There are some areas where modernity has its place, you know. One cannot afford to be slack in identifying contemporary scoundrels.'

'There aren't yet many holes in that photograph of our present government.'

Lambie Crump shook his head. 'I fear Ricketts and – just very occasionally – Henry Potbury are the only members of staff who now keep up this tradition. Potbury usually misses, and it has to be admitted that Ricketts is rather mired in the past. Apart from Lloyd George, whom his predecessor taught him to hate, he mostly aims his darts at Clement Attlee.'

'So this place no longer fulfils its traditional purpose, which I presume – on the Japanese principle – is of stress relief.'

'Come again?'

'I understand Japanese companymen relieve their feelings by throwing missiles at pictures of their seniors.'

'Really. Can't comment on that. *The Wrangler* isn't very interested in the Nipponese. Or in Chinamen for that matter. Oriental preoccupations seem so . . . so . . . grubbily materialistic these days, don't you think?'

He looked put out. 'What you have just said assists in making the playroom idea repellent as well as increasingly pointless. One must confess that were it not for Ricketts one would be tempted to close off this room. It has been rather an irritation to have to rule on whether it is appropriate to instal a blown-up picture of the entire Liberal Democratic Party, selected Conservative apostates or if our venom should be concentrated on New Labour. Ricketts doesn't have a lot of initiative in these matters, you understand. Besides, it makes us appear predictable in our politics, and whatever my colleagues may think, it is my view that we should maintain an open mind.'

'Has it always just been darts?' asked Amiss, who was inspecting what seemed to be very large holes in Napoleon's head.

'Used to be bullets. At one time the entire staff used to have shooting competitions in here. But sometime in the nineteen thirties there was a distressing incident when one assistant editor inflicted an unpleasant flesh wound on a colleague: it was never clear whether it was deliberate or not. After that bullets were replaced by a more plebeian but safer alternative.' He neighed uproariously. 'Come to think of it, you should be grateful for that.'

Amiss, whose ear continued to throb, managed a weak smile.

4

'We have a very small editorial staff,' explained Lambie Crump, as they walked down the stairs. 'Apart from hoi polloi, there are only four. Most of our journal is written by outside contributors, but we do have on the staff a political editor – my deputy – an assistant editor, a part-time literary editor and a kind of odd-job woman. The others you need to know about now, I suppose, are my secretary, Sabrina Trustler-Stomp, who is away at the moment, Marcia and Ben, Miss Mercatroid, whom you've met, Miss Grumshaw, the supervisor of the typewriters and Josiah Ricketts, at whose hands you suffered just now and with whom you'll be working closely; but more of that another time.' If he was aware of Amiss's horrified reaction, he gave no sign of it.

As Lambie Crump stopped at the end of the corridor, he announced portentously: 'Now here is my deputy, Henry Potbury, our distinguished political editor.' He opened the door and together he and Amiss contemplated the form of the room's incumbent, who was sprawled across his desk apparently dead. Amiss's momentary alarm was dispelled by Lambie Crump's heavy sigh, which alerted him to the more mundane reality that Potbury was in a deep sleep.

After a loud greeting from Lambie Crump, Potbury twitched and grunted and finally struggled to an upright position. He gazed at his visitors blearily. Amiss realized that he was drunk. 'Henry Potbury, our senior and most valued editor. Indeed, one should say' – Lambie Crump never lost the opportunity to be portentous, thought Amiss – 'a man whose unparalleled devotion to the mind of Burke has been more than inspirational. One might go further and describe Henry as the lodestar of *The Wrangler* for some thirty years now, a man whose quality of thought has always transcended . . .'

As he paused to find the *mot juste*, Amiss observed that the recipient of this elegant bouquet seemed unimpressed. And as Lambie Crump continued with '. . . all vulgar corruptions . . .' Potbury slowly slipped down into his chair and fell once again into a deep sleep. Within seconds he was snoring.

Lambie Crump looked at him with distaste. 'Alas, in some respects my colleague adheres too closely to the customs and practices of the eighteenth century in which he is so at home.' He set his lips primly. 'One accepts that if we are traditionalists, we must live with tradition. And while as his editor, one might wish for Potbury to have the virtues of the past without its vices, that is perhaps a touch unreasonable.' He sighed. 'Let us proceed to one of his more temperate colleagues.'

'Ah, here is Wilfred Parry.' An exquisite youth in a white suit looked up from his Georgian desk and laid down his fountain pen. 'Good afternoon, Willie.'

'One is always sorry to interrupt, Wilfred, but you will, I know, wish to meet Robert Amiss, who will be joining us on Monday to tidy us up a bit.'

'In what sense?'

'Management, administration, that sort of thing.'

Parry's eyes swept over Amiss in the manner of a busy duchess being presented with a new housemaid. 'Hello.' He turned towards Lambie Crump. 'I'm writing what I hope you will feel is a rather inspired dissection of Tottman's latest. Thought it might make a good lead for next week.'

'Splendid, splendid,' said Lambie Crump, showing no more interest in the downfall of Tottman than Parry showed in the rise of Amiss. 'In a bit of a hurry. Must move on.'

'Any chance of a word later?'

'Doubt it, Wilfred. Doubt it. Have to disappear early. Rather hush-hush weekend, don't you know.'

'Wilfred's keen,' he explained to Amiss as they proceeded

down another corridor. 'But it is possible to be too keen. Sometimes one has the feeling he has little or no understanding of the constant strain on someone in my position.' He opened another door. This time he did not usher Amiss in, having clearly taken the view that it would be foolish to try to circumnavigate the stacks of newspapers, magazines and other paper debris that covered almost the entire floor.

Through a haze of smoke, the room's two inhabitants could just be seen behind the piles of paper, the coffee mugs, the tennis balls and the other assorted objects that littered their desks. Lambie Crump's nose wrinkled in distaste at the smell of tobacco: the man was chewing on a pipe; the woman was smoking a roll-up. Both were intently absorbed in reading that week's *Wrangler*.

'Good afternoon, Marcia and Ben. Here is Robert Amiss, who will joining us on Monday.'

They looked up suspiciously.

'Doing what?' asked Marcia.

Lambie Crump waved a hand vaguely. 'Making one's life easier, one trusts,' he said grandly. 'Taking a bit of the administrative burden away. You know the kind of thing.'

As their eyes strayed back to their *Wrangler*s, Marcia suddenly emitted a yell. 'I knew it, I knew it, I knew it!' she bellowed. 'We should never have let him correct the proofs himself.' She leaped to her feet, tripped over a pile of newspapers, picked herself up and stormed over to Ben, throwing the offending magazine in front of him and jabbing the top right-hand corner. 'Look at that. Just look at that. Makes me feel positively suicidal.'

'Oh my Gawd,' said Ben. 'That's a bloody catastrophe.' They gazed at each other in mute, shared horror.

'What is it?' asked Lambie Crump, sounding weary rather than apprehensive. Marcia picked up the magazine and in the sepulchral tones of a BBC newsreader announcing the death of a national icon read: 'We could have done with less contributors with a penchant for the mawkish . . .' She looked up and asked dully, 'How could he? How could he? How could he?' Her voice rose and she stamped her foot. 'Fewer! Fewer!

25

Fewer! How often do I have to tell that platinum-headed git about where to stick his misapplied lesses . . . ?'

'Along with his misplaced onlies,' added Ben.

'Oh dear, yes, yes, yes, mmm,' said Lambie Crump, to whom they were paying no attention. 'Must be off now, goodbye.' As he shut the door they heard Marcia's voice rise in hysteria. Amiss looked at Lambie Crump and raised an eyebrow. 'These are not bog-standard coolies, you understand. It is because of them that *The Wrangler* has a reputation for being more free of errors than any similar journal here or in the United States. But that brings with it for the rest of us the penalty that an error like "Aegean" being substituted for "Augean" – which happened recently – is a tragedy sufficient to cause lamentations for days. And then, of course, there will be the hysterical reaction to the arrival on Monday of one of those letters.'

'What letters?'

Lambie Crump sighed deeply. 'We have a reader who has taken it upon himself for the last twenty years to read every line of the journal to check it for errors. It's become a kind of primaeval duel between him and Ben and Marcia.

'On a good week a letter comes saying, "ten out of ten". When there are errors, they come listed and with references. It makes it more piquant that no one knows who the fellow is: the letters are anonymous. And he picks up factual errors as well, which are also Marcia and Ben's responsibility. Sadly, the dear things cope badly with failure.'

He stopped. 'Now let me think. Who's next? Oh yes. I almost forgot.' He doubled back on his tracks. 'Here is Phoebe Somerfield's lair.'

Located between Potbury's palatial room and Ben and Marcia's spacious midden, Miss Somerfield's office was tiny, but tidy and apparently well organized, with rows of books, neatly stacked magazines and files, and a cabinet that was not bursting at its seams. The lady herself was in her early fifties, small, spare and bespectacled, and her typewriter was clacking busily. 'Moonlighting again, Phoebe?' enquired Lambie Crump genially.

'Just something for the World Service,' she said crisply. 'Do you mind if I get on with it?'

'Just wanted to introduce our new management wallah, Robert Amiss.'

She looked at Amiss without interest, but nodded politely and recommended typing. Lambie Crump closed the door behind them. 'Bit of a martinet, Phoebe, really. Doesn't think of anything except work.'

'What's her job exactly?'

'She edits the letters page, writes articles and leaders. Has done for donkey's years.'

'On what?'

'On most things. It cannot be denied that Phoebe is versatile and industrious. But she doesn't get out and about enough. If she's not doing her job here she's hammering out freelance book reviews and scripts and that sort of thing. Good girl, Phoebe. And one would miss her. But not really one of us. Doesn't move in the places one would wish her to. Depressingly austere. And brisk.

'Now to the administrators,' he said as they went down the stairs.

'Didn't you mention an assistant editor?'

Lambie Crump's lips compressed. 'Winterton is not with us at present and is not expected back for a week.' He looked at his watch. 'Scudmore almost certainly isn't around either.' He opened a door and nodded as he closed it again. 'Advertising chappie. Has to have luncheons and all that.' Trying the room next door, he found it also empty. This time he looked annoyed, stalked over to the desk and dialled zero. 'Miss Mercatroid, is Mr Naggiar not about?' His face took on a look of irritation. 'Thank you,' he said as he replaced the receiver. 'Naggiar is our circulation manager, Robert. You will find that he is infrequently on the premises.'

Amiss raised an interrogative eyebrow. 'Running around drumming up business?'

Lambie Crump's neigh sounded bitter. 'As no doubt you will find out, he is rather preoccupied with matters medical.'

27

'He's ill?'

'Let us say one gathers that he has a multiplicity of conditions.' He stopped again. 'Now let me formally introduce you to your assailant.' He threw open the door at the end of the corridor and revealed a vision of Dickensian squalor.

5

'And here is Josiah Ricketts, with whom you will be working closely.'

Amiss stifled the words, 'In here??!!' and tried to keep his facial expression steady. Windowless, the office was lit by fluorescent light. Had it instead been candlelit, it would have borne a close resemblance to what the unreconstructed Scrooge thought appropriate quarters for Bob Cratchit: airless, dark, cramped and very ugly. The walls were lined with shelves of ledgers and the tiny, wizened old man was writing in another at a wooden table, using a long steel pen to produce perfect, copperplate handwriting.

As he saw his visitors, he blotted his ink and clambered painfully to his feet. 'Good afternoon, Mr Lambie Crump, sir,' he said reverentially. And then, recognizing Amiss, he wailed, 'Oh, sir. Are you all right? I don't know how I can ever forgive myself . . .'

As Amiss murmured consolatory words, Lambie Crump waved a dismissive hand. 'Absolutely nothing to worry about, Ricketts. Albeit briefly discomfited, Mr Amiss suffered no more than a small abrasion.' As the wailing continued, Lambie Crump became visibly irritated. 'Pull yourself together, Ricketts. There is no time to waste. My taximeter cabriolet is due in five minutes.

'Now, Mr Amiss is coming to help me. He will be manager of the journal. And you will, of course, give him every assistance you can.'

'Honoured, sir,' said Ricketts. 'It will be a privilege. I can promise you my best endeavours, which I have always tried to give the ladies and gentlemen of *The Wrangler*.'

Amiss resisted the impulse to pat Ricketts on the head. Instead, he bowed. 'I am most grateful to you, Mr Ricketts. I look forward to a happy collaboration.' As they left, he was relieved that although Ricketts was palpitating with deference, at least he had not dropped to his knees.

'Awfully sorry,' said Lambie Crump, whose boredom with his present duties was palpable, 'but it truly is necessary to hasten. Perchance you can introduce yourself around the place on Monday.'

'Just one thing,' asked Amiss. 'Which will be my office?'

Lambie Crump clapped his hand to his head. 'Good heavens,' he said. 'Alas, while that is a fair question, it is not one to which there has been time to give attention.' For a moment he looked nonplussed, then he smiled seraphically and laid a hand on Amiss's shoulder. 'Surely that can be left to you, my dear chap. I'm sure you can sort something out. After all' – his smile widened – 'is that not precisely the kind of thing you're here to deal with?

'Now, will you be so kind as to excuse me? Can you show yourself out?'

'If you don't mind, Willie, I'll hang on and have a little chat with Mr Ricketts about practicalities.'

'Rather you than me, dear boy,' And waving a languid farewell, Lambie Crump disappeared.

By now Ricketts was busily back at work. 'Mr Ricketts,' said Amiss gently. 'Could we have a word?'

'Excuse me just one moment, sir, or I'll lose count.' For the next three minutes, Ricketts continued his task of laboriously counting the contents of a carton of pencils. Then he looked up. 'That's right, sir. They've sent the right amount. You always have to check, you know. That's what Mr Flitter always said: "Take nothing for granted."'

'Do they use a lot of pencils here?'

'Well, I keep the consumption in check, sir. Some of the ladies and gentlemen have no idea of economy. Why, I've known Mr Potbury to ask for as many as four pencils in a week. I have to remind him that they don't grow on trees, you know – pencils.'

'You operate strict economies here, then, Mr Ricketts?'

'I do, sir. I keep a very tight eye indeed on my ladies' and gentlemen's requisites.'

'Like?'

'Oh, there's paper and there's pencils and then there's steel pens – though mind you, that's not a difficulty since I'm the only one who uses them now. We had a bit of a to-do a long time back about biros. The last editor, God bless him, he didn't hold with them. Said it was an affront to decency to have them in the building. Fountain pens or steel pens only, he decreed. Or pencils, of course. But then, sir, you know how it is. It's called progress, I suppose. We had to give in in the end, just like with those machines the typewriting ladies use.'

'So you dispense biros freely now, do you?'

Ricketts giggled conspiratorially. 'I can see you are a one, Mr Amiss. "Freely" indeed. That's not what Mr Flitter trained me to do, I can tell you. There's not one item goes out of this room that's not accounted for.'

'So you are a master of stock control, Mr Ricketts.'

'I don't go along with that fancy language, Mr Amiss. I just count my pencils. That's what Mr Flitter said was my job. And when they ask for one too quickly, I go looking for the one that's missing.'

He looked grave. 'And I can tell you it's the same about copies of *The Wrangler* itself. If you let them get away with it there would be rampant waste. They'd be leaving them all round the place or giving them away for nothing. Ladies and gentlemen with brains are all the same, sir. Not much common sense, if you'll forgive my saying so. You have to keep an eye on them or you wouldn't know what they'd be up to.'

He was warming to his theme. 'I've kept my foot down – just like Mr Flitter did. Twenty-two copies come into this building and no more. That's one each for the staff and two each for the editor and Mr Potbury, just in case they have to give the extra away to someone important.' Ricketts emitted an arresting sound, which was made by blowing sharply down his nose while his lips were compressed. It indicated, as far as Amiss could see, a statement that once again the forces of order had overcome those of anarchy.

'Mr Ricketts, I need help.'

'You want me to issue you, sir, with pencil and paper?'

'More than that. I need a room.'

Ricketts looked at him incredulously. 'I'm sorry, sir. But they're all full. They all have their uses, you see.'

'But if I am to work here, Mr Ricketts, I must have an office.'

Seeing the aghast expression on Ricketts's face and his hand clutching at his chest, Amiss intervened swiftly. 'Now, Mr Ricketts, I'm sure everything is as it should be and we'll find some way out of this that won't upset anybody or anything. Why don't you take me around the building and show me all the rooms, what is kept where and so on. Then we'll see if there's any little corner I might squeeze into.'

Ricketts's agitation began to wane. 'Just as long as you're not thinking of changing things, sir.'

'Rest assured, Mr Ricketts, that just like Mr Burke, I'm against making changes for change's sake. I won't be doing anything that doesn't make us all happier.'

Looking at him half with alarm and half with a burgeoning trust, Ricketts left his desk and tottered towards the door.

The rooms unoccupied by people were certainly full. One was entirely devoted to bound copies of *The Wrangler*, another to spares, which Ricketts, Flitter and their predecessors had gathered up every week and preserved. Then there were rooms full of Georgian and Victorian furniture, presumably displaced by the modernizing process of the 1960s, and even a whole room devoted to broken furniture, which Ricketts explained would be repaired when the editor thought it a good idea.

Amiss made no comment on anything except to grunt reassuringly every time Ricketts assured him that this or that room was sacrosanct. 'No one here likes anything to change, Mr Amiss,' was Ricketts's parting shot. 'I'm sure you're right,' said Amiss. 'Now don't worry about anything, Mr Ricketts. You'll hardly know I'm here.'

Where would we be, he reflected, without the humane lie?

'Though hardly a great proponent of revolution myself,' Amiss reported to Rachel that evening, 'I found myself badly in need of someone who wasn't completely reactionary. The only one who seemed a possible candidate was the young door-opener, Jason, whose taste in reading material at least was contemporary. I requested Miss Mercatroid to allow me to borrow him for a couple of minutes and took him outside for a brief walk. Having ascertained that he was bright and bored I arranged to meet him in a pub after hours.

'"Can I wear me normal clothes, or must I go like this?" he asked.

'My heart bled for him. I think I'd sooner wear a frock in a pub than go dressed like that. So he turned up in his tracksuit and trainers and we had an amicable couple of pints, and he's coming in at the weekend to help me make a nest for myself by Monday.'

'Won't that give the organization a corporate heart attack?'

'No one will care except Ricketts, and I know how to fix him. I'll tell him it was that or move in with him. The territorial implications of that should do the job.'

6

Amiss sat in his office on Monday morning, delighted with what he and Jason had accomplished. Though modest in size, the room was magnificently furnished. The removal of spare *Wrangler*s to the back of the room housing bound *Wrangler*s had freed up quarters with ample room for a fine Georgian desk with a green leather top of the kind he had always coveted, a Victorian leather armchair, a wooden filing cabinet that was not too unsightly and a few portraits of *Wrangler*-approved luminaries to remind him what his politics were supposed to be. He had had a shock halfway through Saturday morning, when Lambie Crump, wearing a perfectly foul pair of yellow corduroy trousers and an orange tweed jacket, hurried down the fire escape past the window of the room they were raiding. But Jason had explained that there was nothing sinister about this: it was merely Lambie Crump's preferred route to the outside world from his flat. 'Off to breakfast, probably. And then to shoot things.'

It was with a feeling of real achievement that Amiss left Ricketts, who had taken only half an hour of reassurance to come to terms with this new dispensation, and set off to the Monday morning editorial conference to which Lambie Crump had graciously invited him.

Henry Potbury, looking sober, was already there, as were Wilfred Parry and Phoebe Somerfield. During the next few minutes there trickled in a well-known philosopher of extreme right-wing views, a backbench Tory MP and notorious gossip who specialized in writing amusingly of the vulgarities of his colleagues, and a very young woman who was simultaneously so good-looking and clever and had a mind so well furnished as to make Amiss feel old and jealous.

The main subject was law and order and disagreement was profound, though expressed with extreme courtesy: opinions ranged between those of relative moderation (zero tolerance of crime, more rigorous discipline in schools, boot camps) to those of the philosopher, who was keen for the reintroduction of the stocks, as well as corporal and capital punishment. Lambie Crump sat there with an urbane smile and for most purposes let them fight it out. At the end, he summed up fluently enough and went for the middle path. However much one might abhor the New Labour government, he announced, the fact was that on this issue they were making sense and should be encouraged. Miss Somerfield was charged with writing the leader.

Amiss enjoyed himself. The proceedings reminded him of evenings at Oxford when the more pretentious of his colleagues began showing off in the Junior Common Room. With the exception of the philosopher, who indulged in an anti-immigrant rant, and Henry Potbury, who got angry about some misdemeanor of the foreign secretary's, he detected little passion among the participants. Phoebe Somerfield spoke only to skewer flights of fancy with well-aimed statistics, while the others seemed happily engaged in a familiar intellectual exercise: they fenced with each other and occasionally scored a point, but for most purposes they were almost in a 'Look-at-us-aren't-we-clever?' conspiracy.

At midday Tozer arrived with champagne and the meeting broke up. The Tory MP disappeared with Henry Potbury; Phoebe Somerfield, who seemed to have been allocated at least a third of the work, scuttled off, while the others stood round sipping and gossiping. Amiss was introduced to Clement Webber, the philosopher, and the clever and beautiful Amaryllis Vercoe. When Webber heard the word 'manager', he gazed at Amiss incredulously and said, 'So they're letting the technicians in now.' Unable to think of an appropriate reply, Amiss decided to leave. As he opened the door, he heard Amaryllis Vercoe asking, 'Where's Dwight?' and Lambie Crump replying shortly that he was damned if he knew.

Amiss headed for the administration corridor, knocked on the first door and followed the instruction to enter.

'May I introduce myself?'

The circulation manager, who was listlessly opening a pile of envelopes with a silver paperknife, looked up and smiled wanly. 'Come in.'

He put down the knife, winced, extended his arm to its full length and opened and shut his fist a couple of times.

Amiss stood in front of his desk. 'You're George Naggiar, aren't you? I'm Robert Amiss. Just starting today as manager.'

Naggiar pushed back his chair and stood up gingerly. As he straightened himself he emitted an 'ouch', inhaled sharply through his teeth and grimaced with pain. 'Sorry. Knee's bad today.'

Amiss put out his hand, but Naggiar shook his head. 'Afraid I can't shake hands. Bit of a problem with my right arm. But do sit down.'

Amiss looked at the solitary chair, whose seat was covered with envelopes. Naggiar waved at it carelessly. 'Just put the stuff on the floor.'

Amiss obeyed, sat down and contemplated his host, who with another grimace resumed his seat.

'I was sorry to miss you on Friday when Mr Lambie Crump took me around to perform the introductions,' said Amiss.

'Yes, that was too bad. I was at the hospital.'

'Your knee or your arm?' asked Amiss sympathetically.

Naggiar looked amused. 'Oh, no. Neither of those on Friday. That was my ulcer. It was playing up a bit and I had to talk to the consultant about whether we should go for laser treatment. But he reckons I should play it carefully, not exert myself too much, avoid anything stressful and it'll settle itself down again.'

'Sounds sensible.'

'So what will you be doing?' asked Naggiar, valiantly trying to keep the boredom out of his voice.

'Taking some of the burden off Mr Lambie Crump and I hope off some of the rest of you. But initially I'll just be listening: I don't want to be precipitate, so I thought that for the moment I'd spend a week or so getting some kind of grip on how the place runs.'

'Runs? It doesn't really run. It just jogs along.'

'I'd appreciate knowing how, though.'

'What do you want to know?'

'Well, for instance, I'd be grateful if you could take me through the methods by which you persuade people to become subscribers, to renew their subscriptions, how you deal with complaints procedures and all that sort of thing.'

Naggiar looked at him in some bewilderment. 'We don't solicit subscribers. This is a journal with a sense of its own dignity. We simply make it possible for people to subscribe if they wish. As you will see in *The Wrangler*, there is a form they can fill in and send to me; then they will be sent the journal. But we don't go in for . . . marketing ourselves.'

Amiss tried not to look incredulous. 'Fine, fine. I understand. But for a start if you could just show me how those who do apply are dealt with, it would help.'

Naggiar looked at his watch. 'Can't be today, I'm afraid. Got to go to my chiropractor.'

'For your knee?'

He laughed scornfully. 'Nothing he can do for my knee – not for either knee, if it comes to that. They're like the dark side of the moon, my knees, my consultant says. All pitted and scarred. When they get really bad the only thing for them is bed rest. No, it's for my back that I have to go to the chiropractor.' He moved his shoulders about a bit and winced. 'Otherwise I'd be a cripple.'

'So you'll be out for a couple of hours?'

Naggiar looked surprised. 'No, no. I go at lunchtime and can't get back. He's an hour and a half away, my chiropractor.'

'Isn't that very inconvenient for you?'

Naggiar shrugged. 'What can you do? When you find someone who understands you who then moves, you've no choice but to follow. But tomorrow will be all right.'

'Shall I drop in about' – Amiss hazarded a guess – 'nine-thirty?'

Naggiar laughed derisively. 'How can I get in at nine-thirty? I can't travel in rush hour. Standing's terrible for my knees. Ten-thirty's more realistic.'

'Fine,' said Amiss. 'Thank you very much, I'll be here.'

Scudmore was a different proposition altogether. 'Delighted to see you, my boy,' he said as he bounded around the desk emitting bonhomie from every pore. 'Delighted to see some young blood come into this place for once. Could do with a bit of company.' He jabbed Amiss in the ribs. 'Take a drink, do you?'

'Oh yes. Frequently.'

'Man after my own heart, eh what?' Scudmore looked at his watch. 'Fancy a noggin this lunchtime?'

'Thanks very much. Could we perhaps combine it with work? I'm rather anxious to find out about the advertising department.'

Scudmore emitted a jolly laugh. 'Department? I'm the department.' He thumped his chest. 'I think I can truly say that every ad we get in this place is as a result of my work and my work alone. I can tell you nobody's ever lunched for *The Wrangler* the way I have.' His laugh boomed out again. 'Tell you what. Why don't I show you how it's done? We'll go off to one of my regular haunts and see if we can see any of the boys.'

'What are all these?' asked Rachel, pointing to the pile of books beside Amiss's armchair. She removed herself from his embrace and took off her coat.

'Newspaper histories culled from the London Library.'

'You *are* taking this seriously, aren't you? So how were your first days? Sorry I wasn't here.'

'Interesting and complicated. Tell you over dinner. Meanwhile, how did you and the minister get on in Brussels?'

'Apart from the fact that he misread his brief at a crucial moment and almost gave the Commission a concession that would have added another ten million quid a year to our contribution, it went fine. He's quite good company really when he gets off his high horse. And he is serious about what he believes in.'

'You've found an idealistic politician? Come now, Rach, are you losing your marbles?'

'They're not all the same,' she said stiffly, then looked at her watch. 'God. It's eight o'clock already. Is there anything to eat?'

'Yes,' said Amiss smugly. 'One advantage of this job is that pretty well everyone buggers off early so I can do shopping. Come on into the kitchen, have a gin and tonic and I'll put on the steak.'

'It's incredible,' Rachel said later, as he poured out the last of the wine. 'Lord whatshisname must be mad to have allowed it to go on like that. How could he?'

'He's no more reason than anyone else to realize how time has moved on. Now I am rather more in touch with the modern world than Lord Papworth, and I grasped these guys were throwbacks, but it wasn't actually until I settled down and read and skimmed a few newspaper histories that I realized to what extent *The Wrangler* was out of its time.'

'But I thought you'd already read its history.'

'*The Wrangler* history was written by the sort of person who believes anyone to do with administration is below stairs and beneath contempt; it concentrated wholly on editorial. You wouldn't have known that the paper couldn't have come out without the assistance of printers, distributors, advertisers or anyone else. As Lambie Crump observed to me more than once: "The management people are a race apart." And that editorial cast of mind explains why they've been left quietly to rot for decades, and to preserve – as if in aspic – most of the methods of the nineteen thirties.'

He leaned back in his chair. 'Take Scudmore, for instance. He learned his craft at the feet of one of the greatest advertising canvassers of the nineteen thirties, who picked up advertisements in the manner of the time by spending hours in City pubs buying drinks for those who bought space in which to publish their company results.

'He later graduated to chatting up advertising agencies as they blossomed, and taking the odd mate to dinner. But these days there's much more to this job than bonhomie. You have to be able to answer the questions that all these thrusting young advertising executives ask about the age profile and class breakdown of the readership. That requires scientific questionnaires and all sorts of balls-aching marketing techniques which – needless to say – have never been tried out on *Wrangler* subscribers. So Scudmore gets ads only for old times' sake, or because some enterprising person actually beats on the door begging to be allowed to insert an ad – for port or cashmere scarves or handmade shoes – that might be expected to appeal to fogeys.

'It was really sad on Monday with poor old Scudmore. He took me to a wine bar and explained proudly it was the haunt of the Perkins Telford and AJD Advertising Agency. But only one person spoke to him. The place was entirely full of people sitting around drinking designer water and stabbing at the odd leaf of arugula.

'Such people look at Scudmore and they see a boozy old remnant of the bad old days when people tottered back to work slightly pissed, making decisions that were based on friendship and sentiment rather than greed. These guys don't drink any more: cocaine is in, alcohol is out and with it people like Scudmore. My job – if you'll forgive me sounding like one of those prats – is to ensure that *The Wrangler* doesn't go the same way.'

'It doesn't sound as if it deserves to survive,' she said. 'If it wasn't that you need the job and we need the income, I'd probably hope you fail.'

Amiss felt suddenly depressed.

7

It was five o'clock on Thursday evening, *The Wrangler* had gone to press and Amiss was bored. He decided to investigate Henry Potbury, who welcomed him with a big smile.

'Come in, my dear chap. Sit yourself down and let us have a tincture. Would you be so kind as to fetch the bottle from that cupboard beside you?'

Amiss opened the doors and looked with respect at the array of bottles within. He reckoned there must have been a couple of dozen, including, at first glance, gin, sherry, vodka, port and several kinds of whisky. 'Which bottle would you like?'

'Would Scotch suit you?'

'Admirably,' said Amiss, as he passed the bottle across the desk. 'But I'll have just a small one, Mr Potbury.'

'Henry, please. And forgive me, but I don't know your name. Or even, come to think of it, who you are.'

'Robert Amiss. I've been brought in as manager. You might have seen me at the Monday meeting.'

'Of course, of course. I do apologize. I fear that age, drink and New Labour have taken their toll.' Potbury bellowed with laughter, half filled two tumblers and handed one to Amiss, who poured water to the top of the glass and sipped the mixture gingerly.

'Of course, I remember your face from the Monday meeting, but we weren't introduced properly. So welcome to *The Wrangler* and all that.' He waved his glass jovially. 'What exactly are you here to do?'

Amiss spared him the knowledge that he had been too

pissed on the previous Friday to remember their first meeting and instead went patiently through his patter.

'Can I be of any help? I fear I know little of the other side of things here. All I do is churn out words.'

'You could tell me something of the ethos of the paper,' said Amiss artlessly. 'Like our relations with the government, for instance. Are we just implacably opposed because they're Labour?'

'No, no, dear boy. We always hated Labour – as, of course, we hated socialists in general – but we hate New Labour even more.'

'Because?'

'Because it's like having Gladstone back.' Potbury's great eyebrows moved to meet each other, giving to his face a look of deep dejection. 'Sanctimonious, high-minded bull-shit, inimical to everything that makes life worth living. It's going to be the most depressing government we've had for a hundred and ten years.'

'Wasn't the post-war Labour government a bit like that? And come on, Henry, surely Mrs Thatcher was as high-minded and censorious as they come.'

'It's different now, my boy. Of course Old Labour could be priggish; I admit that under Maggie there was precious little sense of *joie de vivre*; and when it came to sanctimoniousness the Liberals always used to win hands down. But New Labour combine all the worst of all of them. They sit there in their fastnesses in Hampstead and Islington drizzling their extra virgin olive oil and balsamic vinegar over their radiccio, planning to meet up in Tuscany during the summer and instructing all the rest of us how to behave.'

'Not too different from Thatcher when it comes to core values, though?'

'Oh yes, I grant you that. She was big on duty and respon-sibility and industriousness too. But she had been brought up to these values and believed them. This crew have adopted them as election-winning rhetoric to cover the hollowness of their centre. And what's more, the old girl was a lot more tolerant than this lot. Always forgave the womanizers, the drunks and didn't grudge her husband his gin.' He drained his glass. 'For heaven's sake, Maggie didn't marry a puritan. All these New Labour buggers marry mirror images of themselves. And it's almost required of them that they mix only with their own kind. We've got the narrowest ruling elite we've ever had.'

'But they're quite an efficient government in many ways, Henry.'

'Efficient? I don't care about efficiency. Hitler was efficient. What I want is a government that leaves us alone.'

'Surely . . .' interjected Amiss.

Potbury raised a fat hand. 'I know what you're going to say. You're going to say that under Maggie the nanny state extended its grip, but I would say to you the difference between her and Tony Blair is that she didn't want it to. She was trapped by forces like the EU which even she could not control, yet she truly wanted to roll back the frontiers of the state. God help us, if we hadn't had her, things would have been infinitely worse.'

He gazed at Amiss indignantly. 'Who are these buggers, anyway? And what have any of them ever done? They're all career politicians. Except of course the countless lawyers that infest their ranks.' He paused for effect and then said with deliberation. 'There is no lower form of life.'

'Henry, what have you ever done other than be a journalist?'

'Ah ha, a fair point, my boy, a fair point. I have never been anything other than a hack. However, I will plead in mitigation that I've never claimed that my calling is a glorious one and I have never condemned the sins of others – only their lack of intellectual rigour.'

'And sanctimoniousness,' said Amiss mildly.

'Oh, of course I have to condemn the puritan sins.' Potbury began to get agitated. 'Because puritan sins are by definition totalitarian. Puritans don't understand the concept of "live and let live". They're meddlers, all of them. Whereas all we want is to be left alone to go to hell in our own way.'

*   *   *

An hour later, after the conclusion of the tirade against liberalism that had followed the diatribe against puritanism, Amiss decided to tear himself away. As he stood up, Potbury, by now in high good humour, chuckled. 'Whatever you do, don't miss next Monday's meeting.'

Amiss sat down again.

'Why not?'

'Winterton's back.'

'The assistant editor? What's so significant about that?'

'He and Willie loathe each other.'

'But why then did Willie give him the job?'

'He was his protégé initially. Fetch another bottle, will you?'

Amiss did so guiltily. 'Here you are, Henry. But don't pour me any until I've checked at home. Hang on one minute. Don't lose your thread.'

Having learned from his answering service to his mingled relief and regret that Rachel was working late, he accepted another whisky. 'OK, Henry. Tell me all about it.'

'It is not unamusing, really.' Potbury snorted. 'On Willie's last trip to the States he came back raving about this brilliant young man whom he just had to have to liven up the political coverage. He would pay for himself as he'd be able to write so much on American as well as domestic politics that we could cut down on the freelancers.

'Dwight Winterton was a paragon, and a really useful paragon at that. He was one of those hybrids, half English and half American, brought up in the States but with frequent visits to Europe, went to Harvard and was then a Rhodes scholar at Oxford. Hugely well informed about politics and history. Right little prodigy, in fact. And nice, with it. I think Willie saw him as someone who could succeed me when I fall down the stairs or get cirrhosis of the liver or come to some other discreditable end.' He laughed.

'So?'

'It's been a disaster.'

'Why. Is he not as bright as Willie thought?'

'Oh, yes. He's hugely bright. Mad, of course, like most

44

young right-wingers, wanting to stuff children back up chimneys, start a preemptive war against Germany, and take back India with ten battalions. All that sort of thing. But that's all right. He's young. He'll settle.'

'So are their differences political?'

'No. It's just that they hate each other.'

'Why?'

'They're a bit like a couple who had a one-night stand, flew to Las Vegas the following day to get married and found two days later not only that they were incompatible in their habits but that they hated each other's values, and what's more, he just wanted her for sex and she just wanted him for money.'

'That's an arrangement that I understood quite often worked – for short periods anyway.'

'Not as short as this one,' said Henry with a snort. 'Dwight Winterton arrived to a hero's welcome and within a fortnight they were fighting like cat and dog at the Monday meeting.

'Essentially, Dwight quickly discovered that Willie is a self-indulgent poseur and Willie discovered that Winterton despised him and would like his job. And if there is one kind of person Willie can't stand, it's someone bright who wants to be editor of *The Wrangler*.'

He paused and contemplated what was left in his glass. 'It's compounded by the fact that Dwight has principles and Willie has none, and because Willie, though he's lazy, is pernickety, and Dwight, though he's industrious, is slapdash. So Willie has countless opportunities to niggle and patronize and worst of all rewrite, which Dwight absolutely hates.

'And then Willie is driven mad by Dwight's habit of going AWOL because he's decided to go off and see what Yorkshire or Northern Ireland are like. Willie resents this because he rightly fears that Dwight is building up a network and is growing in authority, but he can't stop him because Dwight doesn't even claim expenses. He's got private money. So since Dwight gets the work done, Willie has no ground on which to fight.'

'Can't Willie just fire him?'

'Dwight might sue. He *is* American, after all. And I doubt if Willie would have the trustees on his side if it came to a showdown. To do my colleagues justice . . .'

'Your colleagues?'

'Yes. Didn't you know? I'm a trustee. It's one of the reasons Willie puts up with me. The other two are a couple of pompous old Establishment bores, but they do believe in fair play and though they're often taken in by Willie, he knows he'd have a lot of explaining to do if he sacked a brilliant and prolific journalist. And of course, knowing this, Dwight goes ever more his own way and grins as Willie squirms. Willie is left with petulance as almost his only weapon.'

Amiss began to feel rather gloomy. 'Are you telling me that Willie's no good?'

'Willie could have been good, but he chose otherwise. Essentially, early on he gave up on intellectual rigour and integrity. He can write elegantly, I grant you, and his mind is at least half furnished. But when it comes to the crunch, duchesses and cabinet ministers will always take precedence over truth. Hence *The Wrangler*'s line on New Labour: it attacks because it has to, but as far as Willie can fix it, attacks in ways that do not wound.'

'But I've seen some pretty ferocious criticism in recent months, Henry.'

'Ah yes, but never by Willie. Willie can always flutter his hands at the Downing Street would-be press censors and tell them that I cannot be controlled, so it's not his fault. But if you look at anything he writes you'll find that more and more those he criticizes in New Labour are those our new rulers are happy to see thrown to the wolves. And as far as possible, depending what his colleagues will put up with, he tries to make the anonymous leaders as inoffensive as possible.

'In his heart and in his soul Willie Lambie Crump is an apparatchik who would love to drag this journal towards total support of the government of Anthony Blair. However, I will continue to make this as difficult for him as I can.'

'Is it just you against him?'

'Phoebe follows the party line because she has little choice.

She would not be listened to, even though she has one of the best brains we've had since the war. Amaryllis Vercoe is bright and thinks like us, but she's rather shallow, and anyway, has little clout with Willie. Clement Webber shouts a lot and then goes back to Oxford. So apart from me, the challenge is coming from Dwight, who is everything Willie is not: intellectually curious, vigorous, original and energetic. Dwight will make imaginative and intellectual leaps into the unknown, yet he retains an instinctive understanding of the essence of the Burkean conservative. Willie skims along the surface: Dwight dives underneath it.'

He poured another slug of whisky, and ignoring Amiss's shake of the head, poured some into his glass too. 'If things get worse, I'll have to try and topple Willie: we've got to get back to the glory days when *The Wrangler* thrilled with iconoclasm and intellectual daring.'

'You're actually trying to bring about a change of editor?'

'It's too early yet, but I'm considering future steps.'

Amiss cursed inwardly when the phone rang.

'What? Now? Already?' Potbury looked at his watch. 'My dear, I do apologize. You're absolutely right. I was caught in an agreeable conversation and quite forgot where I was. I shall see you as soon as I can get to you.' Downing his whisky, he lumbered to his feet. 'Forgive me . . . I'm sorry, but I've forgotten your name again.'

'Robert.'

'Forgive me, Robert. I'm delighted you've joined us and I look forward to many more conversations in this room and elsewhere. Drop in any time and if I'm asleep wake me up.' He grinned, and stopping only to pick up the jacket that lay in the corner, left with more speed than Amiss would have given him credit for.

Petulance was much in evidence at the meeting next Monday. Gone was the harmony of the previous week, when the emperor Lambie Crump had held forth when he wished and enjoyed the intellectual ping-pong played by the others when he wanted a rest. The offender was the weedy, bespectacled, impish Dwight Winterton, who gazed innocently at Lambie Crump as he artlessly explained that the sweeping statement he had just made about the French economy had no basis in reality and was totally contradicted by what he, Winterton, had picked up on his visit the previous week to his French stockbroking chum.

Later, Winterton broke into an excited account of his visit to a Welsh eisteddfod, described how he had been made an honorary Druid, and produced an article he had written at the weekend. Lambie Crump clearly ached to tell him to stuff it, but decorum and self-protection had to prevail. Winterton's account had been so amusing that no one in his right mind could think of denying it to *Wrangler* readers. To Amiss, who was getting sicker of Lambie Crump's self-regarding posturings by the day, it was as much as he could do to keep a straight face.

When afterwards, Dwight Winterton chatted to him in a friendly way over champagne and suggested lunch or dinner sometime, Amiss realized he must be careful. He could see Lambie Crump gazing fixedly over at them. 'Good to meet you, Dwight,' he said quickly. 'Let's talk soon.' And pausing only to curry favour with Lambie Crump by asking if he could spare some time later on to give him a word of advice, he headed for the door. As he was leaving, Potbury caught his eye and gave him an enormous wink, which Amiss prayed Lambie Crump had not noticed.

8

Detective Sergeant Ellis Pooley finished his cheese, placed his knife in the centre of the plate, picked a few crumbs off the tablecloth, dropped them beside the knife and took another small sip of claret. 'Very nice indeed. Thank you very much.'

He looked around the room appreciatively. 'I must say, Rachel, how delighted I am to see Robert at last living in a place that is both clean and comfortable. You've had a most civilizing effect on him.'

'Suburbanizing, you mean,' said Amiss, and then caught himself guiltily. 'Sorry, Rach. You know I didn't mean that.'

'I'm not so sure you didn't.' Rachel collected the plates and carried them over to the sink. 'There are moments, Ellis, when I fear that whether he knows it or not, deep down Robert is bored. Life's too straightforward for him.'

'For goodness sake.' Pooley sounded irritated. 'Ever since I first met you, Robert, you've been wailing because you didn't like where you lived or you didn't have a proper job or Rachel was out of reach or you didn't have a penny. Do you mean that now you haven't any of those problems you're looking for new ones?'

Amiss interrupted hastily. 'Rachel's exaggerating. Everything's fine.' He scratched his ear. 'I suppose I could just do with a little bit more excitement at work.'

'Being manager of such a peculiar institution as *The Wrangler* sounds pretty interesting.'

'It is, but in many respects, rather lacking in challenge. A journal as small as that shouldn't need someone like me.'

'Well, why have they got you then?'

'Because things are in such a mess that they need me. Another proprietor would bring in accountants and management consultants. This one's too gentlemanly for that. My job is simply to do accountants' and consultants' dirty work in a gentlemanly manner.'

Pooley looked at him dubiously. 'But you're absolutely useless with money.'

'I'm useless,' said Amiss stiffly, 'with *my* money. But while I may be personally profligate, I am capable of exercising prudence and perspicacity . . .' He stopped. 'What a lot of "ps".'

'Try adding "pompous",' suggested Rachel.

Amiss ignored her. '. . . when I'm dealing with that of others. I'll have you know I've cut costs substantially without firing people or lowering morale.'

Pooley looked incredulous. 'I didn't think such a thing was possible.'

'When you go into a place that is still operating according to the customs and practices of the nineteen thirties that is not too difficult. For instance, simply by spending a few hundred pounds on a fax machine I've saved us a fortune.'

Pooley looked puzzled.

'Ah, I forgot this was going to take a leap of the imagination.' Amiss rose and thoughtfully began to open another bottle of claret. 'Picture if you will –' he said, having tried and failed to persuade his friend to accept a refill, 'an office in which the most modern piece of equipment is a stout manual typewriter manufactured in nineteen sixty-seven, the telephones are splendid nineteen thirties Bakelite models with circular dials and the filing cabinets are ancient and wooden and creak a lot and are jammed with yellowing dusty files so tightly packed that it requires exceptional strength to get anything in or out. Indeed, Marcia Whitaker, who is *inter alia* a fact-checker, has biceps that put me to shame.

'In the midst of this, Josiah Ricketts, who is known as the office clerk, conducts his business along the lines that he was taught when recruited in the nineteen forties by one Albert Flitter, who had joined the paper as an office boy in nineteen fifteen, had risen to the giddy heights of office manager and had a deep reverence for doing things the way the ladies and gentlemen had liked them.

'True, the phones were slightly modernized, admittedly, Ricketts was prevailed upon to allow senior members of staff to have one each and when equipment like the typewriter collapsed did perforce purchase a more or less up-to-date model, but "newfangled" was a dirty word, so with anything newfangled, Ricketts would not have to do. And the idle sods of editors couldn't be bothered intervening.'

'Goodness,' said Pooley, absentmindedly holding out his glass for a refill. 'But how do they communicate with printers and the rest of it?'

'Essentially by recreating the postal system of long ago through the use of couriers. Until after the war, Ricketts explained to me nostalgically, it used to be possible for a contributor to post his copy at nine o'clock in the evening. It would be on the desk of the editor at eight the following morning, amendments were sent to the printers by the nine o'clock post, received by them at midday and the proof would be with the contributor by late afternoon. The major concession since then has been that the proofreader-cum-fact-checker, Ben Baines, is also available to take copy over the phone.'

'Come on,' said Pooley, 'you're not seriously telling me that contributors are prepared to put up with having to read their stuff out loud rather than send a fax.'

'Listen, Ellis, I don't think you understand the status of *The Wrangler*. They pay contributors a pittance, but in fact have no need to pay them at all. Politicians and journalists would pay to be published in *The Wrangler* because of the lustre of the name and the fact that anyone who is anyone on the Right has been reading it for almost two centuries. All this daftness merely adds to its appeal.'

'What made anyone choose you to modernize this outfit? I mean, dammit, you're a technological moron.'

'By the standards of *The Wrangler*, I'm right at the cutting edge of technology. They don't want somebody like you, Ellis, with your Internet and websites and access to ninety-five billion pieces of worthless information that you waste your time over. They want somebody to take them by the hand slowly and gently and lead them into the mid-twentieth century. It is my skills as a communicator that are enabling me tenderly to make Marcia, Ben and the rest of the staff love gentle change. The proprietor wants to reduce his losses – not give his paper a corporate nervous breakdown.

'I've taken as my motto a cartoon I once saw of a demonstration by the Moderate Party, who were marching down the street chanting, "What do we want? Gradual change. When do we want it? In due course."'

The doorbell rang loudly and did not stop. As Amiss ran to answer it, Rachel put her hand to her head. 'Does she have to do that?'

'No,' said Pooley. 'But she always does.'

'I quite like Jack,' said Rachel, 'but sometimes I wonder why.'

The baroness entered at speed, pulled off her black cloak and threw it into the corner. Rachel stood up, retrieved it and went out and hung it up in the hall.

'What's the matter with that girl?' asked the baroness. 'She's not on duty now. I'm not a foreigner. Rachel! Rachel! Stop fussing around and come back here.'

Pausing only to clap Pooley hard on the back, she fell into the chair beside him. 'What have you had to eat?'

'Cassoulet,' said Amiss.

'And very good it was too,' observed Pooley.

'Thank you,' said Rachel as she returned and nodded at her visitor. 'There's plenty left, Jack. Want some?'

'Is it made with goose fat?'

'We're not telling you,' said Amiss. 'Do you want some or not?'

'Not. I had the fattest of fat lunches today, so I'll settle for claret and cheese. What have you got?'

'Since I knew you might drop in, I trekked off to the health food shop and bought extremely aged organically produced cheddar.'

'Hmmmm. I'll give it a try. How old's the claret?'

'Nineteen ninety-four.'

'That's so young, drinking it's almost child abuse.'

'Jack, I don't give a fuck if you eat and drink nothing. Yes or no to the claret.'

'I suppose I'll have to make do.'

She gazed at her companions. 'What's the matter? Why are you so quiet?'

'Because you're so noisy,' said Pooley. 'It's good to see you, Jack. Now listen to Robert's account of how he's modernizing *The Wrangler*.'

'God, how boring. You make him sound like one of those dreary ministers who keep telling us to shape up for the new millennium.'

She took a draught of wine, smacked her lips and greedily tucked into the cheese. 'Not bad. All right, then. Get on with it.'

Amiss gave her a two-paragraph update and continued. 'So my approach is to make progress by gentleness and stealth. I've only been there two months and already the staff have come to terms with a simple photocopying machine, a fax and an efficient, up-to-date and cheap telephone system. I've changed nothing that didn't absolutely have to be changed, their jobs are made easier and I've persuaded them that they are being freed from drudgery to concentrate on more important areas such as – in the case of Ben and Marcia – making the journal ever more accurate.'

'That's all very well, but so far you can't even have saved enough to pay your own salary,' pointed out Pooley.

'I've saved it three times over already just by getting rid of the supervisor and four of the five typists (or typewriters, as the editor calls them), giving the other one a simple word processor that she loves as intensely as Adam did his liddle mop in *Cold Comfort Farm* and persuading Sabrina Trustler-Stomp – '

'Who?'

'Sabrina Trustler-Stomp, who works for Lambie Crump. I've been told he's never had a secretary who was not well in with the aristocracy and had at least a double-barrelled name. Anyway, I took Sabrina out for a jolly dinner one evening and persuaded her that her life would be more rewarding if she learned a) to type and b) to use a computer. She isn't with us much, having a contract that allows her time off for Ascot, Henley and God knows what, but now, when she's around, she helps out quite enthusiastically. Thinks it's all ever so much fun.'

'But you got rid of the old ladies. I thought there were to be no redundancies.'

'They were all happy to leave, being in their seventies and hanging on there really out of a sense of duty, knowing they were the only people left in London who knew how to use manual typewriters and carbon paper and who didn't mind retyping the same document with amendments fifteen times over, which, with all the staff wrangling about changes in the articles, often happened: with a word processor, four or five hours can be saved. So I wooed them with soft words and a generous pay-off. Miss Grumshaw, the supervisor, told me she'd been putting off her retirement for years because no one else could have done her job.'

Rachel knew the story and was thinking of something else, but the others were rapt. 'Bugger me,' said the baroness. 'This makes me look like Bill Gates.' She seized the bottle and poured claret into her own glass. Pointedly, but without her noticing, Amiss topped up everyone else's.

'Then, too, there was the little matter of keeping a master-list of subscribers without ever bothering to check on expiry dates. Every month subscribers were asked to renew their subscriptions if they had run out and were relied upon to be efficient, honest and loyal enough to send money if it was owed. As a guess, I think we've been giving away at least three thousand free subscriptions a year.'

'This is ridiculous, Robert,' said Pooley. 'You must be making it up. Just because the methods were old-fashioned doesn't have to mean that they were completely incompetent.'

'They were. We had a labour-intensive, out-of-date system

combined with administrative incompetence of a kind which the civil service never dreamed of.'

'I doubt that,' said Pooley loftily.

'You've got a nerve,' said the baroness indignantly. 'I knew halfwits in the civil service, but they were never as thick as cops. What about the antiquated filing methods that allowed the Yorkshire Ripper to run amok with impunity for so long?'

'I've been daring enough to get a computer into the subscription department,' went on Amiss. 'Young Jason mastered it within a few days. So now he's happy and the savings are spectacular. Naggiar, the subscriptions manager, doesn't give a toss as long as he's allowed to go on doing buggerall.'

'Any cigars?' enquired the baroness.

'No.'

'Pity.' She felt around in a pocket, extracted pipe and tobacco and began to fill the one with the other.

'Advertising was a bigger struggle. Scudmore is a nice man but as much as a disaster as the malingering Naggiar and much harder to do anything about. It was my good fortune that he collapsed with a heart attack four weeks ago and will not be back. I brought in someone at a third of the salary, who doubled the advertising in his first month.'

As the baroness lit an enormous lighter and aimed it at her tobacco, Pooley hastily moved his chair a couple of feet away. She sucked noisily for a few moments, grunted with satisfaction and then looked up at Amiss. 'Well, I'll say for you, my lad, that you've certainly followed to the ultimate the great old precept that the way to be a success is to succeed a failure. What more has to be done before you put yourself out of business?'

'Plenty, but I won't bore you with an accounts clerk who thinks it impertinent to ask anyone for a receipt, or a system of perks that ensures that no journalist ever travels other than first class – even by air – not to speak of the editor's habit of hiring a first-class cook and butler several times a week to entertain people to what he calls luncheon, or even the distinguished wine cellar which is augmented annually to the tune of five or ten thou a year.'

'How soon can I come to lunch?' asked the baroness.

'I'll ask Willie and ring you tomorrow: he's been at me to ask you. But are you sure you can put up with him for the sake of the food?'

'I want to meet him properly.'

'Why?' asked Amiss suspiciously.

'Never you mind. Now, have there been any mutterings against you yet?'

'Most of them realize they're lucky not to have got some ghastly whizz-kid intent on wholesale revolution.'

'And the gentle owner?'

'Very happy. Since he doesn't mind losing money as long as it doesn't run into six figures, I've already exceeded his expectations. Indeed, he gave me a pay rise the other week.'

'But no contract,' said Rachel.

'It wasn't appropriate to ask, Rach. You know that.'

'You haven't dealt with the really crucial problem yet,' said the baroness.

'What's that?' asked Pooley.

'Willie Crump's lack of intellectual rigour.'

'Jesus, Jack. That isn't part of my job description.'

'Well, you must make it so.'

'You should talk to Henry Potbury. He goes on about that a lot.'

'He's right. *The Wrangler* is too valuable to be allowed to coast. That young whatshisname . . .'

'Dwight Winterton?'

'Yes. He's OK. And Potbury when he's good is good. But I'm worried that there's a loss of direction. If you ask me, Willie Crump's sucking up to New Labour.'

'You might be right. He's been shifting ground. There have been a lot of fights about that.'

'Willie isn't going to stay in the wilderness for perhaps ten years. Courtiers need courts. And I'll bet Willie Crump wants a peerage.'

'Hadn't thought of that, Jack. You could just be right.'

'What's the circulation of *The Wrangler* anyway?' asked Pooley.

'Only about thirty thousand. I want to have a modest advertising campaign but Willie thinks that would be vulgar. "We speak to the *crème de la crème*" he explained. "We have no need of the rest." As indeed he doesn't, while Papworth foots the bill. But I have no remit to do anything about this. Henry's doing what he can to work on him.'

'I know Henry Potbury,' said the baroness. 'Knew him well at one time. Had a bit of a fling, indeed. He'll never be able to do anything now. Past it. So you'll have to.'

'I can't.'

'Then I may have to myself. Someone has to challenge this bloody government.'

'Don't you dare get involved.'

'Try stopping me,' said the baroness.

'Disaffected.'

'What?' said Pooley, who was nervously watching the road. 'Who? Which?'

'Rachel. Didn't you notice?'

'No.' Pooley winced as the baroness accelerated through a changing traffic light. 'I think everything's going terribly well for them both. It's very encouraging that Robert's got a real job and is taking it seriously and Rachel's doing so well . . .'

'Ellis Pooley, are you blind or just so crazed with lust for Mary Lou Denslow that you can't see what's happening to our friends?'

'Well, what do you think is happening?'

'Rachel's become too serious for him. You mark my words, she wants somebody who's going to make a name for himself and forge a brilliant career and all those other things. She doesn't want a drifter.'

'He's not drifting any more. Surely that's the point. He's enjoying sorting out this mad disorder . . .'

'And will be bored when order's been restored; then he'll want to move on.'

'But surely he'll be able to get a much bigger job then? Can't he progress to managing something much more important?'

'He won't be interested in that, Ellis. If all he wanted was a sensible challenging job with career prospects he would have gone back into the civil service ages ago.' The tyres screeched as she cornered sharply. Pooley pretended not to notice.

'The fact is that he's developed a taste for the bizarre and the macabre and by now is about as inclined towards a steady career as was Phillip Marlowe. The best hope is that fans of his like me and Charlie Papworth and Bertie Ormerod keep spreading the word and finding him a never-ending supply of disaster zones to home in on.'

'You've worried me, Jack. You've really worried me. I was hopeful.'

'For heaven's sake, Ellis, why do you want Robert to turn into everybody else? I've always known this about him. He grumbles about his life and deludes himself he wants to live sensibly, but he's always going to want adventure. And that doesn't suit Rachel. Her patience is already wearing thin.'

'I hope you're wrong. I want Robert to be settled and happy.'

'I want him to be interested,' said the baroness. 'That's what makes him happy. And as for you' – she turned and looked at him – 'the sooner you go off with Mary Lou for a long, long idyll of madness and passion, the better.'

The look of embarrassment on Pooley's face as he contemplated this prospect made her rock with laughter so vigorously that she almost drove the car off the road.

9

Henry Potbury's bulbous face peered around Amiss's door. 'A word with you, my dear chap.'

'Of course, Henry.'

Amiss installed Potbury in the leather armchair. 'Coffee? I'm afraid I've nothing stronger.'

'No, no, my dear chap. Even I draw the line at drinking alcohol before noon.' He stopped and considered that statement. 'Well, that is, in the normal course of events I do.'

'So what's on your mind?'

'I think Willie's finally gone potty.'

'How can you tell?'

'Rang me up six sheets to the wind last night, raved at me for about five minutes about the iniquities of Dwight Winterton, whom he described as a treacherous kike, told me I was a drunken oaf and made some disparaging reference to you as the northern fellow who counts the spoons.'

'How . . . ?' asked Amiss.

Potbury snorted. 'How was I sober enough to know this? Because my ferocious Aunt Hortense was staying last night, that's why, and fear of her tongue always reduces my alcohol intake by about eighty per cent.'

'That wasn't my question. I wanted to know how you identified me as the chap who counts the spoons?'

'Because you are really when it comes to it,' said Potbury in a reasonable tone. 'Not a bad description of you, at all, if I may say so.'

'So how did you respond to all this?'

'There wasn't really time to say much. I expostulated a couple of times, but the flood just continued.'

'Doesn't sound very like Willie.'

'No, he's usually pretty ept at keeping his temper. But I'd say the general praise for that piece of Dwight's he tried to spike last week sent him to the bottle.'

'Kike's a bit much, though. I wouldn't have put him down as anti-semitic.'

'Scratch Willie and you find a shit.'

'And what had I done to upset him?'

'Oh nothing, it was just because you, along with Dwight, had had a pat on the back from m'Lud Papworth. If there's one thing Willie can't stand, it's Charlie Papworth saying anything nice about anyone else.'

'But why was he ringing you to carry on about it?'

'Who else has he got, my dear boy?'

'Mrs Willie?'

'Come on, surely you know that Mrs Willie – or rather, to be precise, the Honourable Mrs Willie – departed airhead held high several years ago because she couldn't put up with Willie's insufferable superciliousness, sexlessness and God knows what else. Knowing how loudly and widely she complained about him within the smart set, those whom he would consider eligible haven't exactly been queuing up to succeed her. It's not, after all, as if he were rich or well connected.'

'Is there no little Lambie Crump?'

Potbury shuddered. 'Oh, really. What an unpleasant thought. Can't you see it? Blond ringlets and a lace collar.' He pulled himself out of the chair. 'Drink later? Something I'd like to talk to you about at leisure. And I've got something to knock off before lunch.'

'Sure. I'll call in during the afternoon.'

A full-scale row was in progress as Amiss put his head around the door of the midden shared by Marcia and Ben.

'Rubbish, it's Robert Peel.'

'You silly old woman!' screamed Ben. 'How often do I have

to tell you your knowledge of the nineteenth century is so bloody 'opeless as to be a national scandal. That was never said by Robert fuckin' Peel. It was said twenty bleedin' years later by Benjamin shaggin' Disraeli.'

A tennis ball flew from Marcia's desk and whizzed by Ben's ear. 'You've got amnesia again, you stupid bugger.' Marcia's voice rose to a screech. 'Don't you remember in Gash's biography where it says that . . .'

Amiss was so used by now to the passion and inordinate length of these exchanges that he had learned to barge in. 'Good morning, Marcia. Good morning, Ben,' he said suavely, and the altercation stopped immediately as they greeted him warmly. He walked gingerly along the narrow path that wove between the massed paper columns. 'May I sit down?'

They nodded.

Amiss perched himself on a pile of magazines that looked solid enough to serve as a temporary seat. 'I've been thinking . . .'

They eyed him warily, but without hostility, for despite all their initial shock at the boldness of various of his past suggestions, they had come to accept that he was on their side and that the quality of their lives had improved since his arrival.

'You need more room.'

Marcia perked up considerably. 'We've always thought that. Are you thinking of giving us a bigger office?'

'Steady on, Marcia. We have to dwell in the realms of the possible. I'm just thinking of making this bigger by getting –' He stopped hastily, recognizing that he'd almost put his foot completely into it. '. . . by moving some of our archives from out of your way and hiring you some help to sort out the papers.' Drowned out by a crescendo of protest, but with a calm born of experience he sat quietly until the soprano and basso profundo drew to a close.

'I quite see what you're concerned about, and you can be sure . . .'

The phone rang and Marcia answered. 'It's Willie, Robert. He wants an urgent word.'

'Talk to you later,' said Amiss. 'And remember, there's nothing to worry about.'

61

'What do you mean, Gash?' Ben was already shouting, as Amiss opened the door. 'It's all in Blake's *Disraeli*, if you'd 'ave 'ad the wit to look at it before makin' such a prat of yourself by attributin' . . .'

Amiss closed the door softly and left them to it.

Lambie Crump looked commendably well for a man who had been at the bottle the night before. And, to Amiss's relief, he did not appear to be nurturing a grievance. In fact, he sounded ingratiating.

'Ah, Robert, how kind of you to come so quickly. You know Lady Troutbeck is coming to luncheon today?'

'Yes, indeed, Willie.'

'Alas, something has come up that makes it impossible for me to see her. Albeit it is not possible to explain what it is, it can be intimated to the baroness that the matter concerns people not a million miles removed from Downing Street.'

'Do you mean you're cancelling? She won't take that well.'

'No, no. No such thing. Just that it will be necessary for you to be the host on this occasion. And to deal with the tedious practicalities of her column.'

'What column?'

'Ah, me, one has so much on one's mind that these things sometimes slip it. Lady Troutbeck and I happily coincided at the opera the other night and agreed that she should become a columnist.'

Amiss clutched his hair. 'You cannot be serious. She's to the right of Attila the Hun.'

Lambie Crump looked at Amiss in bafflement. 'You defame a remarkable woman. The Duke of Ormerod, whom she was accompanying, told me that she is an outstanding educational thinker and has proved to be a great modernizer at St Martha's.'

'Yes, but . . .'

Lambie Crump put his palms together, rested his chin on the tips of his fingers and looked grave. 'It seems you dislike the baroness.'

'No, no. Of course not. Actually, I'm very fond of her.'

Lambie Crump sat bolt upright in his chair. 'Well then, can you enlighten one as to what particularly is perturbing you?'

'Jack Troutbeck,' said Amiss, with heavy deliberation, 'is fine in her place. By which I mean somewhere she either owns or which is big enough to accommodate her.

'At St Martha's, her benevolent tyranny has made the college a resounding success. And in the House of Lords – which has proven historically that it can cope insouciantly with even the barking mad – she causes no problems at all. I just have a feeling that involving her in an enterprise this size would be rather like inviting Moby Dick to come for a dip in one's garden pond. At the very least, you might reasonably expect a considerable amount of displacement.'

Lambie Crump had lost interest. 'Look, Robert, one is faced with this hush-hush business, and as well it's press day. You must yourself resolve your esoteric fears. Lady Troutbeck is to be a columnist – not a member of staff – so the analogy with Moby Dick does not apply. Just make sure she knows one has been called away on affairs of state. Keep her happy, tell her all she needs to know and give a gentle steer on our ethos and all that.'

Amiss rose. 'The term "gentle steer" in the context of Jack Troutbeck is singularly inappropriate. However, I will do the best I can.'

'Splendid, splendid, splendid. Just my idea of what a magazine office should be like.'

'You mean two centuries out of date.'

'I mean redolent of a great past and in no way disfigured by the fripperies of a less gracious age.' She peered at the slightly threadbare Persian rug on which Amiss had lain bleeding a few months previous. 'Ah, very good, very good. I want one of those. What's more, I would very, very much like that refectory table in place of the decrepit piece of Victoriana we have in St Martha's as our high table at present.' She sighed. 'Why can't I have everything I want?'

Amiss ignored her. 'Over there you will see a portrait of our founder.'

'Ah, splendid. Seymour Spragge himself. What an excellent old boy. I remember with keen pleasure an essay of his on the perils of paying too much heed to the clamouring of the ignorant – a subject to which I propose to address myself in a series I'm thinking of doing on why all constitutional change is bad.' She beamed. 'I'm going to enjoy being a columnist, stirring things up and getting the lefties fuming.' She put her head on one side. 'What do you think, Robert? Is this a good moment for a piece on why all liberals are boring?'

'Thanks. That includes me.'

'Not in essentials, dear boy. As you well know, you're a Tory at heart, yet you pathetically insist on draping around you the tatters of your childhood liberalism to hide the glorious body of your true faith. Now summon that chap with the champagne and show me some more defunct editors.'

'I don't think for one moment that your views will be acceptable to Willie, especially the way he's been drifting of late,' said Amiss over coffee and brandy, and in the baroness's case, a fat cigar.

'Too true. I'm going to give him a few bad nights.'

'Presumably you hid from him the fact that you're an appalling old reactionary.'

'Certainly. Once we spotted him, Bertie and I conspired to keep it quiet that I'm' – she wagged her finger at Amiss – 'a libertarian, not a reactionary. In fact, Bertie was the one who suggested the column.'

'What exactly do you mean when you say you're a libertarian?'

'That I'm in favour of people having the liberty to do anything that gives them pleasure unless it does harm to other people.'

'Hah! I've never noticed you exercising that self-denying ordinance when you're parking illicitly, throwing your weight around on motorways or generally getting your own way at other people's expense.'

The baroness smirked. 'I'm different.'

Amiss sighed. 'My philosophy of life is that once expressed by the Eton schoolteacher who on seeing a boy peeing over the gallery on to his schoolfellows below, asked: "Where would we be if every boy did that?"'

'Jolly good philosophy,' said the baroness. 'All for it. Doesn't apply to me, though. I work on the principle that the other boys won't do that, so I can.'

'So that explains why you admit to having enjoyed opium but are against legalizing drugs?'

'Exactly. I'm in favour of drugs for me because I'd know how to use them.'

'Just you?'

'Come, now. I'm not that unreasonable. People like me would be OK. But you don't think I'm in favour of making drugs available to just anybody, do you?'

'Seems rather an elitist argument?'

'Of course it's an elitist argument, you idiot. I'm an elitist.' She jabbed him in the chest. 'You're all right most of the time, Robert, but you really do have ferocious attacks of priggishness. You've been away from my direct influence for too long.'

Amiss changed tack. 'So what will the Troutbeck column be about, then? Turning the clock back at the millennium?'

'You really are too simple-minded, my boy. I'm not against change per se. Like Wellington, I believe that one has to accept it when there is no choice.' She brooded for a moment. 'Though sometimes I wonder if he wasn't perhaps a little precipitate when it came to Catholic Emancipation.'

'Oh, for God's sake, you needn't practise being preposterous on me. It's wasted.'

'You think I don't mean it, don't you?' She laughed triumphantly. 'I really do believe that all change is bad. Except, of course, when it is change I want.'

'Because what is good for you is good for the nation.'

'Precisely. You've got it in one.'

'So what will your column be recommending?'

'Oh, the usual: abolishing the blasphemy laws, legalizing

prostitution, withdrawing from the European Union, hanging on to Scotland, Wales and Northern Ireland whether they like it or not.'

'I'm surprised you don't want to take the Republic of Ireland back into the United Kingdom.'

'Oh, I'd like that ideally, of course,' she said cheerfully. 'But it's just not possible to move in and take them over these days, I'm afraid. They'd kick up a terrible fuss. Sometimes games aren't worth candles. Though it would definitely be the best for everyone. Their trains haven't run on time since we left and we need them to liven us up.'

'Will you be dealing with reform of the House of Lords?'

'Reform indeed.' She snorted. 'These buggers are trying to destroy us. Certainly I'll be touching on that. I'm thinking of leading a campaign to recapture the powers of the Lords stolen from them by Lloyd George in nineteen twelve.'

Amiss stood up. 'I think I've had as much as I can stand of your political views, Jack. And so will Willie when he sees the first column. He'll refuse to print it.'

'No, he won't. He was so besotted after the performance Bertie and I put up that he agreed to give me a free hand. We'll draw up the contract now and you can get him to sign it this afternoon.'

'He won't, if I tell him what you're really like.'

'But you won't. You'd hate to spoil the fun.'

She stubbed out her cigar and pushed back her chair. 'OK. To business.'

'How the hell will she find the time?' asked Rachel.

Amiss stopped chopping onions and laid down his knife. 'How much time do you think it takes to be a columnist?'

'I don't know, but presumably it'll take her a half day or so every week to write the article and then, of course, there's the reading and thinking time and the rest of it.'

'When I was trying to deter her I pointed that out, so she took a particular pleasure in proving me wrong. Having mentioned that Ben used to take copy before we acquired a fax, she announced breezily that she much preferred to dictate and would now do so. It was all done in twenty minutes. Of course I'd forgotten that when she was in the civil service she was notorious for dictating blistering memos off the top of her head.'

'And was it any good?'

''Fraid so. Resounding with blood and thunder at the expense of the chattering classes.' He added the onions to the contents of the pan. 'Remember, she's got enough outrageous opinions that they come fully formed like Athena out of the head of Zeus. Ben was deeply impressed. Said she was as fast as anyone he'd taken copy from in thirty years.'

'Pleased with herself, was she?'

'Delighted. Apparently she's been getting a bit bored recently because everything's been going too well.'

Rachel looked up from mixing the salad. 'So she'll be looking for something mad to drag you into.'

'Oh, come now, Rach. That's hardly fair.'

'It's completely fair. And I'm sick of it. You seem determined to fritter your life away dancing to the tune of that egomaniac.'

'But she's a great life-enhancer.'

'It says something about your life that it needs to be enhanced like that.'

A frost settled over the kitchen, which did not dissipate until Amiss cut his finger and cursed loudly. By the time Rachel had done her ministering-angel duty with the sticking plaster, cordial relations had been restored. She unbent and related a story of office intrigue which Amiss enjoyed and responded to satisfactorily.

'We've got the makings of a pretty promising intrigue too,' he remarked over dinner. 'I had a very interesting gossip with Henry Potbury.'

'That old soak.'

'Yes, but he's a nice old soak, Rachel, and a gifted old soak and to me a kind old soak.'

'Each to his own,' said Rachel. 'But at least that explains why you're . . .' She stopped.

'Why I'm what?'

'Let's say *half* pissed.'

'Hardly that, Rach. And be fair. It was a day when through no fault of my own I had lunch with Jack, as well as having to consort with Henry. I'm only the littlest bit pissed really, which is pretty impressive in the circs.' He reached out and gave her a hug. 'Come on, it's hardly a big deal, is it? Just because you're always as sober as a judge . . . Sorry. Bad analogy. If you think about it, it's nonsensical to say sober as a judge. Lots of judges get pissed. In fact, the legal profession is full of piss-artists. What about sober as a Jew? I've never known a Jewish drunk.'

'I don't quite see that it makes sense for a Jew to be described as being sober as a Jew. Though I accept the validity of the analogy. We're brought up to be moderate drinkers. So, however, are many lawyers. You're making very sweeping statements.'

'Don't tell me. New Labour lawyers are moderate too.'

As he saw her irritated look, he bit back an appeal to her to stop being a prig and gave her another hug. 'Let's stop bickering. As I was about to say before I interrupted myself, Henry tells me that Papworth wants to dissolve the trust or at least amend the power of the trustees.'

'I thought that was impossible.'

'Apparently not. Difficult yes. But if the trustees themselves are amenable, it would be reasonably straightforward.'

'And if they're not?'

'More difficult, but still possible if the lawyers are smart enough.'

'So why does Lord Papworth want to break the trust?'

'Sorry. Wrong Papworth. It's Piers, the son and heir, who wants to sell the journal. And who's going to be idiot enough to take on *The Wrangler* with the constraints that have been bleeding the Papworths dry?'

'But why should the trustees cooperate?'

'Henry certainly won't. He says he's not too sure of his fellow trustees, though. He said Lord Hogwood and Sir Augustus Adderly are total wankers and mesmerized by Willie, out of whose arse they think the sun shines. So if he's for it, they almost certainly will be too.'

'But why would he be for it? From all you've told me, it's really in his interests to keep the arrangement he's got.'

'True, true. But Henry's so suspicious of Willie that he thinks he wouldn't put it past him, if the bribe was right, to change his position.'

'Sounds pretty paranoid.'

'Maybe he is. I don't know. But I do know that Piers Papworth has been leaning on Henry and was extremely cross with him for being so totally opposed.'

'He should approach him when he's drunk,' said Rachel. 'Presumably he'd sign anything then.'

'Henry's a good man, Rachel. You'd like him.'

'I doubt it, Robert. I doubt it very much.'

10

Wrangler parties were not just famous but notorious, being known not simply for the quality of drink and food provided at the expense of Lord Papworth – champagne punch, Russian vodka and caviar were the staples – but because over the years invitations had acquired a cachet that made them sought after by every snob in London with literary pretensions.

The journal's politics pulled in the aristocracy hand over fist, bringing in their train the social-climbing Right and those of the Left who adored the frisson of rubbing shoulders with enemies of noble birth. At *Wrangler* parties were to be found choleric columnists of the far Right and paranoid conspiracy theorists from journals on the far Left.

Politicians particularly loved being known to be present: invitations marked them out from fellow MPs as men of letters. 'Didn't see you at *The Wrangler* party,' an MP who wrote occasional essays on his gritty childhood in the dark north would observe to a despised fellow politico who had hoped to be invited because he wrote the odd book review. He would watch with glee as this upstart with pretensions to be a pillar of the literary Left squirmed and muttered unconvincingly about having been otherwise occupied.

Six or seven glasses of *Wrangler* punch was guaranteed to strip away the veneer of civilization so carefully cultivated by those who sold their exaggerated and hyped-up opinions for a living. The occasion when the antique president of a right-wing Think Tank ennobled by Margaret Thatcher for the rigorousness of his condemnation of all that was liberal denounced a competitor – whose road-to-Damascus conversion at the lady's feet had taken him overnight in one swift vault across the political spectrum – of being an ideological counter-jumper, stayed in the memory of those present for many years to come. Indeed it stayed in the memory of many who hadn't been there at all but thought they had, so graphic were the accounts at literary dinner parties of the unedifying wrestling match between two old buffers who had taken no exercise in years.

Since both of them were monumentally unpopular, and most of audience were in a state of happy alcoholic irresponsibility, no efforts had initially been made to pull them apart; the moment when the accuser lost his wig and the defendant his trousers raised an almighty cheer. It had been the bright idea of Lord Fortescue, a noted dog breeder, to empty over the heads of both contenders the contents of a punch bowl. 'Always works,' he said complacently, as the two let go of each other abruptly, and – blinded and winded – allowed the kinder among the audience to help them to their feet.

Six weeks before D-day, Lambie Crump had summoned Amiss to discuss the guest list. Into the third hour Amiss was very fed up, for it was clear he had no role other than as an audience. His remark that if the unprecedented decision was being taken to ask the whole Cabinet, it seemed strange to invite only half a dozen Conservatives, was met with an abrupt, 'Well, that is how it will be.' Lambie Crump seemed merely to want an audience as he drooled over the names of the previous year, appended giggling comment or reminiscence, and sometimes struck people out willy-nilly because they were passé, vulgar or just not amusing any more. But Amiss had put up with it uncomplainingly, this being the occasion when he had at last exacted from Lambie Crump the long-resisted concession to replace Jason by an entryphone and allow the lad to train for computer duties in the subscription department. Lambie Crump had fought a last rearguard action by insisting that Miss Mercatroid would never put up with such a loss, but Amiss had been able to cite her in support, for he had already bribed her with a therapeutic chair that would no longer leave her back in nightly agony.

Having covertly examined the account books for the previous year, Amiss had discovered that the party had cost more than £30,000. Discreet enquiries about the caterers had revealed that they were a couple of sprigs of the aristocracy who were highly efficient, commercially astute in using their names and contacts, but extremely expensive.

The day after the guest-list discussion, having ascertained that Lambie Crump was in a good mood because he was off to a ducal household for the weekend, Amiss called into his office and asked hesitantly: 'Do we have to have the Gascoignes catering for the party? Aren't they a little on the pricey side?'

Lambie Crump looked at him aghast. 'What are you suggesting?'

'Just a little shopping round.'

'You seek to turn *The Wrangler* party into a cheap-wine-and-nasty-vol-au-vent affair?'

'No, of course I don't. I just thought we might find people who could give our guests food and drink just as good for rather less than one hundred pounds a head.'

'This is very disturbing. Lady Amanda Gascoigne is a personal friend. She knows how to do things. Now about that proposal of yours to' – he looked at the piece of paper in front of him and with distaste said – 'acquire comptometers and in other regards alter some of our accounting practices, one would wish to consider it in a calm frame of mind.'

Amiss recognized a bargain when it was being offered to him. 'OK, Willie. I wouldn't wish to upset you. If you like, I'll sort out the details of the party with Lady Amanda.'

Lambie Crump smiled. 'You'll find her quite delightful.'

'Even there,' Amiss reported to Rachel, 'I managed to cut the bill by twenty per cent by persuading Lady Amanda the guests wouldn't notice if she substituted Iranian for Russian caviar and used a cheaper champagne than Krug and just a three-star brandy for the punch. I asked her not to tell Willie about this, because he found economies so wearisome and vulgar and Lady Amanda – who has a sharp eye for the main chance – agreed without demur. "Willie likes nothing but the best," she said, "but sometimes, of course, that is the enemy of the good. Dear old Willie doesn't quite live in the real world."'

'It's still an awful waste of money,' said Rachel.

'But it's fun. And it's traditional. And Papworth doesn't grudge it.'

'It's still inexcusable to spend so much.'

'Oh, for God's sake, Rachel, do you have to take on the puritanism of your new masters?'

'Since you went to *The Wrangler*, Robert, you seem to think that anyone who doesn't get drunk and throw money around is a life-denying puritan and a bore. Fortunately, my colleagues still think I'm good company. Now, if you'll excuse me, I'm going to the study to catch up with some work.'

The weather was fine, the guests were happily disporting themselves inside and outside *The Wrangler* offices and there were no signs that anyone had noticed any diminution in the quality of the food or drink. Amiss was in a benign frame of mind. He had had a happy reunion with the Duke of Ormerod, had been flirted with by a luscious young hackette who seemed to think a manager was a person of consequence, had eavesdropped on half a dozen entertaining conversations and was about to insinuate himself into the group surrounding two truculent old novelists, when from behind came a tap on the shoulder and a, 'My dear Robert,' and he turned to see Lord Papworth, who had in tow a middle-aged man whose large ears and Roman nose suggested a close family relationship.

'This is my son, Piers, Robert. Piers, here is Robert Amiss, the manager, who has done so much over the past few months to stem the losses here.'

'Not enough,' said Piers Papworth, as they shook hands. 'Sorry, that sounds ungracious, but the extravagance of this party always pisses me off. Look at that.' He gestured towards one of Lady Amanda's uniformed waitresses, who was tempting a nearby group with a tray of blinis, while behind her stood another, carrying a silver jug of punch. 'Presumably the Papworth estate has to pay extra to have pretty ones.'

'I don't think so,' said Amiss. 'I can't imagine Lady Amanda Gascoigne ever contemplated hiring anyone plain.'

'Last fucking straw,' said Piers Papworth. 'Us adding to the ill-gotten gains of the bloody Gascoignes,' and with a nod he elbowed his way through a gaggle of critics and disappeared into the crowd.

Lord Papworth shrugged resignedly. 'Sorry, Robert. It's not that Piers doesn't appreciate what you've done. It's just that he won't be satisfied until *The Wrangler* operates at a profit.'

Amiss looked over his shoulder. 'In that case, he'd better take a contract out on Willie.'

'Don't tempt him. Or me, for that matter. I'm finding his political line harder and harder to take.'

'You're not alone. You could probably share the cost of the hitman with several others.'

'I take comfort from that thought.' He looked around him covertly. 'A word in your ear, Robert. Is Willie drinking a lot?'

'Why do you ask?'

'I had the most peculiar phone call from him last week. Raving about all of you. Yet when I alluded to it a few days later he didn't seem to know what I was talking about. Obviously I said I must have been mistaken and didn't push it. Chap had clearly forgotten all about it.'

'There have been a few incidents of that kind. Henry and I have had two or three such calls.'

'Keep an eye on it, will you? It's bad enough having the deputy permanently soused without having the editor making abusive drunken phone calls. Oh, dear. Oh, dear. I hope tonight goes all right. Now, if you'll forgive me . . .'

As Lord Papworth took off, Amiss's arm was gripped firmly and he was pulled into a corner by Baroness Troutbeck.

'What do you want, Jack?'

'Shut up and listen.' The focus of her attention was a tall, angular thirtysomething in an expensive fuchsia suit, with thick gold jewellery on her ears and neck, a huge diamond on her right hand and hair so big, blonde and expensively cut as to have walked straight off the set of a Hollywood soap opera. She was made up to match: the fuchsia lipstick and matching talons were alarming in their stridency. In a harsh Australian accent with American overtones, she was mesmerizing Wilfred Parry, the willowy young academic and part-time *Wrangler* literary editor, whom Amiss had come to loathe

Parry's credentials as a promising member of a famous English department required him to hide his true instincts by dressing up the traditional in obfuscatory cant and making it seem original in a world of post-structuralists, post-modernists and post-revisionists. He was, in Amiss's view, striving to be the first post-fogey – a position that allowed him to dress, think and share the prejudices of fogeys while maintaining a position of ineffable academic and intellectual superiority.

The baroness was watching enraptured. Amiss quickly saw why.

'So you're devoting your life to books,' said the fuchsia woman to Parry. 'I think that's great. I think that's really great. I think books are wonderful. I love books. Books are my companions, books are my friends. Friends are good too, friends are great. And when your books are your friends, you've always got friends. Don't you agree with me, Wilf?'

'Yes,' he stammered.

Amiss – who had never seen Wilfred Parry at a loss for the word that would illustrate his cleverness – chortled inwardly.

'Now have you got any poems about friendship that are your particular favourites?'

'Nothing comes to mind,' he said defensively.

'Come on, come on,' she said. 'A bloke like you must have lots at your fingertips. Who's your favourite poet?'

Parry froze. 'Er, er. Perhaps William Empson.'

'Who? Never heard of him. That's the trouble with you intellectuals. You're not interested in the common people. In what ordinary people relate to. What's this bastard ever written about friendship?'

'Er, I don't know.' Wilfred, who could see that a small crowd had gathered, was beginning to look desperate. 'Not the sort of thing he writes about really.'

'Name me someone else you like who does.'

Amiss was almost beginning to feel sorry for Parry, who looked as if he had gone beyond the stage of being able to think about anything.

'What about Tennyson?' she barked.

'I suppose there is an argument . . .'

'What do you mean an argument? Wasn't "In Memoriam" the best poem about friendship ever written?' She jabbed him in the chest.

'Er, yes. I know what you mean.'

'Do you? And here's another poet for you. What do you think of the lines: "Alas, the friendship that begins in spring / Is often gone before the summer's out."? Come on. Whatdaya think of them?'

An expression of mingled embarrassment and fear crossed Parry's face.

'Er . . .'

'You didn't like them? But they mean a lot to me. My mother wrote them. But you're looking down your nose at them, aren't you?'

'No, no. They were fine. Very moving.'

Fuchsia burst out laughing and slapped him on the back. 'You know what you are? You're full of bullshit. Those lines are crap. You know they're crap. I know they're crap. Why don't you just come straight out with it the way we do in Oz? What a bunch of sissies you pommies are!' And pausing only to look at him and emit a loud snigger, she turned on her four-inch heels and went to find another victim.

Pale and perspiring, Parry caught Amiss's eye, and giving him a sickly smile, tottered away.

'Who is that splendid creature?' demanded the baroness.

'No idea.'

'Find out.'

'I'm not your errand boy, Jack.'

'Yes, you are. And I need to know. I smell money and at

St Martha's we can always do with plenty more of that. If she's as rich as she looks I'll ask her down.'

'Sharon McGregor,' said Lambie Crump.

'Who?'

'A visitor from the Antipodes. Her manners have the exuberance of those colonies.'

'You can say that again,' said Amiss, observing the lady patting on the head a famous ex-editor of a national institution and asking him how he filled his days now that he was past it.

'My, my,' said the baroness when Amiss reported the news. 'Serious money, indeed: I'd better mount a charm offensive. What are you doing for dinner after this?'

'Going out with Papworth.'

'Can I come?'

'No. It's an annual event sacrosanct to editorial and Monday meeting attendees.'

'Monday, then. Seven o'clock, Lords lobby and we'll go on somewhere.' Without waiting to hear his answer, she took off and cut a merciless swathe through the crowd, pushing human obstacles to left and right. Interrupting the conversation without a by-your-leave she whispered in Sharon McGregor's ear and was rewarded with a large beam and a slap on the back. Without a backward glance, they headed towards the fire escape, leaving the elderly sage gazing after them pop-eyed and incredulous.

As befitted a host, Amiss hastened to his side and introduced himself. 'Lovely to meet you,' said the sage as his eyes swivelled to peer over Amiss's shoulder. Within five seconds, with a, 'Must be off, I'm afraid,' he had walked away to talk to someone more important.

11

As Clement Webber came to the end of an ill-tempered diatribe about cushy prisons, Amiss cut in.

'Where's Henry?'

'I've no idea,' said Lambie Crump.

'Nor have I,' said Amiss. Dwight Winterton and Wilfred Parry shook their heads, Amaryllis Vercoe and Clement Webber looked blank, Bill and Marcia continued their private argument and Phoebe Somerfield studied the menu.

'We can't start without Henry, can we?' asked Papworth. 'I don't think he's missed one of these dinners in thirty years.'

'Might he not have gone home?' suggested a bored Parry.

'Henry gone home, when there is conviviality at hand?' interjected Winterton. 'Impossible.'

'Could he have forgotten where we were going?' asked Amiss.

'Hardly,' said Papworth. 'We've been here every year for the past five years.'

'It's just that he can be a little forgetful when he's been drinking,' said Amiss hesitantly.

'Not that forgetful,' said Lambie Crump sourly. 'He always knows where the next drink is to be found. He has probably taken a better offer.'

'I suppose,' offered Amiss, 'it's just conceivable that he might have nodded off in Percy Square.'

'Passed out, you mean?' said Lambie Crump. 'Better leave him.'

Amiss rose. 'I'll ring his office just in case.' He was back in three minutes to report an unanswered telephone.

Lambie Crump shrugged.

'We'd better start without him,' said Papworth.

'Do,' said Amiss. 'But just to relieve my mind I'll pop back to the office. It'll only take ten minutes. It'd be a shame for Henry to miss this because he'd fallen asleep.'

'He'll be a bore,' said Lambie Crump.

'Never mind that,' said Papworth. 'Thanks, Robert.'

The extent of the mess in the dining room momentarily took Amiss aback, but then he remembered that part of his cost-cutting deal with Lady Amanda had been that her staff would be removed at nine o'clock to help with another function so the clearing-up would be left until early morning.

Seeing no Potbury, he ran downstairs to check his office. Just in case Potbury had been too drunk to find it, Amiss looked into all the other rooms. As he closed Ricketts's door he remembered their first encounter and headed back upstairs to the playroom. There was Potbury, slumped amid a sea of glasses, with his head in a silver punch bowl.

Frantically, Amiss pulled his head out of the liquid, laid him on the floor on his face and thumped him on the back. Some liquid came up, but Potbury stayed supine and made no sound. When eventually Amiss rolled him over on his front he was left in no doubt that Henry Potbury had died as he had lived – drowned in alcohol. His face was bloated and purple and his eyes were staring.

Having tried and failed to feel Potbury's pulse, Amiss realized there was nothing left to do except ring for an ambulance, the police and Lord Papworth.

The press loved Henry Potbury's death. Never tiring of writing about their own kind, journalists were thrilled to have the excuse of sudden death to promote Potbury beyond the confines of the obituary page and on to the front pages. Even the tabloids splashed it, for it was on a poor day for news and since the death of Princess Diana their staple fodder was no longer available to fill empty spaces. Their coverage was unkind: Potbury was self-evidently a nob writing for a nob's journal, so they went as close as they dared to making his death sound funny, with various puns about Potbury, pot and potty.

It was another twenty-four hours before the broadsheets could really go to town on Potbury as a great columnist of his time and produce acres of reminiscences from every old and middle-aged British columnist about wonderful days in El Vino's and memorable toots abroad. It was quite clear that the press in general – perhaps with the exception of Potbury's friends – were hoping that he had been murdered or at the very least had committed suicide so that the story could run and run.

The autopsy was inconclusive. And after a few cursory enquiries, the police inspector in charge rang Amiss to tell him that foul play was not suspected.

'It's definite, Willie. They're treating it as an accident. Apparently he was drunk enough to have slid in there and simply drowned.'

Lambie Crump passed his hand over his forehead in one of his more affected *fin-de-siècle* gestures. 'What a relief! What a huge relief! It would really have been intolerable to have those . . . those . . . buffoons trampling all over the psyche of *The Wrangler*. Now perhaps we can return to some semblance of normality. It is a major achievement that the journal came out this week: the strain has been so intense.'

Amiss forebore to mention that there was precious little thanks due to Lambie Crump himself that the journal had appeared at all: most credit was due to Dwight Winterton and Phoebe Somerfield. Lambie Crump's only contribution had been an admittedly elegant but ultimately shallow appreciation of Henry.

Winterton, however, was disappointed. 'How dreary,' he drawled. 'A murder investigation would have been rather fun, don't you think? It would really have put the wind up New Willie and there's nowhere I'd prefer the wind than up Willie. Besides, they seem to have been rather indolent in deciding so quickly on an accident. What do you think?'

'I don't know, Dwight. There was no obvious motive – none of the normal ones anyway. Nobody wanted his job, he'd almost no money, and presumably sex wasn't an angle.'

'I don't know about that, Robert. I quite want his job as Willie's deputy. Though of course I won't get it, so there wouldn't have been a lot of point in knocking off Henry.'

'Still, you'll have a higher profile.'

'True. But I would need a little more reason to kill someone I rather liked. Have you thought about sexual jealousy as a motive?'

'Sexual jealousy?'

'Yes. There's the matter of Henry and Marcia to be considered.'

'Henry and Marcia?'

'Robert, are you going to stop repeating everything I say. Yes. Henry and Marcia.'

'They were having an affair?'

'Indeed they were. I caught them in a clinch in his room. He was a bit embarrassed and asked me to keep my mouth shut. Which I did until now.'

Amiss shook his head. 'I shouldn't have thought Henry could do the necessary. However, there's no doubt that sex is a department that is always full of surprises. The most unlikely people are at it, at the most unlikely ages, in the most unlikely condition . . .'

'And in the most unlikely manner.'

'True. Yet Henry and Marcia as an item is a trifle hard to come to terms with.'

The truth of Winterton's story was confirmed by the surprisingly youthful and good-looking Mrs Henry Potbury. Over a drink with Amiss, who had come to talk about practicalities, she burst into outraged denunciation of her husband and his infidelities – particularly with those she persisted in calling his *Wrangler* totties. 'Henry was an unspeakable old lush,' she said. 'But at least he was my old lush. I could tolerate his drunkenness. I could tolerate him coming home frequently in an absolute stupor, falling into bed and snoring all night.

I could stand the fact that he made a public exhibition of himself on many occasions and I had to drag him out of parties and make him ring up the next day to grovel.'

She laughed ruefully. 'Sometimes he involved me in scenes that would make most wives unable to show their faces in public for months, but I had got to a stage when I was beyond embarrassment. What I found very hard to bear was the combination of drunkenness and rampant philandering. It's one thing to be a philanderer if you know how to cover it up. One of my tenets is that the least a philanderer owes his wife is discretion, but clever as Henry was, he was no exception to the rule that drunkenness and discretion do not go together, so I had no option but to know about several of his inamoratas, and that I resented. Which is why I'm keeping the funeral private and am not contemplating a memorial service for a few months: I might get angry if I saw any of them.'

'I understand.'

'The hardest – or to be precise – the second hardest to bear was Marcia. Not that I have anything against her personally, but she should have had more sense. Thou shouldst not philander with a colleague, especially when you know his wife, more especially when you know he's a drunk and above all when you know that he makes a habit of this sort of thing. What's more, it is particularly stupid when someone as jealous as Ben is liable to find out.'

'Ben?'

'Surely you know about Marcia and Ben?'

'What?'

'They've been living together for about thirty years, and when it comes to jealousy, from what I've heard, Ben makes Othello look like a proponent of open marriage.'

'I don't know why I didn't know that, but I didn't.' Amiss rubbed his eyes. 'Next thing you'll be telling me that Lambie Crump and Josiah Ricketts are lovers.'

'No. But Henry and Amaryllis were.'

This caused Amiss to sit bolt upright. 'That's too much. You're having me on.'

'That's no way to talk to a widow,' said Amelia Potbury –

to Amiss's relief breaking into laughter. 'I assure you when you're married to somebody like Henry you don't need to make up stories.'

'But Amaryllis!'

'Meaning she's young and beautiful, and bright and well born and all the rest of that sickening mixture. So she is. Clearly you hadn't realized that Henry was actually very attractive to women. Don't ask me why. I never found a rational explanation for it, even though I was myself one of his victims.'

'I'll take your word for it,' said Amiss. He struggled to repress a feeling of deep resentment at his friend Henry. Having admired Amaryllis from afar, Amiss had never thought that he himself would have had a chance with her, even had he been in the market. It did not make it any easier that Henry had scored.

'You don't think, do you, Amelia, that Ben might have done anything violent?'

'To Henry, you mean? Oh, if he'd found out about Marcia, yes, quite possibly. Though I'd expect him to beat Henry up in those circumstances. I can't see Ben doing anything sneaky. But then it's always possible that he was presented with an irresistible target when he saw Henry plastered beside a full punch bowl.'

She looked at him seriously over her big glasses.

'I wouldn't want it pursued, Robert. If Henry got rubbed out for being a philanderer, frankly he had it coming. Much as I loved the old goat, I wouldn't want revenge.'

'Umm,' said Amiss.

12

Despite Amelia's relaxed view of murder, Amiss arranged to meet his friend Detective Chief Superintendent Jim Milton the following evening. The first hour was spent on catching up on news, for Milton was just back from America, where he had spent three months unpaid leave visiting his wife, and he knew nothing of *The Wrangler*, beyond having heard of Henry Potbury's mishap.

'I think he might have been murdered, Jim.'

'My colleagues don't.'

'Yes, but they show little sign of having thought much about it. Seem to want to get Henry out of the in-tray and into the out-tray.'

'We're all bureaucrats now. However, if you think differently, I'll pay attention. Not that I've any chance of persuading them to reconsider unless you've got a very strong argument.'

'I haven't really. I'm just uneasy. And I liked Henry so much I feel I owe it to him to make sure his death is taken seriously.'

'Tell me about him.'

'Brilliant journalist, who was less and less productive because of the booze. He'd been associated with *The Wrangler* from his time at Oxford in the nineteen fifties when he wrote such witty and penetrating stuff in student magazines that the then editor invited him to write a series of "Letters from an Undergraduate". He was an immediate success and when he came down he was offered a job straightaway. Although he was tempted away a couple of times to highly paid jobs elsewhere, he always kept relations friendly and would do the odd think-piece or book review. Really, *The Wrangler* was where his heart was.'

'So when he got fed up with elsewhere, he'd let himself be persuaded to come back?'

'Persuaded and bribed. But he was worth it. Until the last few years, apparently, you could rely on him every week for, say, one of the anonymous leaders, a signed article and maybe an important book review. And he was utterly brilliant at the Monday meetings.'

'The what?'

'The meeting of editorial staff and some outside contributors every Monday to discuss the line to be taken on the week. He was the intellectual driving force, full of ideas and with a brilliant way of twisting the news to provide a focus for an onslaught on ill-considered reform.'

'Why wasn't he made editor?'

'The proprietor wanted him, but the trustees wanted Willie Lambie Crump and overruled him. Lord Papworth then made Henry the staff trustee as a kind of consolation prize. But disappointment contributed towards Henry taking to the bottle and he started to go slowly downhill.'

'Why wasn't he fired?'

'Lifetime contract. Couldn't be fired until he was sixty at the earliest.'

'Sounds as though Papworth had a good motive for killing him. Or you, come to think of it, if it's cost-cutting you're at.'

'I loved Henry,' said Amiss. 'He was the person I most enjoyed at *The Wrangler*. We had some great bibulous lunches and even more bibulous dinners: he was riotous company until he fell asleep. Great iconoclast and a magical anecdotalist, awash with wonderful mad stories of the wild days of Fleet Street before it was destroyed by the move of newspapers to Docklands and what he denounced as the long march towards the puritan dawn.

'I don't believe that anywhere throughout the present newspaper world nowadays there's a room into which you could go at four o'clock in the afternoon and sit down and drink and talk ideas.'

'So who do you think might have killed him?'

'In his professional life, I can only think that it could have been to do with his performance as a trustee. First, he bitterly opposed Lambie Crump's recent lurch towards New Labour and away from the journal's core belief in the evolution of institutions. And second, he would have virulently opposed any attempt to change the terms of the trust in such a way as to make the journal vulnerable to the whims of a proprietor.'

'So you think the editor or the proprietor had a vested interest in getting rid of him?'

'Lambie Crump, yes. Though I doubt if he'd have the balls. Charlie Papworth, no. It was his son who wanted the trust altered. Not him.'

'Not very strong reasons for suspecting murder, then.'

'I grant you that. I'm just not happy. And I wish the police had given the idea more house-room.'

'I'll talk to someone.'

'Thanks, Jim. Now tell me about America.'

'Interesting. And it provided the opportunity for Ann and me at last to make our decision.'

Amiss waited.

'We're going to get a divorce.'

'Oh, Jim. I'm very sorry. I like Ann so much.'

'So do I. And she seems to like me too. But it's no use.'

'Was it just geography in the end?'

'More than that. I couldn't do what she wanted. I don't just mean that she wanted me to move to America. That was really an excuse. What she really wanted was for me to give up a career that she had come to despise. And to show I had the balls to make a go of a new line of work in a totally new environment.'

'And don't you?'

'I don't want to. Maybe I'm opting for safety. Or maybe the truth is simply that with all my grumblings and resentments about the way the Met has gone I'm doing something I think I do well and don't want to leave the field clear for the bastards. So I won't and I don't and I think it's unreasonable of Ann to force me to choose between her and my profession and my country.

'America and I wouldn't suit. Ann loves it because it throbs with energy and it's given her a completely new career. I'm too English in my bones to adapt, as well as being too much of a policeman to walk away. We were happy together for a long time and we're both grateful for that but the time apart revealed the differences we never faced. Ann is idealistic and emotional: I suppose I'm pragmatic and sceptical.'

Amiss sighed. 'Modern women are very demanding, aren't they? Do you remember the old days, when they didn't necessarily despise us?'

'Too long ago for either of us to remember, surely.' Milton sounded rather bitter.

'Sometimes,' said Amiss dreamily, 'I think we should just sit back and let them take over the world, while we learn to sew and lie on chaise longues eating chocolates.'

'We wouldn't look good in negligees.'

'Anyway, they won't give us that option,' said Amiss. 'They want us to be chefs in the kitchen, wimps in the living room, studs in the bedroom and masters of the universe outside the home. Tell you what. Let's get pissed. Ann's ditched you, Rachel's away doing important things and tomorrow's Saturday.'

'You're on,' said Milton, and signalled to the barman.

'It's a shame about Ann and Jim,' said Rachel. 'Though I suppose it's inevitable when they view things so differently. Personally, I agree with her that he should have done the courageous thing.'

'But he's a good policeman, and, mostly, he loves the job.'

'Perhaps so. But he's never known anything else.'

'You're always complaining that the trouble with me is that I didn't stick with a career.'

'You took the career-flexibility path to extremes, however.'

'I suppose that's true. Anyway, the other thing is that Jim's seeing if Henry's case can be reopened.'

As soon as the words were out of his mouth, he regretted them.

Rachel stopped peeling potatoes and looked squarely at him. 'Do I gather that you're trying to make a murder out of an accident?' She dried her hands and walked over to him. 'Let's sit down for a minute.' They sat down at the kitchen table and she took his hands in hers.

'Robert, I know you think I'm being very crabby recently and I know we're looking at things differently. I'm sorry for my part in all that. But I'm angry now because it seems that when the conditions for a murder mystery don't exist, you need to create them.'

'Are you suggesting I murdered Henry in order to make my job more interesting?'

'I wish you wouldn't always be flippant. What I mean is that everybody seems to think Henry died as a result of an accident, but for some reason you are determined to prove otherwise.'

'But there's a chance it wasn't an accident. And if it wasn't, I want that known. I think that's the least I can do for Henry.'

Rachel got up. 'What's the use?' she asked, and went back to the sink.

13

'Hmmm,' said the baroness. 'Maybe you're right, but you'll need a lot more evidence. You'll have to sniff around. Now, do you want to know how I got on with Sharon McGregor?'

'Should I? I hadn't really thought about it. The last I saw of you both, you appeared to be in cahoots, but later events put that out of my mind.'

'You should want to know about her. She's going to matter to you.'

'Tell me then.'

'We went off to dinner and she thought I was wonderful, naturally. I've got her coming down to a St Martha's feast soon. I'm hoping for great things – i.e. large cheques – from her if I play her right.'

'What things? Who is she?'

'Surely you've heard of her? She's one of the richest women in Australia. Correction – one of the richest *people*.'

'How did she get it? Inheritance? Divorce settlement?'

'Well, well,' said the baroness. 'I never thought to use such a word to you, my lad, but I feel impelled to point out that you have made a deeply sexist assumption. Our friend Sharon owes nothing to any man, unless you count those she's impoverished on her climb from the gutter to the penthouse. She's some broad, I can tell you.'

'I feel quite embarrassed,' said Amiss. 'I do apologize for my unwanted inference.'

'God, you're so malleable. And apologetic. Why can't you just stand your corner and point out to me that until very recently it was a safe bet that rich women were rich because of their husbands or fathers and that it's PC crap to accuse anyone of sexism for making such an assumption.' She shook her head. 'Let me have men about me that have balls.'

'Oh, shut up and get on with it, Jack. Stop playing games.'

She beamed. 'Have to keep you on the hop. Without plenty of mental gymnastics, how will we defeat the enemy?'

'What enemy?'

She threw out her arms and hit a passing waiter a smart blow. He winced painfully, but she paid no attention. 'There's always an enemy. The important thing is to be fit and ready for him.'

'Or her,' said Amiss.

'When it comes to enemies, I am, as they persist in putting it these days, gender-blind.'

'Anyway, how *did* she make her money?'

'Transport. Started out charging her schoolfellows a knock-down price for driving their cars from parties. Saved enough for a down payment on one of her own and had a fleet of sixty taxis within two years. By her early twenties she was leasing company cars and within five years had moved into buses, coaches, light aircraft and helicopters in the States as well as Australia. Personal fortune of three hundred million as of last count, but she's greedy for more. I expect she's moving in on the UK transport industry. There's plenty of scope.'

'Married?'

'Thinking of ditching Rachel?'

'No, I couldn't marry a woman with fingernails that long. I'd go in fear of my life. She probably uses them to stab people in the back.'

'May I take your order, sir? Madam?' The waiter sounded irritable.

'In due course,' said the baroness firmly. 'But first I need to know the answer to some questions. What fish have you in the bouillabaisse?'

'The usual, I expect.'

She gazed at him reprovingly. 'There's no such thing as the usual ingredients. They change from location to location and chef to chef. If you don't know the answer, go and ask.' Scowling, the waiter departed.

'Poor bugger,' said Amiss. 'What does it matter, Jack?'

'We're talking about food. When it comes to food, everything matters. Now where were we? Oh, yes. I was going to tell you that Sharon wants to buy *The Wrangler*.'

'She *what*?'

'You heard.'

'Why, for God's sake?'

'Well, I can't think she imagines she's going to make money out of it, so she's either dipping her toes into the newspaper business or she's social-climbing. I'm inclined towards the latter, though I have to say . . .'

The waiter returned and took up his position beside her. 'The bouillabaisse, madam. It consists this evening of crab, prawns, cod and salmon.'

'That isn't bouillabaisse. Bouillebaisse is made exclusively with seafish. What you are offering is fish soup. Tell the chef you could be sued under the Trades Descriptions Act.'

The waiter looked at her sullenly.

'Is the salmon wild?' she asked.

He attempted to stare her down. He lost. 'I don't know, madam. I'll go and ask.'

'Jack, why are you tormenting that man?'

'What's the point of being a waiter if you're not interested in food? And besides, I don't like him. He was patronizing me. And you patronize Jack Troutbeck at your peril. Where were we?'

'You were telling me about Sharon McGregor. Surely, she isn't fool enough to want to become seriously involved with newspapers? She hasn't got the kind of money to take on the likes of Rupert Murdoch.'

'She certainly isn't a fool. And I'm sure she doesn't want to take on Rupert Murdoch. What she claimed was that she has an affinity with England because of her immigrant father, so she wants to help preserve that essence of civilized England that is represented by the civilized virtues of *The Wrangler*. Which is obviously all cock. But she might be seeking to rub shoulders with the landed interests none-theless. And why not? If American heiresses could buy up dukes and earls a hundred years ago, why shouldn't self-made Aussies do the same today. She could become the Duchess of something-or-other and still buy up our railways.'

The waiter returned and stood by her elbow.

'Well?' she asked.

'The salmon, madam, is not wild.'

'Tell the chef that in that case he shouldn't be cooking it – not even in soup. Cultivated salmon is bland, tasteless and pointless. I'll have the gravadlax and the dill sauce. But make sure the dill sauce comes in a separate jug. Now for the main course. Is the rabbit . . . ?'

'Wild, madam?' The waiter was beginning to wear a defeated look. 'I doubt it. Shall I ask the chef?'

'Don't bother. It won't be. I'll have a bloody rump steak with plenty of very hot chips.'

'I'm afraid chips aren't on the menu tonight, madam.'

The baroness beamed. 'I'm sure if you tell the chef that Lady Troutbeck is relying on him to provide them, he'll change his mind.'

The waiter clenched his teeth. 'And other vegetables, madam? Shall I bring you a variety?'

'What are they?'

'Our selection includes broccoli, courgettes, cauliflower and carrots.'

'Good God, no. I don't want any of those. See if the chef's got some cabbage. Otherwise I'll just have the chips. And make sure the steak is very, very bloody.'

'Yes, madam.' He turned away.

'Excuse me,' said Amiss. 'I'd like something to eat too.'

'I'm very sorry, sir. I got confused for a moment. What would you like?'

'French onion soup and the navarin of lamb, please.'

The waiter shot him a look of gratitude and tottered away.

The baroness shook her head. 'You let them off too lightly, Robert. Now, where's the wine waiter? I'll torment him by demanding Australian wine. That always drives the Frogs crazy: it's a refined – nay exquisite – form of torture.'

The wine waiter – older and wiser than his colleague – did not rise to the baroness's bait, but enthused with her about her shortlist of wines, commended the vineyard she had selected and averred that he too on occasion felt that the French had something to learn from newer competitors. They beamed and chatted together for several minutes, to the evident bewilderment of the bearer of soup and gravadlax.

'I wonder how they reconcile their impressions of you afterwards,' said Amiss, as the baroness tucked a vast white napkin around her neck and proceeded to tuck in with gusto. 'The first one thinks you're an intolerable old bitch and the second evidently considers you a bit of all right.'

'That's fine with me. If everyone likes you, you're not doing your job. I'm a reasonable woman and if everyone does what I tell them they'll have nothing to complain about. Now eat up, you're looking peaky. And make sure you finish it all up.'

'Dining with you is a bit like having a nursery tea. Did you have a nanny?'

'Of course I had a nanny. Splendid woman. Taught me all I know and stood for no nonsense. Which takes us back to Sharon. I think you'd better expect a bumpy ride if she gets to buy the paper.'

'What can she do if Willie stands firm? He's got the trust behind him.'

'I'll give you ten to one that Willie turns out to be an amoeba. And probably the trustees too. And if they don't, take my word for it, there is no trust that can't be broken. But I don't even think she'll have to try. For every one member of the great and good who'll fight his corner, there are two who'll skulk away with their white flags in the air. You'll see.'

Amiss put down his spoon and sighed. 'Oh dear. And things were going so well. On my side, at least.'

'I think that's usually the moment when it gets dangerous.' She speared the last of the gravadlax, stuffed the remains of the roll in her mouth, chomped vigorously and took a hearty swig of Chardonnay. 'Never mind,' she said consolingly. 'At least it'll be interesting.'

She chuckled evilly and called for the waiter.

Amiss was missing Pooley badly. He could have relied on him to take the keenest interest in every aspect of the Potbury death. For even more than Amiss, Pooley was a man who did not consider a case closed until there was no further room for doubt. But he had disappeared off to staff training college and was out of reach.

As befitted a senior policeman who had been in the job for twenty-five years, Jim Milton was more of a realist. 'You can forget about Henry Potbury as far as we're concerned,' he told Amiss a couple of days after their night out. 'There's nothing doing. I had a word with an old mate who's the supervising superintendent and he showed no interest. Said it's an open-and-shut case and the Met's quite busy enough without following will-o'-the-wisps. I didn't push it because I didn't see any point. And in fact I agree with him. Why don't you forget about it?'

Amiss tried interesting the baroness further, but she was busy and impatient with detail and speculation. And it was obvious that the less said to Rachel the better.

Yet Amiss did not give up. First, he looked at Ben and Marcia closely until he was satisfied that their relationship seemed exactly as it always had been. Indeed, both of them clearly missed Henry a great deal. When Amiss dropped by they were often very happy to reminisce with him about Henry. And if Marcia shed the occasional tear, there was no indication that Ben saw this as anything but an understandable reaction to the sudden death of a valued colleague.

One evening Amaryllis Vercoe called in and Amiss invited her to the pub. She showed little interest in talking about Henry, preferring to flirt outrageously. While Amiss affected not to notice, he was secretly very pleased, though he had enough sense to grasp that a woman who might fancy Henry Potbury just possibly might fancy anyone.

'Is Amaryllis involved with anyone?' he asked Winterton the next day.

'If you mean, "Is there someone who is – as it were – settled down with her?" then no; she lives alone and appears to have no regular escort. If you mean, "Is there a man in her life?" you've asked the wrong question. There are many men in Amaryllis's life. In fact, it has to be said that she's pretty generous with her favours. Why, has she been giving you the glad eye? I should go for it if she has. She's very good value as well as being the trophy shag of the intellectual Right.'

A crestfallen Amiss tried to look dignified. 'It was just idle curiosity, Dwight. I'm a settled man.' And he withdrew before Winterton could evince his scepticism.

The only line of investigation left,' he said to the baroness when she rang him at work a few days later, 'is the Papworth one.'

'Oh, that would be good. You mean you think Charlie Papworth rubbed Henry out so he could sell the journal.'

'Piers Papworth's my candidate.'

'Um, maybe that's possible. He certainly comes across as a ruthless little bugger.'

'Maybe he's in it with Sharon.'

'How do you propose to find out?'

'There's damn-all I can do, Jack, as you well know. I'm completely stymied. The only people who have any chance of finding out who knocked off poor old Henry – if anyone did – are the cops. And they won't. I can hardly go round all these people demanding to know if they can provide two independent witnesses to prove that they left the gathering while Henry was still alive.'

'Too bad.' She sounded rather bored. 'I've had a run-in with Willie.'

'About what?'

'He made another attempt to persuade me to soften the line. Said I was being unreasonable. Outrageous! I'm the most reasonable woman in the world.'

'What did you say?'

'Told him to get stuffed. I'm not going to be pushed around by Willie Lambie Crump.'

'He is your editor, Jack.'

'I'm not prepared to be mucked about by an unprincipled little turd. And if you remember, I made damn sure that I couldn't be. The contract's watertight. Willie can't do a thing until the year is up. I told him I'd sue the arse off him if he didn't honour the agreement. And I would too. And since I'd enjoy a good court case and he'd crumble in the witness box and he knows it, that put paid to his small rebellion.'

'I'll make a point of avoiding him for a few days. He'll be furious. He went up the wall at what you said about the only honourable class being the landed gentry.'

'Good. Now put me through to Ben. I want to dictate this week's.'

'What's it about?'

'My proposal that henceforward the crown should be passed on to the dimmest and least sensitive of the monarch's children – levels of general thickness to be assessed when they have all reached adulthood. The way the public, the government and the media behave these days, being king or queen's no job for anyone with brains or finer feelings. What you really want is a blockhead as close as possible in IQ to Mr and Mrs Below-Average and with a hide as thick as Tyrannosaurus rex.'

'Or Jack Troutbeck.'

'Absolutely. Now stop gabbling and get Ben.'

'Oh, Mr Amiss, Mr Amiss, come back, come back.'

The voice on the telephone trailed off into a collection of squeaks that Amiss accurately identified as the Ricketts distress call.

'Steady, Mr Ricketts. Steady. I'll be back soon. Now, tell me what's wrong.'

'This man is here and he's looking at everything and shouting at me.'

'What man?'

He heard in the background a nasal voice calling, 'Cut

the crap, Josh, and walk the talk. You heard me. Walk the talk.'

A great wail emanted from Ricketts. 'Oh, please, Mr Amiss. Just come back.'

'All right, Mr Ricketts. All right. I'm coming. Just keep calm and I'll be with you very soon.' Amiss depressed the lever and jabbed the redial button. 'Miss Mercatroid, it's me again. Please put me through to Jason.'

'Mr Amiss, I have a complaint. I have been abused and insulted.'

He tried not to raise his voice. 'Please, Miss Mercatroid, not now. This is important. I'll be back shortly to hear your complaint, but now please get me Jason.

'Jason? Robert. What the hell is going on? I finished a meeting at the printers, responded to a message from Ricketts asking me to call urgently and found him having a fit on the other end of the phone. He was wailing about a man who keeps looking at everything and shouting at him. And now Miss Mercatroid's complaining about being insulted.'

'Some pillock's been going round the building demanding to know everything we do and then being rude.'

'About what?'

'Everything, really.'

'Who is this pillock?'

'All I know is he's called Bett, he's a Yank and Lambie Crump told Ricketts to tell everyone to give him maximum cooperation. And everyone did and now they're all going mad. All except me,' said Jason complacently. 'I'm tougher than the rest of them. And anyway, he wasn't that rude to me.'

'Jason, will you drop what you're doing and go and see Ricketts and try and calm him down. I'll be back within the hour.'

Amiss raced for the station and caught a train with just half a minute to spare. En route he tried to block out pointless speculation by burying himself in the new *Wrangler*. It was dull, apart from the baroness's tirade against drink-driving laws and speed-traps and what she called the Singaporization of Britain, which would shortly lead to heavy fines for those who bet on horses or spent their money foolishly or didn't wash their necks or failed in some other unspecified way to meet the criteria for the New Brit: squeaky-clean, unprincipled, touchy, feely, moderate in everything, regular in his bowel movements and deadly dull. There was nothing from Webber, nothing identifiable from Dwight, some good workman-like pieces from Phoebe and a fawning piece from Lambie Crump on the transformation wrought by the inspirational new government in the public attitude to the benefits of education. He ended his journey apprehensive and depressed.

Miss Mercatroid was crying when Amiss arrived.

'What's the matter, Miss Mercatroid?'

'That dreadful man. He said I could be replaced by a machine.'

'Don't worry, Miss Mercatroid. I'll sort this out.'

He ran upstairs and rushed into Jason's office.

'Update.'

'This Bett guy's told Bill and Marcia the Internet could do most of their job and the grammar-check and spell-check the rest. He's told Sabrina she's a pointless status symbol and Miss Mercatroid that she could be replaced by an automated switchboard and Mr Ricketts has had to lie down in one of the storerooms because he was afraid he was going to have a heart attack after what Bett said to him. What'll we do if he's had one? Will we burn him on a funeral pyre of *Wranglers*?'

'Make sure he's all right. I'm going to find this Bett person. Where do you think he is?'

'I think he's with the editor.'

Amiss ran down the corridor and knocked loudly on Lambie Crump's door.

'Enter.'

Inside, sitting across from Lambie Crump, was a crew-cut thirtysomething wearing jeans, trainers and a T-shirt that bore the legend 'CAN DO' in enormous letters.

'Mr Bett, I presume,' said Amiss.

'Ah, Robert,' said Lambie Crump. 'Hold hard while one performs the requisite introductions. Walter, this is our manager,

Robert Amiss. Robert, this is Walter Bett, who has called in to look around and see what scope there might be for . . .' He paused and furrowed his brow.

'For downsizing and ass-kicking,' proffered Bett.

'At whose request?' asked Amiss.

'Ms Sharon McGregor's.'

'And what has it got to do with her?'

'Now, now, Robert,' said Lambie Crump. 'There is no need to sound perturbed.'

'I am not bloody perturbed. I'm furious. And I want an answer.'

Bett looked at him scornfully. 'She might be buying this dump, so she wants to know the scope for economies. And I can tell you, I'll be telling her there's plenty.'

Amiss's voice became icy. 'By what right, Mr Bett, do you come in and upset my staff as you have done? It would have been courteous to arrange a tour with me. As it is, you appear to have gone through the building like a particularly bad-tempered bull and have caused widespread distress through your rudeness.'

'Don't give me that shit.'

Lambie Crump came in hesitantly. 'Perhaps one should apologize to you, Robert, for the manner in which this was done. But Sharon rang me only last night and one wasn't to know you wouldn't be here this morning.'

'Except that I go to the printers every sodding Friday morning.'

Lambie Crump winced at his language and tone. 'One cannot remember everything. There is so much. In any case, in your absence, it seemed best to pass Mr Bett over to Ricketts. Perhaps one should have pointed out that Ricketts is not robust.'

'I can't hang about all day listening to all this crap. Do you want to hear my opinion or not?'

'Yes, please, Mr Bett. Please, Robert. Give him a minute.'

'Just a minute, then. I need to check that he hasn't actually killed Ricketts off.'

Bett leaped to his feet and strode to the window, displaying his back, which read 'HIT THE GROUND RUNNING'. He jumped up and down a couple of times and then whirled round and jabbed his finger at Amiss and Lambie Crump. 'What's the key?' he cried. 'Ask yourselves. What's the key to success in any organization?' There was a pause. 'I'll tell you. You got to help yourselves individually and collectively.

'Now, what that means is a lean, mean organization with plenty of energetic smarts getting to work at dawn every day shouting, "Hey, this is a can-do day, a can-doody day. A day I score a home run." I want achievers whose personal goals are the goals of the company's owner. What we don't want are any fuddy-duddies looking backwards. I'd fire everyone in admin, except that kid Jason, for a start.'

'No doubt that includes me.'

'No idea what you do. What is it? Come on. Come on. Give.'

'I manage the paper.'

'That means zilch. Put skin on it.'

'Robert is very good at keeping everyone happy,' said Lambie Crump to Amiss's surprise. 'And he has cut costs here a great deal in the last few months.'

'I'm not interested in cost-cutting. I'm interested in cost-slashing. Sharon McGregor doesn't like costs. And she doesn't like passengers. And another thing she doesn't like is stuffiness. My God, today's Friday and you guys haven't even dressed down.'

'I beg your pardon,' said Lambie Crump.

'Cool people dress down on Friday. Shows we're regular guys like everyone else, not stuffed shirts. And it bonds us. Corporate bonding matters. What ya done about that here?' He looked at them. 'Say, look at you two. Why aren't you in tracksuit and sneakers? Show leadership has the confidence to be casual. That's how you bond. Gotta to have the vision thing.'

Lambie Crump emitted a burble of protest. Amiss glowered at Bett. 'You're full of shit,' he said. 'If you're not out of the building within fifteen minutes, you'll be thrown out.' And ignoring Lambie Crump's bleats, he stormed out of the room.

14

A week after the ejection of Bett – a week in which Lambie Crump had displayed some signs of deference towards Amiss – Miss Mercatroid arrived at work wearing a voluminous brown headscarf and announcing her conversion to Islam.

Amiss took her news with equanimity and wished her happiness in her new faith. Winterton giggled. 'It's apposite, if you think about it. We've had New Labour and New Britain, so why not New God? And can I perhaps add to the gaiety of nations by searching out my late father's yarmulke and sporting it around the office in honour, as it were, of Old God.' And Jason predicted trouble ahead. 'Ramadan'll be bad news. She likes her grub, does Miss Mercatroid. Three big meals a day and snacks from the big stash of chocolate bickies in her desk. She's cross enough at the best of times. Wait till she's fasting all day.'

'Let's not worry about trouble ahead. Anyway, you've nothing to fear now you're not sharing the same territory with her any more.'

'I'm grateful for that every day,' said Jason fervently.

When Amiss next passed Miss Mercatroid, she was shaking with outrage over the baroness's column, which unfortunately in the circumstances had selected intransigent British Muslims as a particular target in the course of a savage attack on the suggestion that the next monarch should be defender of all faiths rather than simply of the Church of England.

'I don't know if I can go on working here, Mr Amiss, if this kind of blatant prejudice is to be directed against my religion.'

'Now, Miss Mercatroid, you know that *The Wrangler* is a paper that believes in freedom of speech: it is entitled to criticize anyone it wishes.'

Miss Mercatroid, who seemed to be having a little difficulty in managing her scarf, tossed the end of it indignantly over her shoulder. 'Some things are too sacred to be criticized, Mr Amiss. There are more important issues than freedom of speech and one of them is the worship of Allah.'

'The very point being made here by Lady Troutbeck, Miss Mercatroid, is that this is England – a Christian country – and that it is unreasonable to expect the British monarchy to defend faiths with fundamental principles with which Britain is out of tune – as for instance the notion that religious censorship is in itself a good.'

'I've made my protest, Mr Amiss, and I'll be grateful if you would make it on my behalf to Mr Lambie Crump.'

She tossed her scarf-end haughtily over her shoulder and answered the ringing telephone.

'Does one really have to put up with this?' asked Lambie Crump.

'Morally, legally or practically?'

'Any and all. In her present manifestation, Miss Mercatroid is hardly someone one wishes to guard the entrance to a great, traditional English institution of no small importance.'

'You can't fire her for being becoming a Muslim, Willie. Or not without the most ferocious public outcry and a possibly quite expensive lawsuit.'

Lambie Crump shuddered. 'But she looks so disagreeable. She was never what one might call handsome, but she had a certain angular austerity that added gravitas: now with that hideous scarf tumbling into her eyes she looks ridiculous.'

'I suggest you avert your gaze, Willie. After all, she'll give us an image of tolerance and pluralism. We might as well get what we can out of that.'

*　　*　　*

Tolerance and pluralism were sorely stretched a few days later, when Miss Mercatroid arrived clad in what Jason crudely described as a bin liner, topped with a tightly fitting headdress. Amiss took in this improbable sight and sat down beside her desk. 'Look, Miss Mercatroid, I respect your beliefs. But at work do you really have to dress so . . . so . . . exotically?'

'The word is decently, Mr Amiss. My imam believes strongly in the wearing of the chador. Indeed, by rights my face should be covered, but he's permitting me some licence because it might be an impediment to my job. Who says Islam is not tolerant?'

'If I might make a personal comment, Miss Mercatroid, you were not exactly given to dressing indecently.'

'The sight of hair or an ankle might cause an ungovernable passion in a male colleague.'

Amiss suppressed the desire to remark that in her case the contingency was remote.

'And what's more,' she said, 'I want to be called by my new name.'

'Which is?'

'Fatima, meaning daughter of the Prophet Mohammed.'

'Isn't that rather familiar? We never called you by your Christian – sorry, first name – before.'

'Fatima is now my only name. Please tell Mr Lambie Crump and the others of my wishes.'

'It's no good going on about it, Willie. We've enough trouble on our hands, what with Henry's death and all the rows over our changes of editorial direction and Sharon McGregor hovering without getting embroiled in a discrimination case that would be guaranteed to cause us great embarrassment. You wouldn't want to be in the dock defending us on a charge of maltreating a loyal employee whose only crime is to take her religion seriously.'

Lambie Crump's face took on a peevish little-boy expression. 'Can't you bribe her to leave? Give her early retirement or something?'

'I'll see if there's any mileage in that possibility. But knowing Miss Mercatroid – sorry, Fatima – as I do, I don't think there's a hope in hell. Missionaries are hard to buy off. I fear your only hope is that she oversteps the mark and starts annoying other people by trying to convert them; we could get her on that. But my advice is that you just forget about her. You don't see her often.'

'One will be the laughing stock of Pratt's when this gets out,' said Lambie Crump in a tragic voice.

You probably already are, thought Amiss sourly.

Amiss had gradually slipped into the role of youthful father confessor, as Lambie Crump's drift towards the new British Establishment became more apparent.

'If I even believed he was principled,' said Winterton, 'I wouldn't mind as much. But the shit is doing it because he feels excluded from the corridors of power since the general election. So he's smarming up to New Labour by applauding all the conservative things they do, congratulating them on their political nous and trying to spike any criticism.

'He has even – God help us all – started to praise modernization for modernization's sake.'

Winterton threw a sheaf of typescript across Amiss's desk. 'Look at that.' It was one of Winterton's most merciless and malicious assaults on the government: almost against his will, Amiss found himself laughing out loud. 'Nice one, Dwight,' he said, pushing it back to him.

'Willie spiked it.'

'Spiked that? He must be mad.'

'He's not mad. He's a bad, bad, bad, bad bastard. This is going on all the time now. Come on, Robert. You heard him last Monday morning. He treated Phoebe disgracefully.'

'Agreed.'

'And what about that shouting match with Clement Webber? When Clement was absolutely in the right.'

'Well, he was in the right in the sense that the journal is on the Right and Willie was being on the Left, as it were.'

'God, you're so even-handed, Robert. Have you no political blood in those veins?'

'It got drained out of me in the civil service. I have no opinions left, Dwight. But never mind. You more than make up for me.'

Phoebe Somerfield was next. 'I could put up with being overworked and underpaid because I believed in *The Wrangler*, but I can't stand it now Willie is abandoning everything we stand for with the same insouciance as this government set about meddling with the constitution and breaking up the United Kingdom.'

Amiss listened sympathetically, as for fifteen minutes she poured out a litany of complaints about Lambie Crump's recent decisions. 'Phoebe,' he said at the end, 'don't answer this if you don't want to. I truly am not prying. But how much are you paid?'

'Twenty thousand.'

'Twenty thousand! A year?'

'What do you think I meant? A month?'

'But you could get much more somewhere else.'

'Moving would be difficult for me, Robert. For a start, I've always been here and I'd hate to leave it. Secondly, so much of what I do is anonymous that readers of the journal know very little about me. And anyway, I just don't think I could adapt now to one of those papers where they're full of hate and mistrust and jealousy.' She stopped. 'Mind you, we're beginning to get that way here.'

'But surely Willie should be paying you more than that – far more than that.'

'He says he can't afford it. You know how badly they pay contributors.'

'That's different. Do you know what he pays himself?'

'No. Nobody knows who's paid what. All negotiations are private and with the editor.' She buried her face in her hands. 'I wish I was paid more. I'm sick of doing all that badly paid stuff for the World Service. And you know Willie won't let me write for any other paper.'

'He let Henry.'

She got up. 'Henry was in a strong position,' she said wearily. 'I'm not. Now I've got to get back to work. I've got three leaders to do this week as well as everything else.'

'Can you give me the staff payments ledger, Mr Ricketts?'

'Oh, no, Mr Amiss. I can't do that. You know I can't do that. It's secret.'

Amiss dismissed the notion of arguing with the old idiot. He knew from experience that Ricketts wasn't ready to relinquish to outside eyes anything that Albert Flitter had decreed was for the editor's eyes only. Nor did Amiss want him squealing to Lambie Crump. 'Fair enough, Mr Ricketts. I hadn't realized.'

Ricketts ceased to look like a neurotic squirrel and resumed counting biros. Amiss had long ago rejected any notions of trying to train him to do anything useful or to take away from him such prized duties as the payment of staff and contributors and the recording of various kinds of information that could have been done in a tenth of the time by Jason on his computer. Smiling reassuringly as he left, Amiss headed down the corridor to the room that Jason shared with the malingering Naggiar.

'Where's your boss today?'

Jason grinned. 'He's being tested for allergies. Claims he's having skin trouble. Hardly been in all week.'

Amiss looked appreciatively around the room, which after two months of Jason's arrival was unrecognizable. Papers relating to subscribers were neatly filed in boxes and Jason had almost completed fully computerizing the database so that reminders would go out on time. As it was, the printers were now provided weekly with pre-labelled and franked wrappers.

'I've got some ideas about how to boost circulation,' said Jason. 'Can we talk about them sometime?'

'Sure. But I warn you it's going to take a long time before Lambie Crump agrees to any advertising.'

'Stupid git.'

'You may say that, Jason. I couldn't possibly comment.

Anyway, we have to deal with what we have to deal with. And my immediate problem is practical. Do you by any chance know how to break into a locked filing cabinet? Did your misspent youth equip you with such a useful skill?'

Jason grinned. 'No. But I've got a mate who's sure to. Have you lost the key to your cabinet, or are you trying to break into someone else's?'

'Mr Ricketts's. He's got some records I need to see that he's convinced are top secret. I don't want to give him a heart attack by insisting he disgorge them.'

'Be better if you did, Robert. We don't need the old sod. Any more than we need old Naggiar.'

'You have all the heartlessness of youth, Jason. For now, please do your research and then we can do the deed when Ricketts has gone home.'

'Glad to, Robert.' Jason smiled at him beatifically, for Amiss had transformed his life and his gratitude was boundless.

The staff ledger duly liberated by Jason made fascinating reading. It was clear that whatever tenets of New Labour Lambie Crump now claimed to belive in, equal pay was not one of them. For Phoebe Somerfield not only earned less than a fifth of Lambie Crump's salary, but only just over half that of Dwight Winterton, twenty-five years her junior. Even Ben and Marcia earned more. Outraged, Amiss stormed off to the editor's office.

'Oh goodness, it's nothing to make a fuss about.' Lambie Crump looked at Amiss with distaste. 'One pays what the market requires, does one not? One is not a charitable institution.'

Amiss repressed the first six retorts that came to mind. 'I know it is technically none of my business, Willie, but since I'm the cost-cutter, I'm sure you'll listen to me seriously when I suggest a cost increase. I'm uncomfortable myself earning twice as much as Phoebe and I will tell her so.'

Lambie Crump sat bolt upright. 'You're not seriously contemplating telling her, are you? Nobody tells anyone what they earn. Nobody knows except Ricketts and he doesn't know what he knows. Or does he? You didn't get it from him, did you?'

'No, Willie. As you rightly say, Josiah Ricketts doesn't know what he knows. But I have my sources.'

'What are you asking me to do?'

'Double her salary.'

'Don't be silly. I'm prepared to consider a couple of thousand extra.'

'Willie, if there was any justice you'd give her twenty years of back pay.'

'But it was perfectly well understood when Phoebe came to work here that you could get a first-class woman for the price of a second-class man.'

'What you have in fact is a first-class woman for the price of a fifth-rate man. It's grossly unfair.'

Lambie Crump looked at him petulantly. 'Another five thousand? That's plenty. And even that will make her ask difficult questions.'

'You can tell her all the recent administrative economies have made some money available.'

'Oh, really.' Lambie Crump pouted at his tormenter. 'It just seems such a waste, when she's never complained. Well, not much, anyway.'

'She'll complain a lot more if she finds out what I'm earning, Willie.'

'That's blackmail.'

'Afraid it is.'

'Be under no illusion that one is pleased.'

'You'll get over it,' said Amiss cheerfully. 'Phoebe's still in her office, I think. I'll send her straight up.' He walked out, taking Lambie Crump's silence for consent.

'She saw me after she saw Willie,' reported Amiss to Rachel, 'and burst out crying. As she's usually so private, I hadn't known she was supporting an ailing mother who has to have a paid companion while Phoebe's at work. So money's been ferociously tight. She was so happy. I took her out for a bottle of champagne to celebrate.'

'Good old Robert,' said Rachel. 'Always a bottle rather than a glass.'

He felt suddenly very deflated.

15

'I just thought for curiosity I'd check out how Number Ten views the recent *Wrangler* lurch towards the new Establishment,' said Amiss to Winterton. 'I've got an old civil service colleague working in there.'

'And?'

'Mixed. It was much appreciated that New Labour were getting such surprisingly generous treatment, but Willie's own behaviour makes it unlikely that he's going to become a popular pet.'

'What's he done?'

'Apparently over the past few weeks he's rung up the PM's private secretary, the press secretary and the chief of staff and demanded a peerage from all of them.'

Winterton chuckled maliciously. 'You're kidding. He couldn't do that.'

'Well, he did.'

'Maybe he was sozzled.'

'They didn't seem to think so. Though he was when he rang me at home last week.'

'And me. Long tirade about my iniquities.'

'Much the same as my call, then. You aren't the only one under the lash.'

'And Henry had a few in his time when he was around.'

'I've never seen Willie drunk. Have you?'

'Not in the flesh,' said Winterton. 'Seems to be a recent development. I suppose it might be tension, from all the rows. I think he was nervous for a time that the trustees might come down heavily on him as Henry wanted them to. But of course the other two are spineless creeps who think Willie's God.

'It's all very sad, Robert. He's going to wreck a great institution and there's bugger-all anyone can do about it.' Winterton got up. 'I'd better go off and find some way of saying what I believe in terms that'll pass the muster with New Willie. You've cheered me up a bit anyway. It looks as though he's scored a few own goals. I can stand anything except him becoming Lord Lambie of Crump.'

'I bet he'd drop the "Crump". Watch this space for Lord Lambie of Mayfair.'

'Where the hell is Willie?'

Amiss looked up in surprise at the unprecedented sight of Phoebe Somerfield crashing into his room angrily and without ceremony. 'I'm sorry, Phoebe. I've no idea. I assumed he was in his room by now. Have you tried his flat?'

'There's no answer. I can only guess he was off on one of his nights in the country with toffs and hasn't got back yet. I could strangle him.'

'What's the matter?'

'It's press day and we're looking set fair to produce this week a journal with three blank pages unless I fill them full of whatever we spiked last week. Willie was supposed do a leader and an assessment of the latest collapse in the Northern Irish peace process. It's eleven o'clock and there's no sign of him or what he was supposed to write. And Dwight's up to his ears.'

'You'd better start writing, just in case he doesn't turn up. I'll try to locate him.'

'I've already fucking well written half the goddamn journal,' said Phoebe Somerfield. 'And we've only got an hour and a half left.'

'What is the leader about?'

'The government's U-turn over personal taxation.'

'I'll do that and you do Northern Ireland. How many words?'

111

'Eleven hundred.' She turned to go and then looked back. 'But can you write?'

'You'll have something better than a blank page. And wasn't it you told me the journalist's golden rule was, "Don't get it right. Get it written"?'

She shrugged and disappeared.

After a dash to Lambie Crump's room that yielded a diary that showed him as having been due at the opera in London the previous night, Amiss went back to his office and began to type frantically. Ninety minutes later he delivered the leader to Phoebe Somerfield, who scanned it quickly and then smiled at him. 'I hand it to you. It's OK. In fact, it's better than OK. I didn't realize you were a writer *manqué*.'

'I'm not, Phoebe. But I was once a civil servant and had to write about complex issues simply and quickly.'

'Thanks, anyway,' she said rather gruffly. 'You got me out of a hole. I'll be off now to the printers with Marcia, and if you see that hound Willie, spit in his eye for me, will you?'

'I hope he's all right. After all, he might have had an accident.'

She got up, gathered up her papers and looked squarely at Amiss. 'Frankly, my dear,' she said, 'I don't give a damn.'

Amiss went downstairs and addressed Miss Mercatroid. 'Fatima, are there spare keys to Mr Lambie Crump's flat?'

She peered suspiciously at him. 'There could be.'

'What do you mean, "There could be"?' he asked irritably.

'I mean it depends who's looking for them. Mr Lambie Crump leaves me the keys to let in workmen on occasion. They're not for anyone else.'

'Fatima, Mr Lambie Crump has disappeared and I am fearful that he is ill in his apartment and unable to answer the telephone. Perhaps you might accompany me and we will investigate together.'

That seemed to reassure her that he was not intending to set fire to the Lambie Crump pad or scrawl graffiti all over the walls. 'Very well, Mr Amiss. I shall give you the keys.

Obviously it would be improper for me to accompany to such a place a man to whom I am not related. And even if it were, I could not do so at a time when I am required to be at prayer.'

She handed him a handsome brass key, stood up, looked at him challengingly and with impressive speed prostrated herself across the rug behind her desk. Amiss resisted the temptation to point out that since she was facing west rather than east, it was her feet that were pointing to Mecca; he left her chanting indistinctly but enthusiastically.

As he went up in the lift to the top of the house, he wished he had someone with him. If Lambie Crump was inside, presumably the best scenario was that he was dead drunk and the worst that he had died of a heart attack or been strangled by a rent boy or by some other homicidal visitor.

Amiss resisted the temptation to summon Ben or Jason: there was, after all, only a slim chance that Lambie Crump was on the premises at all. He was very relieved when this assessment proved to be right: the flat was empty of everything except the exquisite furnishings which – to Amiss's by now trained eye – looked to have been liberated from *Wrangler* stocks. Whatever one felt about Lambie Crump, reflected Amiss, one had to admit he had excellent taste, as well as an unerring capacity for finding whatever was most agreeable in the line of the good things of life and acquiring them for himself – preferably at other people's expense.

Of the flat's tenant there was no sign. Everything was neat, the bed was made, there were no dishes in the sink.

Amiss wandered around the flat for a few minutes, assessing Lambie Crump's taste in pictures (English watercolours), books (political biography, nineteenth-century novels, art and travel) and music (obscure opera). Resisting the temptation to look in the wardrobe for any signs of sartorial perversion, he headed virtuously towards the front door, pausing only to admire the view from the window of what Lambie Crump undoubtedly would refer to as his withdrawing room. Urban though the vista was, it was calculated to gladden Lambie Crump's heart, being composed entirely of elegant Georgian houses, unpolluted by any trace of the twentieth century other than the fire escapes forced on ungrateful inhabitants by bossy bureaucrats.

It was as Amiss cast an appraising eye on the fire escape of *The Wrangler*'s building, that he saw down in the garden a flash of white in the middle of an expanse of black. As he tried to identify it, a nasty idea came into his mind. Frantically, he rushed around searching for a door out to the fire escape exit, only to find that access was via the window through which he was looking: climbing out was simple.

Amiss raced down the first flight of stairs: just before he came level with the fourth floor his foot struck violently against something thin and sharp. He was never to know to what primitive instinct he owed his survival, for, as he began to fall, he wrapped his arms around the handrail and held on grimly, thus avoiding plunging like Lambie Crump to his death a hundred feet below.

Amiss's shock was compounded by the sight that met him, when, nauseated and in pain and still clutching the rail, he arrived swaying at the bottom of the fire escape. To his left was the body of Lambie Crump. From his battered and bloody face stared open, sightless eyes.

Although Amiss realized that since Lambie Crump was wearing a dinner jacket, it followed that he had almost certainly been in the garden for more than sixteen hours, he nerved himself nevertheless to feel his pulse: the clammy wrist yielded no sign of life.

Limping to the back door, Amiss staggered to the hall. He had just reached the reception desk when he fainted. When he came to he was lying on the floor with a cushion under his head and Miss Mercatroid dabbing at his brow with a damp handkerchief. As he struggled to sit up she forgot her maidenly modesty, put an arm around him and helped him prop himself against the wall.

'What's the matter with you, Mr Amiss? You look as if you've seen a ghost.'

'I'm afraid that's essentially what I have seen, Fatima. I'm afraid I've bad news. Mr Lambie Crump's body is in the garden. Can you please be very brave and call the police and tell them that.'

With a muttered ejaculation to Allah, Miss Mercatroid followed his instructions swiftly and then rang Jason to instruct him to procure a cup of tea straightaway and bring it to reception. Within five minutes Amiss was on his feet and functioning: his right leg, though bruised and sore, needed no medical attention. Immediately, he put out calls to all the staff to come to reception, where he told them the news.

'How could he have fallen down the stairs?' asked Jason. 'Unless he was pissed, that was.'

'He was ambushed by a trip-wire. I'm afraid we have to face the fact that it's murder. So we're going to have to come to terms with a police investigation and all that that entails. I doubt if this will be an open-and-shut case. Can I just ask all of you to be calm and cooperative?' Seeing tears running down Josiah Ricketts's face, he got up and went over and put his arm around the old man. 'Would you like to lie down for a few minutes, Mr Ricketts? I know this is very upsetting for you.'

Ricketts got out a large handkerchief and mopped his eyes and blew his nose. 'No, thank you, Mr Amiss. I'll be all right. I'll go back to my room now and go on copying the names into the contributors' book. Duty is duty.' And with a bowed head he left.

Winterton grinned sardonically. 'I'm glad Ricketts shed a tear for Willie. He's likely to be the last as well as the first.' No one contradicted him. With what was almost a communal shrug, the staff went back to their offices.

'You were incredibly lucky,' said Milton. 'The wire was still taut: in fact, you've got off fantastically lightly with just a few bruises.'

'I'm incredibly lucky too that you've been given the investigation. How did you fix it?'

'I was there this morning when the decision had to be made

115

and the AC thought I was the man to deal with a high-profile case that would attract lots of media attention. I'm thought to be tactful, you see.'

'Unlike the cops that arrived yesterday. You'd have thought I'd pushed Willie down the stairs, the way they interrogated me. However, I'll stop cribbing. What's the plan?'

'I'm just finishing something off. Then I'll talk to the forensic people, find a sidekick to stand in for Ellis . . .'

'Oh, bugger. Of course he's gone off on his holiday with Mary Lou, hasn't he?'

'Yesterday. Straight after he got back from his training course.'

Amiss sighed. 'Can't be helped. And, anyway, I've got you. Now, do you know anything yet that I don't know?'

'Only that the wire was tied efficiently just three inches above the step, the optimum height. It was intelligently placed halfway down the second flight to take advantage of the momentum Crump would have built up if he was going down the stairs at any speed. At night he had no chance of seeing the wire. His height and thinness was against him too, for he had a less concentrated centre of gravity than had he been short and fat. He went headlong over the handrail and ended up the mangled mess you saw.'

'Wish I hadn't.'

'You should be getting used to such sights by now.'

'You know me, Jim. I'm squeamish.'

'You're alive. That's what matters. I'll be in touch.'

If the newspapers had got excited about Henry Potbury, they went frantic about Willie Lambie Crump. 'Bloody hell,' said Amiss to Winterton, 'I know journalists think they're the chosen people, but they're carrying on about Willie as if they've been robbed of a Messiah. I mean, for God's sake, the *Independent*'s described him as a conviction journalist who boldly risked the wrath of his readers to embrace Tony Blair's vision, and the *Guardian* alleges he was risking his job by shedding the tired and discredited philosophy of a tired and discredited age.'

Admittedly, there were hints of criticism in the papers of the Right: the *Telegraph* even implied that Lambie Crump's desire to be at the centre of political London might have influenced the paper's recent drift away from its core values. But all the papers – including the tabloids – were united in shock that anyone should dream of murdering a member of the Fourth Estate. Indeed, said the *Mirror* darkly, there were strong reasons to suppose that Lambie Crump might have come to his death because – in the best traditions of journalism – he put his beliefs before his safety. And of course the more sensationalist journals and indeed radio and television programmes made much of the fact that his death had followed not long after the violent death of another pillar of *The Wrangler*: police, the public was told, were even now examining the two cases to see if they were by any chance connected.

'Bad business, all this.'

'Certainly is. And not just limited to Willie, I fear. Even the police are now admitting there's a fair chance that Henry was dispatched as well. Seems too much of a coincidence otherwise.'

Lord Papworth shook his head. 'I don't know, Robert. I don't know what to think and I don't know what to do except rejoice that you – at least – have not joined them in the afterlife.'

'And find another editor, presumably, and fast.'

'That's all very well,' said Papworth, 'but I shouldn't think people are actually going to be queuing up to take over from Willie until they're sure it's safe. Only a war correspondent is likely to want to command a ship that appears to have a homicidal maniac among its crew. We'll have to wait until this is all cleared up before we start an editor hunt.'

'I take your point, Charlie. So what will you do? Get Phoebe or Dwight to stand in?'

'Don't think I can. After all, it's not outside the bounds of possibility that one of them murdered Willie – and even Henry. They've got the most obvious motive. Don't want *The Wrangler* to have the stigma of an editor – even if only a temporary one – being charged with murder. Not quite the image of a paper so hot on law and order.'

'If you can't have someone from outside and can't have anyone from inside, Charlie, how is that paper going to come out next week?'

'You're going to take over as editor.'

Amiss was so shocked that he made an incautious gesture and knocked over his tea. The ensuing mopping of himself, the table and the floor occupied a few minutes during which he had time to collect his thoughts. 'I'm honoured, Charlie,' he said as he sat down again, 'but that idea's a non-runner.'

'Give me a better one.'

'There has to be some retired or freelance journalist who'd come in for a few weeks until things are sorted out.'

'Don't want an outsider coming in as a temporary measure, and I don't think anyone would want to either. It's going to require great tact to preside over such an interregnum, and I can't think of any available journalist with such a quality.'

'But, but . . . but . . .'

'But me no buts, Robert. If you haven't an alternative, it has to be you.'

Amiss's mind frantically raced through staff and regular contributors. 'Amaryllis Vercoe?'

'Now you're being silly. How could I put Amaryllis in over Dwight or Phoebe? The whole point with you is that clearly you're a temporary measure and unthreatening. I'll tell them you'll be doing it in cooperation with them, but that you'll have the authority.'

'What are the trustees going to say?'

'Won't have any trouble from them. I rang Doug Hogwood and Gussie Adderly this morning and they told me to do whatever I thought fit. And Jack Troutbeck, of course, was delighted – she being a chum of yours.'

'Jack Troutbeck?'

'Oh, sorry. Didn't I tell you? She's Henry's successor. Appointed as soon as I heard about Willie. I'd been dithering up to then, but this is no time for dithering.'

'Whose idea was that?'

'Mine, but the other two were quite happy. She's a valued contributor with no journalistic ambition – best kind of staff trustee one could have, really. And not knowing her the way I do, they're comforted by her being in the Lords. One of us and all that.'

Amiss brooded and then shook his head. 'I just can't see it, Charlie. I just can't see how editorial will accept a non-journalist.'

'They like you. And it was fortuitous that you wrote that tax leader last week. They know you're capable of being a contributing editor.'

'How did you know about that?'

'Phoebe told me when I tried this idea out on her.'

'What was her reaction?'

'Fine. She'd rather you than Dwight, and Dwight prefers you to Phoebe.' Papworth looked at his watch. 'Got to go home: people coming in for drinks. Right, now to practicalities. Spend what you need. For instance, if you need to hire someone to stand in for you, feel free. Or pay out some decent money to journalists. I don't mind what you do. Just get the journal out.'

'Jolly good,' said the baroness. 'It's very satisfactory that we'll be running the show.'

'Correction, Jack. I'm running the show.'

'I'll be running the trustees. That means I have power of life or death over you. Mind you, I envy you. Always wanted to have a bash at being an editor. Why didn't he appoint me?'

Amiss laughed. 'He did mention on the way out of the Lords that the notion had crossed his mind but he decided you were too barmy. To be precise, he said: "To let someone as opinionated as Jack Troutbeck loose on *The Wrangler* would be like inviting an alcoholic to take over a pub." And I must add, Jack, that apprehensive though I am about this job and anxious though I might be to pass on the poisoned chalice, I agreed with him.'

'You underestimate my prudent streak. But I'm used to

being misunderstood and I'm big enough to rise above it. Now, get cracking and pull *The Wrangler* out of the mire.' The phone went dead.

'It's wonderful news,' said Rachel. She threw her arms around him. 'I'm absolutely delighted. And it's such a good time too. Lambie Crump was taking the paper in the right direction at last and you'll be able to accelerate the pace.'

Amiss looked at her with alarm. 'I'm only a caretaker, Rachel. And what I'm caretaking is a right-wing magazine.'

'I know that. I'm not suggesting you change course any more than Lambie Crump did. Just embrace sensible policies quicker.'

Amiss decided to avoid any argument. 'This week my ambition is to get *The Wrangler* out with no blank pages. Next week I'll be able to think.'

She beamed. 'You'll see. You'll make such a success of it, Papworth might even give you the job permanently.'

'I'll do the best I can.'

She hugged him again. 'Let's go out to the wine bar and have a glass or two – I mean a bottle – of champagne.'

'You're on,' said Amiss.

16

Having neglected to send out a press release to announce his appointment as temporary editor, Amiss had only himself to blame when a Sunday paper broke the news that Lambie Crump had been replaced by a dark horse called Robert Amis (sic), thought to be a little-known member of the wider Amis clan – a rumour which persisted until Martin Amis contemptuously denied it. That newspaper however had done better than the rest of the broadsheets, who had filled a column or two each in speculation about the journalist most likely to succeed Lambie Crump. Many kites were flown: the internal candidates mentioned were Winterton, Amaryllis Vercoe and Wilfred Parry.

Amiss spent much of the weekend on the phone reassuring colleagues and contributors and asking for suggestions on how to proceed. After some dithering, he decided to move into the editor's office: there was no point in starting off being apologetic.

The mood of the Monday meeting was friendly. Wilfred Parry made sycophantic noises, and even Clement Webber came as near to graciousness as could have been expected by saying, 'Well, I suppose you can't be worse than Willie.'

'I hope we can get all this mess sorted out soon,' said Amiss. 'But however long it takes, we need to do the best we can for the journal. I'll be relying on all of you. And you'll understand, won't you, that since we still haven't replaced Henry and I won't be doing much writing, we'll have to use more outsiders.'

'But you'll do some,' said Phoebe.

'What I can. But I have the problem that *The Wrangler*'s politics aren't my politics.'

'What are your politics?'

'I don't really know. I suppose the best way of describing my politics is that they aren't anybody's politics – mostly because I don't like politicians.'

'Presumably you'll be following Willie's drift towards New Labour, then?' said Webber sourly. 'Seeing it's the politics of people with no politics.'

'No, Clement, I won't. I think Willie had got out of touch with the journal's soul and that's what I'm here to nourish.'

'It was the body he liked,' said Winterton, waving at the grandeur that surrounded them. 'Incidently, where is the funeral to be? Westminster Abbey? St Paul's?'

'No. I talked to his brother and he has in mind something rather more modest. We're meeting this evening to talk it through. It looks as if it will be a proper Fleet Street event at St Bride's, probably next Friday – with a memorial service later if there is enough popular demand.'

'Don't hold your breath,' muttered Phoebe Somerfield.

'I dare say I'll be able to help you.'

'I certainly hope so,' said Milton. 'That's what you're here to do.'

'Oh no . . . sir,' said Detective Sergeant Tewkesbury, giving a strong impression that it hurt him to use the title. 'I meant that I'm pretty knowledgeable about the literary world and all that. English is what I read' – he paused again and looked at Milton – 'I mean studied . . . at Oxford.'

Milton tried not to show his irritation. 'I see. So you think you'll understand these people.'

'Oh, I think so. Mind you, I wouldn't read *The Wrangler*. It's very out of date and has values that are of no relevance to Britain as we approach the millennium. I mean, obviously when you're a modernizer you want to read journals that look forward not back. But I know the sort of thing they write about.' He laughed. 'There aren't, I think, very many people in the police force for instance who know about Edmund Burke.'

'There's me,' said Milton.

Tewkesbury started. 'Oh, really, sir. I didn't realize you had been to university.'

'Tewkesbury, even if you've never been to university it is possible to read books. However, let us not get sidetracked. I would of course appreciate any insights you might have to bring to bear on this murder. Feel free to make suggestions.'

Tewkesbury leaned forward and addressed Milton with the air of an Englishman of the old school trying to make a foreigner understand. 'This is an unusual case, concerning unusual people. I have little doubt that the motives are ideological.'

'What makes you think that, Tewkesbury?'

His sergeant assumed a condescending expression that made Milton want to knee him in the groin. 'It's easy,' he said, 'to underestimate the venom of the Right when threatened by progress. I can well see that Lambie Crump's conversion to New Labour would have been a matter that outraged those loyal to the anachronistic beliefs of *The Wrangler*.'

'What are you suggesting? That a bunch of outraged readers got together and murdered Lambie Crump in the name of Edmund Burke.'

'That's a bit far-fetched, sir, if you forgive my saying so. But I shouldn't put it past Clement Webber. He is, after all, fanatically Thatcherite.'

'So, in many respects, is New Labour,' said Milton. 'Now can we please get on with checking alibis.'

'My God, how I miss Ellis.' Milton threw himself on the sofa in Amiss's room and closed his eyes. 'What they've given me in his place . . .'

'Well, what have they given you in his place? Somebody thick?'

'Thick'd be a damn sight better than what I've been given. "He's just the man for you, sir," I was told brightly. "We know

123

you like the clever ones and there's one of the cleverest ones available right now. DS Tewkesbury is a real intellectual."'

Milton covered his face in his hands. 'Drink?' asked Amiss sympathetically. 'Gin and tonic?'

'And plenty of it,' said Milton, with feeling. Amiss went over to the corner cupboard, poured Milton's drink and took it to him.

'Aren't you having one, Robert?'

'Got to meet someone in the pub shortly. Can't afford to get pissed during the week any more now I'm doing a job for which I'm completely unqualified. I've got about ten minutes or so. Tell me what's the matter with him,' asked Amiss.

'Self-satisfied, smartarse git patronizing the poor old copper who hasn't even been to university.'

'You're not just being sensitive about that, Jim, are you?'

'Don't be ridiculous, Robert. When was I ever sensitive about Ellis having been to Cambridge?' He took a large swallow. 'But I can't stand superior prigs.'

'But Ellis is a bit of a prig.'

'Oh, come off it, Robert. He has priggish tendencies, but plenty of imagination and compassion and knows about dark nights of the soul. But this little creep is thoroughly pleased with himself and convinced that the world will be a better place if everyone does what he says. He's the worst kind of arrogant little prat.'

'New Labour?' asked Amiss.

'I've met self-important little Tory prats as well.'

'The only way of dividing the sheep from the goats that makes any sense to me is to classify them as Cavaliers and Roundheads. And New Labour measure up worse than the Tories here. They don't understand that real enjoyment is a good in itself: they partake of the good things of life, but they do so austerely. There's never any suggestion that they're capable of having a riotous time. Everything has to be so fucking moderate. They're so bloody austere they make you almost warm to Bill Clinton. At least he got into trouble through dropping his trousers.'

'So did our foreign secretary.'

'Ah yes. But he showed no signs of enjoyment. Anyway, enough of this. Are you going to slap Sergeant Tewkesbury down?'

'No, I'm not, or not yet anyway. At the risk of sounding as sanctimonious as he is, I do try to get the best out of my staff even if they're personally objectionable. And I suppose he's got brains. I just have to hope that his colleagues knock some of the more objectionable characteristics out of him. Anyway, he's what I'm lumbered with and I'd better make the most of it.'

'So how are you going about this? Will you be interviewing us here? Do you want a room?'

'Not yet. We've got the preliminary statements, and over the next few days we'll be sorting out alibis and all that sort of thing. I want to do some nosing round Lambie Crump's private life. Tewkesbury obviously thinks I'm wasting his valuable time, since he's made up his mind already that the motive is ideological: Crump was slain for going over to New Labour.'

'What do you think?'

'I'm keeping an open mind. Phoebe Somerfield, for instance, from what you've told me, might have had good reason to want to murder him for ripping her off all those years. Or of course like Winterton she might have wanted the editorship.'

'Or Ben or Marcia might have taken vengeance over his wayward way with semicolons.'

'Or Miss Mercatroid might have brought in an Islamic hit squad.'

'And we haven't even considered who had any reason to do for Henry.'

'All in good time, Robert. All in good time. I'll be off now. I'll be in touch, but my guess is we'll be along on Monday.'

Amiss quickly gathered that Joe Crump was not one of his brother's greatest fans. 'I couldn't stomach the Lambie bit, to tell you the truth,' he said to Amiss over pints of beer in the pub around the corner from *The Wrangler*. 'First it was demanding we call him Willie instead of Bill, and then he took

125

my mother's maiden name and tacked it on when he went up to Oxford. Right load of pretentious twaddle, if you ask me. Double-barrelled names with hyphens are bad enough: those without are the last straw.

'Still, I suppose we'll have to respect his wishes and do his service the way he'd want, which no doubt means some fashionable clergyman and lots of poncy High-Church carry-on.' He winced. 'Maybe even incense. And to think the Crumps have always been Presbyterians.'

He swallowed some more beer. 'To be honest,' he said lugubriously. 'I hate the very thought and don't know where to start. I don't even know what hymns he liked. We only ever met every couple of years or so.'

'Can I help?'

'Can you help? What I'd really like you to do is settle the whole business with that vicar.'

'I have a friend who'll sort it all out,' said Amiss. 'She has tame clergy at her beck and call. Now, let me get you another pint.'

The baroness grabbed Amiss's hand. 'Come on. Let's clear out and make a run for El Vino's. I couldn't bear to talk to any of this mob after what I've just been through.'

They slid away from the congregation and walked briskly up Fleet Street. 'We did a bloody good job there, didn't we?' she said. 'Even if it was sickening. It was a stroke of luck that that little prat, Father Fogey, or whatever he calls himself, was able to do the honours. As pretentious as even Willie could have wished.'

'It was splendid,' said Amiss. 'A real one hundred-carat pseud's extravaganza. What did you think of Papworth's encomium?'

'Well, you've got to go a bit over the top at times like that. He produced a prime example of great English hypocrisy with all that bullshit about selfless devotion to a great intellectual tradition.'

'At least he didn't say anything about integrity. I'd have thrown up if he had.'

126

The baroness sniggered. 'I saw at least six people in that church who were at a dinner with me last week where we traded stories of the awful posing and dishonesty of Willie Crump. Still, hypocrisy is the cement that glues us all together.'

She stopped and looked at Amiss. 'Incidentally, don't let this go to your head, but this week's *Wrangler* is the best for months.'

'Really? What was it that . . . ?' But they had arrived at El Vino's and she had already disappeared inside.

'Come on, come on.' She pushed her way through the crowd, Amiss in her train. A triumphant hoot signalled the capturing of a table and two chairs. 'Now, order a bottle of champagne and make it a decent one. We'll drink a sympathetic glass to Crump because even he didn't quite deserve to be murdered and then we'll drink the rest to celebrate the interest that his passing has added to our lives.'

When they had completed the formalities and drunk their toasts, the baroness enquired about Jim Milton. 'Sleuthing well, is he?'

'He's dug thoroughly around Willie's private life in the hope that a demented lover would emerge from the woodwork. But it looks as if the assessment given him by Mrs Lambie Crump – to wit that Willie wasn't interested in sex – may be the correct one. Our Willie wasn't at it with anyone, it would seem, or if he was no one knew about it. And nor does there seem to be any family motive. The parents are dead and the brother a decent bloke.'

'What about money in the case of the brother?'

'You mean does he inherit any?'

'Yep.'

'He certainly didn't expect to. Nor does he need it. He's a successful chiropodist who owns his house and whose kids are independent. In fact, he seemed genuinely surprised when he discovered Willie had left him ten thousand quid.'

'Who got the rest?'

Amiss grinned. 'The Society for Distressed Gentlefolk.'

'You're kidding.'

'I'm not kidding.'

The baroness raised her glass. 'Here's to Willie Crump. He even managed a fogey's will. That's what I call thorough. Nothing else interesting on the private life?'

'No. Willie doesn't seem to have had a private life in the sense of intimate friendships. He knew a lot of people, but they all seemed to be acquaintances. He was the sort of fellow one invited to dinner to make up the numbers, secure that he'd know which forks to use and would have a flow of entertaining gossip: he could be very amusing when he was being bitchy about other people. Or you'd invite him because he expended Papworth's money on entertaining lavishly in his apartment or in smart restaurants: his expense account was huge. Otherwise his social life consisted mainly of attending pretty well every shindig to which he was invited on the literary and political front. One of nature's spongers, was our Willie.'

The baroness had lost interest. 'To business, my lad. You haven't asked about Plutarch.'

'Well, what is there to ask? No doubt you'd tell me if there was anything wrong with her.'

'You're very unfeeling. You haven't seen that magnificent cat for months. Don't you miss her?'

'I don't think "miss" is quite the word,' said Amiss cautiously. 'I notice she's not with me, as it were.'

'I take your point. I notice she's with me.'

'Is she all right, then?'

'In the pink. But we are, perhaps, nearing the time when she should be returning to you.'

'Christ, Jack, you don't mean that, do you? Rachel would go mad.'

'I didn't offer to take her for life. Merely for convalescence after her nasty experience in Westonbury. And that was a long time ago. She's been recovered for months. Some of my colleagues are becoming a little testy.'

Amiss felt a familiar sense of dread enveloping him. 'She's been behaving badly, hasn't she?'

'Nothing that would trouble me, you understand. But there have been, let us say, a few incidents. And the one that caused some distress to a royal personage got her into most people's black books.'

'What happened?'

'She decided to assist in the laying of the foundation stone of the new wing by jumping on the back of the Duchess just as she was turning the sod.'

'Oh dear.'

'Oh dear is right. Her claws were unsheathed at the time.'

'Oh God, oh God.'

'Did nothing for the elegant yellow silk ensemble. It might have proved possible to cleanse the fabric of the blood, but I doubt if the rip could have been invisibly mended. I offered compensation as tactfully as I could, but got a pretty chilly response. I'm sorry to have to say that there were those among my colleagues who suggested that it was time that Plutarch was stiffed.'

'In the heat of the moment, surely? They wouldn't actually do it, would they?'

'I'm not so sure. She's all right while I'm there. And you know I would if necessary lay down my life – and knock off some of my colleagues, for that matter – for that splendid beast. But I have few allies on this one – especially since Mary Lou buggered off to the West Indies – and I'm beginning to fear that one or two of my rougher colleagues just might take the law into their own hands when I next go away for any length of time.'

Amiss gazed at her in horror. 'You mean you're going to send her back to me?'

'Talk it over with Rachel. I'll pass the word round at St Martha's that I'm negotiating Plutarch's release back into the community. That might hold them off for a short time.'

'I couldn't bear it,' said Rachel. 'I really couldn't. I loathe that bloody cat. She's fat, greedy, aggressive, destructive and dangerous. And ugly.'

'Oh, come now, Rach. That's not all quite fair. She's much

better than she used to be. She only causes trouble when she's upset or excited.'

'You forget that I was present when she assaulted that red-haired waitress at St Martha's.'

'It was an honest misunderstanding over the leftovers.'

'I don't care what her motivation was, Robert. The result was hysterics. Call me unreasonable, but I really don't want to share my home with an enormous and savage creature who beats up acquaintances and strangers alike. And what's more, it isn't even as if you liked her.'

'I do have moments of being fond of her. We've been through a lot together and she has guts. In any case, what choice have I if Jack can't keep her any longer?'

'I'm not hardhearted enough to suggest you put her down. But surely you can find an alternative?'

'Rachel, if *you* won't take her for my sake, why would anybody else?'

'I don't know, Robert. I don't know. But you'd better try to find someone.'

17

Milton rang Amiss on Sunday evening to report progress. 'I'm keeping an open mind on Henry Potbury, but since it's easier in his case to determine who had the opportunity to kill him, I've had that checked out assiduously.'

'And . . . ?'

'No one admits to having seen him after eight-fifty, when he was noticed by two waitresses who were collecting their coats from the storeroom off the dining room. You know – the one with the photographs and portraits.'

'The playroom.'

'If you say so. Potbury had apparently tottered in there to take the weight off his feet.'

'Was he conscious?'

'They said he looked sleepy but hadn't actually passed out, and yes, he was sitting in front of a full punch bowl. One of the waitresses suggested that they should take the bowl outside and give people one last round, but the other one reminded her that they had to be at their next venue within twenty minutes, so they let it be.'

'How many people were still there around that time?'

'Lord Papworth, and all those who were going to dinner with him: you, Lambie Crump, Amaryllis Vercoe, Clement Webber, Phoebe Somerfield, Dwight Winterton, Wilfred Parry and Ben and Marcia, as well as a handful of others, including Piers Papworth, Sharon McGregor and Jack Troutbeck. There was also a poet who was so drunk that he had to be helped out of the building by two others and a Cabinet minister who had arrived very late and was talking intently to a journalist.

Nobody can be certain that there weren't some more odds and ends around but a few of them are pretty sure the drink had dried up ten or fifteen minutes earlier and almost everyone had stampeded off to dinners or pubs.'

'And how many of those have alibis for each other?'

'Only the non-*Wrangler* people. Most people had had a few drinks, and in the nature of things at the end of parties there's a lot of rushing round to say goodbye to different people, most people are not exclusively with any one other person and only teetotallers – and I don't think there were any there – have much sense of time.

'Piers Papworth thinks he was with Sharon McGregor at the crucial time but she's not sure if he was there all the time until she left without him to go off to dinner with Jack Troutbeck. And neither of them is clear when or where they parted. Bill and Marcia are pretty sure they were together at that stage of the evening, but they probably would think or say that anyway, wouldn't they?'

'Maybe,' said Amiss, 'but remember their lives are devoted to getting things right, so they're hardly natural liars.'

'Lambie Crump apparently said he was with Lord Papworth all the time but Lord Papworth thinks it was only part of the time and so on and on. You and Amaryllis, in fact, seem to be the only pair that are definitely out of it, since several people observed you in an animated conversation in the corner, and several wondered if you were going to get off together.'

Amiss coloured slightly. 'What a filthy-minded lot my colleagues are. If I remember correctly, we were talking about the government's devolution plans. Enough of that. How easy would it have been to knock off poor Henry?'

'Easyish, from what I can work out. I really wish I could do a reconstruction of all this, but you can't do reconstructions at the end of parties where a lot of alcohol has been consumed – especially if you're trying to do it several weeks later. It all comes down to whether a) somebody saw Potbury going into the store . . . sorry, playroom, and nobody admits to that, b) whether they were aware that the waitresses had all gone home and c) whether they had the opportunity to pop in and do the deed without anyone else observing them. But how could they have known he'd have placed himself obligingly in front of a punch bowl? More likely is that someone might have gone in to talk to Henry, or even just to look for more drink, and having seen his opportunity to kill him, took it. I have to say it all sounds very unlikely.'

'But possible.'

'Yes, certainly possible. You were all apparently by then crowded together around the corner from the main part of the room, so anybody leaving the group would have been thought to be going home, going to the loo or going in search of a drink. But in fact no one noticed anybody.'

'So in theory someone could have killed Henry while the rest of us were around the corner.'

'Yes, or done it later by hiding in the building until everyone left. It looks as though that may well be what happened, since you say when you came back the Chubb lock wasn't on.'

'That's no guide to anything, Jim. Very few of the staff have keys to the building, so if whoever leaves last can't lock up from the outside, that's just too bad: we have to trust to the Yale. You can't easily be tight on security with that kind of crew. We – that is, the few people who care – rely on the fact that what is valuable in the building is not very portable. Even the dumbest cop might become suspicious if he saw people removing furniture from a Mayfair house in the middle of the night.'

'I hope you're right, though I suspect you're not.'

'So how long would it have taken to murder poor old Henry?'

'The estimate is a maximum of three minutes from start to finish. But the risk wasn't very great. If the perpetrator had been caught in flagrante, he could have pulled Henry out and claimed to have saved his life; if he was seen coming out of the room he'd presumably have realized it and would have been able to call for help and rush back in and pull Henry out before anyone else arrived. Even if Henry had been resuscitated, he'd have been unlikely to have had a coherent view of what had happened.'

'So we're not much wiser.'

'No.'

'Any advance on the Lambie Crump conundrum?'

'There's only one lead and it's so tenuous I doubt if it's worth a damn.'

'Which is?'

'Lambie Crump seems to have phoned Papworth when he got home from that drinks party, yet Papworth said he hadn't talked to him for days when he spoke to our people.'

'Really, Jim, the notion of Charlie Papworth murdering Lambie Crump seems absolutely preposterous. He mightn't have liked the business of the trust but you don't really murder for reasons of *noblesse oblige*. Charlie's sensible and he certainly knows that in the great scheme of things, *The Wrangler* is but a grain of sand on the beach.'

'You're probably right. I'll find out. Failing that, it's an open field. Pretty well any of you could have done it – as indeed could anyone who knew his habits.'

'I didn't really know Willie's habits, but like a lot of other people I knew that he often used the fire escape: there are more taxis available near the back gate than there are near the front door.'

'It was a taxi he was in search of the evening he fell down the steps. We know where he was going and when he was due so we can pinpoint the time of his death pretty accurately to around seven o'clock. However, wire could have been put there at any time from when he had last gone down those stairs.'

'It'd be very difficult to do during the daytime, surely,' said Amiss.

'Not that difficult for an inhabitant of *The Wrangler* building. It was perfectly possible to go up to the fourth floor into the storeroom that overlooks the fire escape, climb out and do the business without anyone seeing. Though admittedly forensic can find no evidence that suggests that was what happened.'

'No marks in the dust?'

'No dust to speak of.'

'Our cleaners are very thorough.'

'But of course, as you know, it was also perfectly possible to do the job from the outside at night. Someone merely had to slip that childishly simple lock on the gate and do the business. Or even easier, someone Lambie Crump was entertaining could have gone down the fire escape and set the ambush then.'

'Anything in the diary to indicate if anyone was at his place the night before he was killed?'

'No. His only appointment was an early-evening cocktail party at the Ritz. Of course he might have gone to dinner with someone.'

'Equally likely he stuffed himself on free food as well as free champagne and then went home by himself.'

'Or took someone with him?'

'Possibly. Or someone might have called on him. But if so, they haven't owned up.'

'All wonderfully vague, isn't it? Nobody's ruled out.'

'Unless they were provably away, which none of the obvious suspects were. It's hard to be ruled out for a period of twenty-four hours. Even Professor Webber could in theory have driven from Oxford, though his wife said he was at home that night. And while Ben and Marcia say they were never separated during that period, what's that worth, even if one of them is telling the truth. Either of them could have crept out during the night. As, indeed, presumably could Webber.'

'The thing is, Jim, that while I think it's too much of a coincidence that Henry died like that, I can't think of the faintest reason why anybody would knock off both him and then Lambie Crump except that they wanted promotion.'

'Exactly.'

'And that pretty well narrows it down to Dwight who is, anyway, bright enough to make it anywhere without having to resort to murder.'

'Except at *The Wrangler* under Lambie Crump.'

'But why should he not simply go and work for someone who would appreciate him?'

'Why not indeed? So, since I'm buggered if I can find a

sensible motive for knocking off Potbury and Lambie Crump,
I'm going to focus on Lambie Crump.'

'While not completely ignoring Henry.'

'While not completely ignoring Henry.'

'You've no idea who might have done this?' Milton asked
Lord Papworth, early next morning.

'None. Willie had enemies, but I can't imagine he had
murderous enemies. Just people who didn't like him.'

'Because?'

'Because he wasn't very nice,' said Papworth simply. 'He
was selfish and he didn't think about other people unless
it suited him. For instance, I think he did damn-all to find
and encourage talent. Dwight Winterton fell into his lap. He
didn't treat his staff very well either. He was a shit, really,
was Willie.

'I'm sorry if I sound callous, Chief Superintendent. And
what I'll say in public is different. But I see no point in being
less than frank with you.'

'What was your relationship like?'

'Perfectly civil. But then I had no stomach for a fight. I
resented him for exploiting me and I'd have fired him if I
could, but he had two out of the three trustees in his pocket so
that was that: Willie expended most of his energy in guarding
his own back. But I've put up with the situation and jogged
along and it's been more bearable recently since I've put into
the journal a clever young man who has saved me a lot of
money.'

'But I gather there was a recent sharp difference of opinion
between you and Mr Lambie Crump.'

'Ah yes. You're speaking of the Papworth wars, I suppose.'

'Can you tell me about them, sir?'

'Yes, yes. Certainly. Do you know about the role of the
trustees?'

'In general terms, yes. I know how they protect the editor.'

'Right. Now in a nutshell, I have a difference of opinion

with my heir Piers about our duties towards *The Wrangler*. I regard it as a duty to keep it going with its integrity intact. He thinks it to be an anachronistic burden that we should get rid of to the highest bidder. And under the present terms of the trust, no one would give tuppence for it unless they were looking for ways to lose money.

'So Piers is trying to get the trustees effectively to put themselves out of business, so the journal can be sold un-encumbered when I'm dead and he gets his hands on it. He seems to have found a prospective buyer who is prepared to give him a good price. So, having tried and failed to find a compromise, we're having a legal tussle.'

He cackled. 'It's quite funny, really. I love my son but I take duty seriously, so I'm spending money he would otherwise inherit to try to stop him parting with something I don't really want, which he certainly doesn't want and which would make him financially secure instead of debt-ridden. A sense of duty is an expensive commodity, I can tell you.'

'Do I gather Mr Papworth does not have such a sense, sir?'

'Oh, he does, Chief Superintendent. It's just that his doesn't extend to the journal, only to Papworth Castle, which he loves even more than I do. He will explain it to you himself better than I can, I think. Although he won't be able to do that in person until he gets back from Australia in a few weeks.'

'And Mr Lambie Crump's position on all this was . . . ?'

'Selfish and venal, of course. He was throwing all his weight behind Piers for reasons I don't know. But what I do know is that his motives will not have been honourable. I suppose Piers promised him something or Miss Sharon McGregor, the potential buyer, promised him something. There will certainly have been a practical reason that benefited Willie. There always was.

'I have to admit that whatever reward he had been offered, he deserved. He was certainly Piers's most powerful ally. He'd managed to get those two old blockheads – Adderly and Hogwood – to take Piers's side, and nothing I've said to them could move them, even though they were flying in the face of all their job was supposed to be.'

'And the third trustee?'

'Henry Potbury stood up to all the blandishments and by doing so was certainly slowing things up. We hoped that the delay would put Miss McGregor off. She did not seem a patient woman. And then he died, but fortunately the appointment of his successor was in my gift and I appointed somebody even tougher than him.

'I'm still hoping Lady Troutbeck may be able to win over her new colleagues. She's a persuasive woman.'

'When did you last speak to Mr Lambie Crump?'

'Can't remember. Maybe a week or ten days before his death.'

'Even on the telephone?'

'Even on the telephone.'

'Yet his telephone records, Lord Papworth, say that he phoned you the evening before he died.'

'Really? How extraordinary. When?'

'At ten-fifteen.' Papworth wrinkled up his face in perplexity. 'My goodness, you surprise me, though if you say so I suppose it must be so. Perhaps I am a more forgetful old man than I thought.' He brooded. 'Could it perhaps have been late on in the evening after I had dined well? Could it be that Alzheimer's compounded by alcohol might be at the root of this mystery? Would the operator know if it was a long call?'

'It was short.'

'Then I expect it was something routine. I do apologize, Superintendent. I would not wish to mislead you, but at present such a call is ringing no bell in my addled old mind.'

Milton got up to go. 'I'd be grateful if you'd think about it some more, Lord Papworth. Otherwise, thank you very much. I'll be in touch.'

As they got into the car, he said, 'Tewkesbury, I want you tomorrow extremely tactfully to have a word with the two old boys Papworth had dinner with that night and find out if he had much to drink. Their names were given in his statement.'

Papworth was on the phone an hour later. 'The mystery is resolved, Chief Superintendent. Lambie Crump did indeed ring here the night before he died, but I had gone to bed and my wife took the call.'

'And didn't tell you?'

'She said he said not to bother, it was nothing urgent and he'd catch me on another occasion. So she didn't. I must say this comes as a relief to me. I really was beginning to fear that I was going gaga.'

'Thank you,' said Milton rather dispiritedly. 'If you don't mind, I'll send my sergeant round just to take a formal statement from your wife for the records.'

'Of course, my dear chap.' Milton heard him call: 'Imogen, Imogen, my dear. Can you come to the phone?'

A moment later a crisp voice said: 'Good morning. Will two-thirty this afternoon suit you?'

'Thank you, Lady Papworth. That'll be fine.'

'Good,' she said. 'Goodbye.'

Amiss was reading at his deak when the phone rang.

'I've had a postcard from Mary Lou and Ellis.'

'Good morning, Jack. Saying what?'

'"Scenery magnificent: have spent most of our time studying architectural and archaeological artifacts with the rest of our time devoted to improving books. Love Ellis." Mary Lou's PS reads, "Got him dancing in the market square last night with a clutch of dusky beauties. I'm proud to say he's degenerating by the hour."'

'Excellent,' said Amiss. 'She seems to be doing her stuff. Do you think he'll come back changed?'

'As you well know, people don't change much, just adjust a bit. When he's finished his hol and his hair's fully let down, he'll wash it, set it and pin it up again primly ready for his first day back at work. All one can hope is that Mary Lou frequently gets the opportunity to pull it down again. Anyway, that's not what I'm ringing about. Where have you got to on the Plutarch front?'

'Oh, God.'

'Rachel not thrilled?'

'Rachel not thrilled.'

'College council not thrilled either. Had to nip a rebellion in the bud by saying the matter was being addressed with urgency. That was enough to win her a stay of execution, but only a short stay. If she's found in the library with a dagger in her back I won't be in the least surprised.'

'I'm investigating long-term fostering. But my guess is that the kind of people that like cats don't like Plutarch.'

'Perhaps you need to market her as something else.'

'Like what?'

'A werewolf.'

'Not many people like werewolves.'

'I do.'

'You're unusual.'

'If you say so. I always think I'm Baroness Ordinary myself, but I admit not everyone agrees. But keep at it. I can't guarantee her safety for more than another couple of weeks, so stop wanking. Get fucking.'

The phone went dead. Amiss groaned and went back to reading Dwight Winterton's assault on what he termed New Labour's deracination of Britain. It was harsh, cruel in parts and was bound to bring the Number 10 press secretary down upon Amiss in a rage. Amiss thought he agreed with only a quarter of it, but he passed it to the printers unchanged. He was less kind to a lead review of Wilfred Parry's, out of which he took every pretentious or obfuscatory word.

When the participants in the Monday morning meeting had all arrived, Amiss addressed them. 'The police will be turning up again today to interview some of us.'

'What? Again?' said Phoebe Somerfield.

'You have a better class of cop this time. Detective Chief Superintendent Milton is intelligent and civilized.'

Parry looked down his nose. 'I doubt if that is possible. Anyway, surely there's nothing left for us to say to these people. We don't want plods hanging round *The Wrangler*.'

'Like it or not, Wilfred, we have to cooperate on a murder investigation. Mr Milton needs our help in finding possible motives for Willie's murder. And then, of course, there's the matter of Henry's death, and whether it is possible that he also was killed.'

'What fun,' said Winterton. 'I can't wait. Are we all suspects?'

'Have to be, Dwight. They've found nothing promising in Willie's private life, I gather. So obviously they have to focus on us for a while. They're only . . .'

'. . . doing their job,' chimed in Winterton.

'Exactly. And the easier we make it for them the sooner they'll be out of here.'

'Well, that's blown that,' reported Milton to Amiss. 'Tewkesbury said she was *compos mentis* and very clear about the conversation, which seems to have consisted of no more than two or three minutes of pleasantries.' He sighed. 'Of course, they might be lying. But why should he simply not have admitted to the call in the first instance? It wouldn't have implicated him.'

'Are there any leads at all, Jim?'

'Just forlorn ones. Like will some cab driver respond to the appeal to anyone who picked up or deposited anyone at the end of that alleyway the evening or night before Crump died? All I can do is press on with interviews and hope for the best.'

'I'll take you to your quarters. Jason'll have taken your sergeant there already.'

Amiss led Milton to his old office – now equipped with an extra Sheraton side table for Sergeant Tewkesbury.

'Jason will keep an eye on you, provide you with coffee and anything else you want, and search for people you can't raise on the telephone. Now, if you'll excuse me, I've an appointment.' Remembering the different workplaces and the different jobs in which he had seen Amiss over the previous few years, Milton grinned at his new suavity. Even Tewkesbury seemed impressed. 'He's young and quite bright,' he said grudgingly when Amiss had left to have his argument with Parry about reviewers. 'Even looks normal. I can't imagine why someone like that is prepared to work somewhere like this.'

'The world is full of such mysteries, Tewkesbury. Now, pass me the list and I'll decide in which order to summon our interviewees.'

18

If Miss Mercatroid was to be believed, Lambie Crump had been murdered as a result of some kind of anti-Islamic conspiracy similar to that which she was convinced had caused the deaths of Princess Diana and Dodi Fayed.

'I'm not with you, Miss Mercatroid.'

'Fatima.'

'Fatima. Why should anybody murder Mr Lambie Crump because you're a Muslim?'

'It isn't just that,' she said darkly. 'A couple of weeks ago an Islamic scholar had a letter in *The Wrangler* saying that Islam would triumph in Britain because Christians lacked conviction. This could be the backlash. Why, they may be trying to exterminate everyone on this paper.'

'Who is they? The Archbishop of Canterbury?'

'Not necessarily. But he might be part of it.'

'She continued in this vein for the best part of an hour,' reported Milton wearily to Amiss later on. 'It was almost – but not quite – worth it to have Tewkesbury forced to take notes throughout.'

'And who does she think are the actual perpetrators?'

'She talks darkly of security services serving the evil designs of the royal family and the British government. I think Freemasons were mentioned, and, of course, an international Jewish conspiracy featured somewhere.'

'Do you mean she's fingering Dwight?'

'Don't think so. I don't even know if she knows he's Jewish. She certainly never mentioned him. Anyway, I don't propose to waste any more time on her. She's bonkers. The Muslims have my sympathy.'

'Now don't worry, Mr Ricketts. Don't worry. There's nothing to be afraid of.'

Ricketts's squeaks diminished somewhat in volume and intensity.

'I hear, Mr Ricketts, that you are the longest-serving member of *The Wrangler*'s staff, so you'll have known Mr Lambie Crump for many years. Can you tell us what you thought of him?'

The squeaking started again, accompanied this time by the wringing of hands. Milton waited patiently.

'Sir, he was the editor. And there is no greater honour than to be editor of this great journal. And, like the other three editors whom I had the privilege and honour to work for, he was a great gentleman.'

'Yes, yes. I quite understand, Mr Ricketts. But perhaps you might be able to tell me how he got on with the rest of the staff? Would you say that the atmosphere was harmonious and friendly, between, for instance, Mr Lambie Crump and Mr Winterton?'

Ricketts looked shocked. 'I'm sorry, sir. I'm only the clerk. I wouldn't presume to know how editorial does its job. I count my pencils and I write in my ledgers, and all I know is that all the ladies and gentlemen are very nice to me. Very affable. Sometimes they even have a joke with me. Why, poor Mr Potbury used to say to me, "Mr Ricketts, Mr Ricketts, I suppose you've come to confiscate my extra pencil."'

Milton looked at him dully. 'So you've no ideas or information about the circumstances of Mr Lambie Crump's death? You didn't see anything, or hear anything, that might be relevant.'

'Oh, no, sir. Nothing.'

'Very well,' said Milton flatly. 'Thank you very much, Mr Ricketts. That's all for now.'

Tewkesbury looked after the departing little figure with scorn. 'Really, sir,' he said when the door had closed, 'it seems to me absolutely extraordinary that anywhere could tolerate a person like that these days. He's not just anachronistic, he's a throwback to the Victorian period and utterly valueless.'

'I can see Ricketts's deficiencies as well as you can, Tewkesbury. But you should not overlook his virtues too. Honesty, loyalty, industry and – dare I say it – humility, have their place. Now I'm going to call Miss Somerfield.'

'Can you give me one sensible reason why I might have wanted to kill Lambie Crump?' asked Phoebe Somerfield impatiently.

'No. But it would be helpful if you'd answer my questions anyway, Miss Somerfield. That's why I'm here and I've got to start somewhere.'

'Oh, very well.' She began ticking off her fingers. 'Sex, greed, ambition, revenge: they're the usual motives, aren't they? Well, neither Willie nor I ever had the faintest interest in each other in any area at all – let alone sex. Greed's out as well. I don't make any money as a result of Willie's death; indeed it's worth mentioning that he recently gave me a massive pay increase. Ambition is a non-starter. I can't see anything changing under a new editor. Revenge? For what? Now, does that satisfy you? I'm busy.'

Milton leaned forward. 'Miss Somerfield, this is a murder enquiry. Murder enquiries inevitably are inconvenient for those involved. I must ask you, please, to take my questions with a good grace. In turn, I promise you that I will try not to waste your time.'

She put her head on one side and stared at him appraisingly. 'OK. That seems fair enough.'

'Can you tell me, please, about your relationship with Mr Lambie Crump, when you came to know him and how you got on together?'

'I came to work here thirty years ago straight from university. Willie arrived a decade later from a newspaper where I gather he hadn't done particularly well and spent the next five years scheming to get the editor's job.'

'How did he scheme?'

'Snuggling up to the trustees mostly: consulting them, taking them to dinner and discovering and pandering to their prejudices in what he said and wrote.'

'You have three trustees?'

'Yes, but it was the two GGs he was smarming up to.'

'GGs?'

'Great-and-Goods. We have one staff trustee and two well-known outsiders who are essentially self-perpetuating because they choose their successors, who seem inevitably to be from the most spineless representatives of the British Establishment: vain and wimpish old men who are suckers for types like Willie Lambie Crump.'

'Are those two still alive?'

'No, though looking at their heirs you'd hardly be able to tell the difference. M'Lord Hogwood and Sir Augustus Adderly haven't any backbone or judgement either.'

'Who was then the other trustee?'

'The literary editor, who lived, breathed and wrote in a waft of Victorian letters. I can only suppose he was made a trustee because he was not a blind bit of use.'

'So what happened?'

'Gavin Wells, our then editor, was losing his grip slightly. Tended to turn up in the office drunk sometimes after lunch. Now, he still did the job reasonably well, the journal came out on time and there was no reason for the trustees even to have known unless Willie told them. And in the normal course of events they probably wouldn't have minded much. In those days, journalists were allowed to be a bit raffish and badly behaved.

'However, there was the matter of Gavin's savage attacks on aspects of Establishment behaviour. The trustees saw him as the severest critic of the Right and failed to grasp that he was also its best friend. So with Willie dropping poison in their ears they geared themselves up to the "a-word-in-your-ear-my-dear-chap-don't-you-think-perhaps-it's-time-to-make-way-for-someone-else?" version of the bum's rush. So exit Gavin and enter Willie.

'It wasn't a nice way to treat someone who had given him

146

a second chance and always been encouraging and kind, but then Willie wasn't a nice person.'

'How would you describe your relationship with him?'

'Distant. He dished out the work and I did it.'

'Would you describe him as a considerate employer?'

Phoebe Somerfield let out a yelp of laughter. 'What a hilarious idea. Willie had a very simple view of employees. They were there to do his work as well as their own, while he got the credit. It was one of the reasons he was so keen to keep all the leaders anonymous. It enabled him to take the credit for any that attracted praise, and to cover up how little work he actually did.'

'But was he considerate in terms of pay and benefits and so on?'

'For some reason that is quite beyond my understanding, having paid me very little for years, Willie doubled my salary a few weeks ago. I know Robert Amiss had something to do with it, but I can't imagine how he persuaded Willie. But double it he did, so I suppose you could say he was treating me twice as well as usual.'

'Are you likely to succeed him as editor?'

She laughed again – this time scornfully. '*The Wrangler* is not the sort of place that would choose somebody like me.'

'I understand there were tensions within the paper over a change of direction which Mr Lambie Crump appeared to be conducting.'

'No doubt of that. A vivid example of Willie's lack of scruple.'

'You minded, then?'

'I minded. But I don't murder people, even if I disagree with them. I hoped it would be just a passing phase. As indeed, it has proved to be.'

'And do you think any of your colleagues might have minded enough to murder?'

'None, Mr Milton. With all our failings, journalists are somewhat more tolerant than that. I think you'll have to look elsewhere.'

*   *   *

When she had left, Tewkesbury looked solemnly at Milton. 'Of course there is one exception to the ideological argument. I mean, if you look at who has gained most from the death of Lambie Crump, it is Robert Amiss, whom we haven't yet talked to at any length.'

'I've talked to him at considerable length.'

'But there's no record of the conversation, sir.'

'No. I didn't consider it necessary. He hadn't any information other than what he gave in his original statements. And he has no more idea than we have why anyone should have wished to murder either Potbury or Crump.'

'But he would really seem to be our Number One suspect, wouldn't he? He had the best opportunity to murder Potbury, if Potbury was murdered. And it's pretty suspicious that he hit the same obstacle as Lambie Crump but didn't fall. And then he ends up as editor.'

'Two problems there, Sergeant. Why should he have gone out of his way to discover Lambie Crump's body? And how could he have known he would become editor? Or, to be precise, acting editor. He's only holding the fort, after all.'

'He could have decided it would be a clever bluff to find the body.'

'The cleverness is lost on me, Sergeant. However, go on. How do you deal with the fact that he cannot have expected to become editor?'

'That's what he says, sir.'

'That's what Lord Papworth says.'

'But how can he have known what Amiss was thinking?'

'He knows that the solution of having him as editor hadn't occurred to any of the others he consulted, so it would have been bizarre for Amiss to have gone to such lengths for such an incredibly long shot. And, incidentally, he tried hard to turn the job down.'

'Or appeared to, sir.'

Milton felt weary. 'Tewkesbury, it is admirable that you explore every option, however improbable. But I really recommend that you forget this one. Apart from anything else,

I've know Robert Amiss for some years. And indeed he has in the past been of considerable assistance to us. In so far as one can say it of anyone, he's above suspicion.'

'In so far as one can say it of anyone, sir. So we should not rule him out.'

Visions of head-butting this git floated wistfully through Milton's mind. Instead, he said, 'Thank you for that advice, Sergeant. I shall bear it in mind.'

Irony, he noticed, was lost on Tewkesbury, who sat back looking pleased with himself. Milton dialled Winterton's number.

'Wilfred Parry and Dwight Winterton were as useless as Phoebe Somerfield,' reported Milton to Amiss. 'Parry didn't seem to have a clue about anything. He genuinely didn't seem to know about Piers Papworth and the trustees and he certainly had no motive for knocking off Lambie Crump, with whom he said he had always got on well. You've obviously been upsetting him: he said *The Wrangler* was going to pot now that an arrogant amateur was throwing his weight about. I never thought I'd hear you described as arrogant.'

Amiss chuckled. 'He's going to be more upset when I've finished with him. Willie had let him use the literary pages to promote himself, his chums and those he wanted to get on the right side of. I've just begun the process of clipping his wings, and if he doesn't play ball he'll be out.'

Milton gazed at him in amazement. 'You're certainly toughening up fast.'

'Wilfred makes it easy. He's such a pretentious shit. I threw back at him today a sneering and pseudy denunciation of Trollope as a pedestrian clock-watcher and told him if he didn't understand that the glory of Trollope is his humanity, he shouldn't be writing for *The Wrangler*. Bugger him. Anyway, how did you find Dwight?'

'Amusing, but he didn't know any more than you'd already told me. Tewkesbury couldn't stand him, of course, and now has him as Number One ideological suspect. Now I want to talk to Ben and Marcia and just want your advice on whether to see them them together or apart.'

'Depends what you're looking for. That is, if you're seeking to trip them up on alibis or whatever – as presumably you fuzz always do – you will prefer to see them separately, but if you want news, views or opinions, my guess is you're better off with the two of them together. I've had the odd conversation with them individually and it's been dull. They spark off each other like gunpowder and matches.

'I'd suggest too that it might do no harm to see them on their own territory. They're more relaxed there.'

'OK,' said Milton equably. 'Thanks, Robert.' And with a, 'be seeing you,' he went back to his office and dialled 14. 'Mr Baines?'

'That's me,' said a voice, which sounded extremely cheerful despite the shout of 'halfwit' coming from further away.

'Chief Superintendent Milton here. Would it possible for me and my colleague to pop in and see you and Miss Whitaker?'

'Yes, sure. Any time.'

'Thank you, Mr Baines. My colleague and I will be along shortly.'

Tewkesbury looked at him with bafflement. 'Do I gather, sir, that we're going to the room of these two . . . proofreaders? Yet more senior people came here. Isn't that a little . . .'

'. . . Egalitarian, Tewkesbury? I thought you'd be in favour of that. What's bothering you?'

'It just seemed inappropriate to me, sir.'

'I'm not with you, Tewkesbury. I thought snobbery had been abolished along with everything else, under the government of which you are so proud.'

Tewkesbury looked at him resentfully. Milton felt a stab of guilt at the realization that he was beginning to sound like a gung ho right-winger. 'I'm sorry, Sergeant. I was just pulling your leg. Perhaps I should explain that I have been advised that these people will talk best on their own territory. So that's where I'm going to see them.'

'Advised by . . . ?'

'Robert Amiss.'

'And you don't think that he had an ulterior motive?'

'No, I don't. And I really don't wish to have this conversation once more. You're clutching at straws. If you're going to be a successful policeman, you have got to let your pet theories go, along with your prejudices. And you have to have the humility to listen to people who know things you don't and have qualities you don't have. Among the virtues which are undervalued by the police are intuition and imagination and I commend them to you. And one of the reasons I trust the judgement of Robert Amiss is that he has shown himself to have considerable stores of both. I have also always found him trustworthy.'

He stood up. 'Now, are you coming with me?'

'Yes, sir,' said Tewkesbury. He sounded almost meek.

Milton knocked and was bade 'enter' by a contralto and bass duo. He looked around him disbelievingly at the vast spread of paper and the fog of smoke. 'I'm Chief Superintendent Milton and this is Sergeant Tewkesbury.'

'Just call us Ben and Marcia,' said the small man who peered over the huge desk. 'Do sit down.'

'Thank you, but . . .'

'Tell them where to sit, you silly bugger,' said the hennaed woman. 'How are they supposed to know?'

'Well,' said Ben, considering the matter judiciously, 'if I were you, Chief Superintendent, I would perch over there on the *Financial Times* pile while your sergeant sits opposite you on *The Economist*.'

Tewkesbury looked nervously at the pile to which he was directed.

'It's all right, Sergeant,' said Marcia. 'You've got a small enough bum to be accommodated here.'

Milton seated himself easily, Tewkesbury gingerly. As a militant anti-smoker, he was clearly in a state of outrage. Ben and Marcia looked at them benignly.

'Sorry to disturb you . . .'

'But you're conducting an investigation,' said Ben.

151

'Into the recent unfortunate incidents,' proffered Marcia.

'Concerning our late lamented employer,' said Ben. 'William Lambie Crump, gentleman of letters . . .'

'And boulevardier,' added Marcia.

They both burst into sniggers.

'It sounds to me,' said Milton mildly, 'as if you don't lament him much.'

'Mourn,' said Ben. 'Lament isn't a transitive verb.'

'Yes, it is,' said Marcia.

'No, it isn't.'

'It fucking is.'

Ben started to shout as loudly as Marcia, and then caught sight of Tewkesbury's horrified face. 'I'll look it up,' he said in a mollifying tone.

There was a pause in the proceedings for a few moments, and then, in a chastened voice, he said, 'Sorry, Marcia. Don't know what got into me. It's both, of course.'

He threw down the dictionary and turned his attention back to Milton. 'Where were we?'

Milton tried and failed not to smile. 'You were not lamenting him.'

Ben smiled back. 'That's right.'

'Though we miss him a bit,' said Marcia.

'We were used to him,' said Ben.

'You can miss anyone when you get used to them,' said Marcia.

'Even if you don't like them.'

Marcia considered the statement judiciously. 'Even if you despise them.'

Ben nodded. 'It was different with Henry.'

Marcia nodded. 'We lament him.'

'Really,' added Ben, 'when you come to think of it, if you're making comparisons, Willie Lambie Crump wasn't fit to breathe the same air as Henry.'

'Henry was a great man,' offered Marcia.

'With style and substance . . .'

'And bottom.'

They sniggered appreciatively once more.

152

Milton thought it was time he joined the conversation. 'Do you think Henry Potbury was murdered?'

'Put it this way,' said Ben. 'Anyone who murdered Henry was a bastard.'

'Like anyone who murdered Lambie Crump was a public benefactor,' said Marcia.

'Therefore,' added Ben, 'it's just a question of looking for bastards with a motive to kill Henry.'

'If there aren't any,' pointed out Marcia, 'it means he wasn't murdered.'

'Any suggestions?'

Marcia and Ben looked at each other, Ben compressed his lips. 'You want a list of bastards or a list of bastards with motives.'

'Preferably the latter.'

'Can't help you with motives,' he said.

Marcia nodded. 'Can't help you much with bastards either.'

'We don't get involved with office politics.'

'Really, the only serious bastard we knew round here was Willie himself, but I'm buggered if I can think of any reason why he might have wanted to get rid of Henry.'

'There's Wilfred Parry,' said Marcia thoughtfully.

'Doesn't really count. You only think he's a bastard because he's so supercilious.'

'I suppose you're right. He wouldn't rob his dying granny.'

'Unlike Willie.'

Milton came in again. 'Do you know about the attempt to change the terms of the trust?'

'Yes,' said Marcia, and, 'No,' said Ben, simultaneously. He looked at her suspiciously. 'What are you talking about, you old bag?'

'Oh, come on, you idiot. You must remember that. Henry mentioned it.'

'When? What? I don't remember.'

Milton wondered if he were imagining it or if Marcia really looked nervous.

'I don't know when. Maybe some time he came in here.

Maybe at the party. I'm sure I remember him saying some-thing about an attempt to water down the trust that he said he'd see off if it killed him.'

'If you heard it, how come I didn't? Or didn't you tell me?'

'Search me,' said Marcia. 'I only remembered it now the chief superintendent said it. I suppose I just forgot about it.'

Ben glowered at her. 'It would be just like you, stupid bitch. Bloody can't remember anything, can you? I mean, for God's sake, fancy forgetting the Finnish employment statistics.'

'I didn't forget them, you miserable old sod,' said Marcia, her voice rising with every word. 'I was merely wrong by one per cent.'

'Being wrong is forgetting,' said Ben.

'Please,' said Milton, in a relaxed voice. 'Do you mind if we get back to what we were talking about?' He observed to his pleasure that Tewkesbury was looking increasingly ill at ease. 'Do either of you think there might have been someone with a vested interest in getting Henry Potbury out of the way because of the business of the trust?'

'Haven't a fucking clue, mate,' said Ben amiably. 'Since I never heard of it before now, owing to this old cow having a head like a colander, I wouldn't have any theories about it, would I?'

'And you?' asked Milton of Marcia.

'All I know is he said he'd see them off. He wasn't mak-ing a fuss or anything, so I never gave it another thought till now.'

'And Lambie Crump?'

They looked at each other and shrugged. 'Well, we've talked about it, obviously,' said Ben.

'Incessantly,' said Marcia.

'Ad infinitum,' said Ben.

'And the upshot is . . .' said Marcia.

'Bugger-all,' said Ben. 'He was a greedy, lazy git and pom-pous to boot.'

'No doubt about that.'

'But not murder material, I should have thought.'

'Not bloody worth the price of the wire,' said Ben.

'Oh, come on, that's a bit unkind,' said Marcia. 'He had some good qualities.'

'Like what?'

'He let us be.'

'That's because he was lackadaisical. That's not a good quality. He was just too shagging lazy to care.' He stared at her. 'What's getting into you, girl? Don't start getting sentimental just cos the cops are here or they'll think it suspicious.'

'Speak as freely as you like, Marcia,' said Milton.

'Sorry. I had an attack of tact for a minute. The truth is we're quite glad Willie's dead.'

'Bloody well saved *The Wrangler*. Who'd have wanted to read it with Henry dead, Dwight castrated, Phoebe reined back, the literary pages getting more and more pseudy by the week and his lordship's weekly leader brown-nosing the government?'

'It was only Troutbeck,' said Marcia, 'would make anyone want to pick up a copy of the bloody thing the way it was getting.'

'Look at this,' said Ben and produced a letter in crabbed handwriting. 'This is from a geezer who writes to us every week if there's any errors. He's fanatical about standards on *The Wrangler*. It came last Monday.'

He passed it to Milton, who, for Tewkesbury's benefit, read out the entire document. '"Ha-ha. Fucked up on the Finns, didn't you?"'

Marcia pouted. Ben looked triumphant.

'"'Focussed' for 'focused'. How often do I have to tell you?"'

Ben interrupted. 'I wish the bugger wasn't anonymous. For years I've been wanting to have that out with him. He's no more right than we are.'

Milton continued. '"OK otherwise, so nine out of ten. PS. I don't know how much longer I'm going to do this now *The Wrangler*'s gone to hell. Someone should fire your editor."'

Tewkesbury was shaking his head. 'This person is obviously deranged.'

'Why?' asked Ben. 'Because he thought Lambie Crump should be sacked?'

'Of course not. Because he writes anonymous letters like this.'

'What's wrong with that?' asked Marcia.

'It's the action of a fanatic.'

'Naw, it isn't,' said Ben. 'He's just a pedant with time on his hands.'

'It's the sort of thing Ben would do in retirement,' said Marcia. 'Only he'd be ruder.'

'But why should he stay anonymous?' asked Tewkesbury. 'It's hardly the action of an honest man.'

'Maybe he's simply not sociable,' said Marcia. 'Doesn't want to answer letters or argue.'

'Just wants the satisfaction of keeping us up to the mark,' added Ben. 'Seems quite reasonable to me.'

'Well, not to me,' said Tewkesbury. 'I find it very suspicious.'

Ben eyed him with distaste. 'You're just one of these gits thinks anyone different from himself is mad. So you think this guy is mad enough to have knocked off Lambie Crump because of declining standards.'

'It's a hypothesis,' said Tewkesbury huffily.

'A bloody stupid one, if you ask me.'

'And me.'

'The guy's as sane as I am.'

'For what that's worth,' said Marcia.

'A bleeding sight saner than you, mate. At least I can tell my Finns from my Swedes.'

Milton stood up. 'Many thanks to you both. We appreciate your help.'

He led his discomfited sergeant away.

19

'Can I pick your brains,' asked Milton, 'or is this a bad time?'

'No, it's fine. Rachel's at an official dinner, I've just finished a disgusting take-away, I'm delighted to have an excuse not to tackle the essay Wilfred Parry gave me this evening and I had a particularly crazy encounter before I left that I'm longing to tell someone about.'

'What happened?'

'After everyone except me had left, Miss Mercatroid – a.k.a. Fatima – decided to remove the portraits from the reception area. Apparently her imam has been cutting up pretty rough on the issue of representational art.'

'But those portraits look as if they weigh a ton.'

'They do. Which is why when I found her she was lying spreadeagled under a sombre picture of the third Marquis of Salisbury, who has not been improved by the encounter.'

'What did you do?'

'What could I do, except remove his lordship and run for the first-aid kit? After she had sorted herself out and recovered her breath we had a little chat.'

'And?'

'I felt it was time for the young master to become stern-faced. I waxed eloquent about our heritage, not to speak of the likely cost of repairing M'Lord Salisbury, and explained what I required to forget about this incident. Faced with the news that she had to choose between me and the imam on this and one or two other matters, she chose me. Or rather, she chose her job: I think she grasped the point that the imam does not actually need to be told about her workplace in all its gory detail. So the bonus was that she agreed to keep her hands off our portraits and sculptures, stop disconcerting visitors by praying to Mecca in the reception area and shut up about pork and alcohol.'

'My goodness, you never have a dull moment.'

'And what about you. What's bothering you?'

'I just can't understand how Lambie Crump could have been getting plastered so often during the last few months and making those phone calls, yet nobody's ever reported seeing him drunk. Second, I can't understand why he would have been so foolish as to make – apparently sober – those disastrous begging phone calls to Number Ten.'

'I can't help with the first, except that the calls I experienced and heard about were lateish in the evening, and it's perfectly possible that Willie sometimes got sozzled on his own after coming home from a social event.

'As to the second? Well, when I was in the civil service I found it to be commonplace for businessmen, in particular, to go virtually on their knees to influential officials looking for knighthoods – let alone peerages. Admittedly they usually claimed they were doing this because their wives wanted to be Lady Thingummy and such honours meant nothing to them – an excuse Willie didn't have – but still, beg they did.

'I expect his line was the other popular one, viz, that he was seized with a desire to serve his country by working selflessly for it in the House of Lords. And it may be that he realized that if you don't tout for honours, you often get overlooked. Yet I would have expected that Willie would have gone about things in a more sophisticated manner, by dropping a word discreetly in a friendly ear and having its owner make the case in the right quarters.'

'I think I'll call on Downing Street tomorrow,' said Milton. 'And just to punish Tewkesbury, I shan't take him.'

'That's very harsh, Jim, isn't it? The equivalent of refusing to take Miss Mercatroid – sorry, Fatima – with you to Mecca.'

'I'm not just dim,' said Milton. 'I'm cruel too.'

He called into Amiss's office mid-morning. 'Curiouser and curiouser. The recipients of the calls all remembered them clearly, which says a lot, since they're so incredibly busy and take dozens of phone calls every day. They all give a similar account and none of them thinks Lambie Crump was pissed, though they're not ruling out the possibility that he had had a few. But there seems certainly to have been none of the slurring you and other *Wrangler* people reported. The general theme in all calls was the same: the huge contribution he could make in the Lords as a working peer, which he considered so important that he would give up *The Wrangler*.'

'Which seems odd in itself, since it suits the government to have *The Wrangler* on side and their only chance of that was under Willie. Unless they calculated he might turn against them if he hadn't got his peerage?'

'Yes, but by then they'd have had another year of favourable coverage out of him. Maybe he could have been played along for some time until the journal's course had been so far changed that it would have been hard for a new editor to do a volte-face.' Milton looked at his notes.

'Two of them mentioned how irritating he was.'

'Willie was always irritating.'

'Yes, but if you're ringing such a PC stronghold of swinging modernity as New Labour's Number Ten is, would you really not censor some of your affectations of language?'

'Like what?'

'"I could pop into a taximeter cabriolet immediately and call on you for ten minutes", was one example.'

'He always said "taximeter cabriolet", like he said "wireless" and "gramophone".'

'To the Prime Minister's press secretary? When he's praising the administration's passion for modernizing?'

'I've never known if he actually used language like that consciously or unconsciously, but I take your point. Hardly helpful.'

'He told the PM's chief of staff that they badly needed new

talent in the Lords, which these days was altogether too full of ghastly women wearing vulgar attire and sporting gaudy baubles. And he told his private secretary that since it might help to counter the view that the PM had surrounded himself by bully boys, the acquisition of a gentleman might be no bad idea.'

'Oh, Jim, this is preposterous. You'd think he was trying to wreck his chances.'

'Precisely. That's exactly what he did. The Number Ten view of him changed dramatically as a result.'

'Good God,' said Amiss. 'Of course, that's it.'

'You're thinking what I'm thinking.'

'Yes. And I bet we agree on the likely culprit.'

It took Tewkesbury the best part of a morning to track down a Harvard don who knew Dwight Winterton well. 'Great guy,' he said. 'Mad as a coot, but a first-rate mind, great company and a brilliant mimic.'

'Many thanks,' said Tewkesbury. 'That's all I needed to know.'

'What's the problem?' asked the don in a tone of alarm. 'Is he in trouble?'

'No, no,' said Tewkesbury. 'Goodbye.' He put the phone down. 'He's a brilliant mimic, sir.'

Milton, who had been leafing through interview reports in increasing frustration, looked up. 'Says who?'

'His Harvard history tutor.'

'Did you cover your tracks?'

'How do you mean, sir.'

'Like telling him you were just checking up that you had the right Winterton.'

'Eh?'

'Oh, never mind. Just fetch me Winterton, wherever he is, before he gets a tip-off.'

Tewkesbury spent most of the afternoon vainly searching for Winterton, who had gone to lunch with a civil service mole and then disappeared to read in the London Library.

When he finally sloped back to the office, Miss Mercatroid, as instructed, sent him straight to Milton.

'What can have been going on in my absence, Mr Milton?' he asked, as he sat down. 'Why am I in such urgent demand? No more cadavers, I trust, just when we were settling down?'

'Mr Winterton,' said Milton, 'you are, I hear, a formidable mimic.'

Winterton looked him straight in the eyes. There was a long pause and then he grinned. 'I suppose, Mr Milton, this is where you would like me to start guiltily, blush to the roots of my hair, clutch at wherever it is my heart is supposed to be located and cry, "Who told you that?", thus making it clear that I've been keeping it a secret that, yes, I have a certain facility in that department. So instead I shall confound your expectation and instead say, "It's a fair cop, guv." I impersonated Lambie Crump in several phone calls to my colleagues. I thought you'd eventually twig that since there was no other evidence he ever got pissed, he was unlikely to be making nuisance phone calls.'

'May I ask why you did this?'

'Malice and fun, Mr Milton. It relieved my feelings of rage to have him appear to behave like an uncouth, drunken prat, and there was the amusing bonus of listening to my colleagues coping with their deranged editor.'

'And how did they?'

'Let's see. Robert, of course, was diplomatic, Wilfred was obsequious, Henry expostulated and argued angrily – especially when he was drunk himself, Ricketts – '

'You didn't call Ricketts,' interrupted Milton, despite himself.

'I did, but I thought better of it three sentences in. Couldn't cope with the whimpers and wails of, "Oh, no, Mr Lambie Crump, sir. What are you saying? I don't understand." I stopped in mid-rant, launched into sober Crumpspeak and explained that I was just perpetrating a small jest by pretending to be inebriated.'

Winterton adopted a high-pitched falsetto. '"Oh, Mr Lambie Crump, sir. Thank you, sir. I'm sorry, sir, that I was taken in for a moment and became a little upset. But it was a very good joke, sir. I know that you ladies and gentlemen always like your little jokes." And the poor old sod followed with a forced "ha-ha", that would have melted the steeliest of hearts.'

'Who else did you call?'

'The usual suspects. There was a wonderful row with Clement Webber, which I wish I'd taped. Amaryllis was a bit of a disappointment, being pissed herself that night and only half listening. Ben and Marcia were a particular hoot, because they were on two different extensions and plunged into a row between themselves over the pseudo-Crump's assertion that there had been more errors in March than in April.'

'Was that it?'

Winterton thought. 'Apart from Lord Papworth, who was courteous, there was Milady Troutbeck.' He laughed.

'How did she deal with it?'

'Swiftly. "Bugger off, Willie," she said, and put the phone down.'

'No one guessed?'

'No, because I had sneakily never mimicked anyone to any of my colleagues. I thought that in a new job it was wise, perhaps, to keep this card up my sleeve in case I needed it. And I was glad I had. Willie was driving me mad, and getting at him this way got a lot of the venom out of my system, while damaging the bastard at the same time by enhancing his reputation for selfishness and double-dealing.'

'Hardly responsible behaviour, though.'

'Indeed, Mr Milton. Hardly responsible. I thank you for the moral guidance.' He burst into a convincing imitation of Tony Blair. 'Responsibility, maturity, compassion, vision, giving. Ask not what you can have but what you can give.' He reverted to his own voice. 'All missing during those calls, I'm ashamed to say.'

Milton's lip twitched. Tewkesbury looked disapproving and Winterton broke into a broad grin.

'So much for your colleagues, Mr Winterton. Now, did you make calls to anyone outside *The Wrangler*?'

Winterton looked appraisingly at Milton. 'Do you already

know, I wonder. I'd better tell you the lot, hadn't I? Otherwise you'll find out about them anyway and think I'm underhand and that would never do. And besides, it doesn't matter now.

'I did two impersonations of Lambie Crump. For his colleagues, who knew him very well, it was always Drunk Willie, because the slurrings covered up any slight failings in my impersonation. With acquaintances and strangers of course I could do a sober Crump. What I decided to do was from sheer spite to try to scupper his chances of a peerage by making unhelpful calls to Number Ten, Downing Street. And I enjoyed every minute. It was great fun to wind up those PC know-alls.'

'But would it not have been of benefit to you, Mr Winterton, to have had him elevated to such a position? Wouldn't he have been compromised as editor and have had to leave the paper?'

'I don't know that he would, Mr Milton. From what Henry Potbury told me about his fellow trustees, Lambie Crump would have been allowed to stay on even if he had become the Prime Minister's official catamite. Anyway, I didn't care. I just wanted to spike his chances of becoming Lord Arselicker of NewLab the way he spiked my articles.'

Tewkesbury looked even more disapproving. Milton tried not to show how much he was beginning to like Winterton.

20

'I wish I could kill off Tewkesbury's obsession with ideological motives once and for all. I've made some progress. He's given up on Phoebe Somerfield as a suspect on that front and has been pretty shaken on Winterton since he discovered he was doing well screwing Crump up by other means, but now he's clinging to the notion of Professor Webber as prime ideological suspect and we're going to Oxford to see him tomorrow.'

Amiss grinned. 'Make sure you neglect no opportunity to get them talking to each other.'

'Sounds promising. I'll do what I can.'

Milton looked up from his file as Tewkesbury drove into North Oxford. 'Tell me, Sergeant, I know you don't like Webber for political reasons, but do you dislike him personally?'

'I never met him, but I didn't like what I heard about him in Oxford. Mad as well as reactionary, I understand.'

'Still, it helps that you know something of him. And after all, it's a bond that he teaches at your alma mater. Feel free to join in the interview.'

The car pulled up outside a large villa and the two policemen got out. Milton looked with some distaste at his colleague, who had taken to applying gel to his expensively coiffed hair, which was brown, with artful blond streaks. It was not, he realized, as they opened the gate, that he cared about the gel, the dye, the haircut or the money – just that since he couldn't stand Tewkesbury, everything about him was irritating.

A large and portly man with small, green staring eyes greeted them impatiently at the door of his North Oxford villa and led them briskly into a large study. 'Now, what do you want to know?' He looked at his watch. 'I've only an hour.'

'I hope that will be ample time, Professor Webber. May I introduce Sergeant Tewkesbury, who remembers you from his Oxford days.'

Webber looked positively pleasant. 'You were a student of mine?'

'No, Professor Webber,' said Tewkesbury. 'I read English.'

Webber's face darkened. 'Good God, what an absolute waste of your time and the taxpayers' money. They're a collection of Marxists, pseuds, mad feminists, halfwits, crazed structuralists and neo- and post- this and that who have nothing in common except that they're all wankers. You'll have emerged from Oxford more ignorant and stupid than when you arrived. Why didn't you have the sense to take a real subject, like classics – or, of course, philosophy? I would have stretched a point to include history until it was taken over by that shower of dreary and pretentious – '

Pleased though he was to see Tewkesbury looking both aggrieved and embarrassed, duty required Milton to interrupt. 'Professor Webber, you're a busy man. Could we perhaps get down to business?'

'What do you want to know?'

'We'd be grateful for your view on why anyone would have wanted to murder Mr Lambie Crump, or – as is also possible – Mr Potbury.'

'Henry I can't help you on – in his professional life, that is. I imagine there may well have been people who were fed up with his drunkenness and philandering, but all those of us connected with *The Wrangler* liked Henry Potbury. He'd a good mind and was an honest man. But as for that little creep Lambie Crump.' Webber began to turn puce. He clenched his fists and waved them wildly over his head. 'By the time he died, I would think that at least' – he paused and began to count on his fingers –' one, two, three, four, five of us would have been prepared to contemplate doing him in. And I can tell you that I would have had no difficulty in justifying his murder to my ethics group.'

'The five were?'

'Winterton, Phoebe Somerfield, Amaryllis Vercoe, me and probably Amiss.'

Tewkesbury broke in excitedly. 'Do you mean, Professor Webber, that you can see an ideological reason for Robert Amiss to have wanted Lambie Crump out of the way?'

Webber looked at him in bewilderment. 'Ideological? Pull yourself together, you stupid boy. What are you talking about? What's ideology got to do with it?'

Tewkesbury began to stammer slightly. 'It's j-j-just that I've noticed a discrepancy here. Now, you admit that it was ideology that was at the root of the disagreements you and your colleagues had with Lambie Crump. Yet Amiss has always denied feeling sufficiently angry about the change in *The Wrangler*'s political line for it to constitute a motive for murder.'

Webber bounced angrily in his chair. 'What a load of clap-trap.' He looked at Milton. 'What sort of morons are you taking into the police force these days? I don't know what world this person is living in. But what can you expect when he read English under that crowd of addle-pated, venal fools who jabber platitudes and think that to use obscure terminology and peddle tenth-rate ideas makes you an intellectual?' He glared at Tewkesbury like an enraged lizard. 'Ideology my arse. This is England, not fucking Cambodia. We don't kill each other over ideology. At *The Wrangler*, ideological arguments are our intellectual bread and butter – our *raison d'être*. It's called debate. Something you wouldn't understand, coming from an environment where they all vie with each other to impose their own pet orthodoxy: mediocre minds hate dissent.'

'Really, Professor Webber, you're being very unfair. There are many fine minds in the English faculty.'

'What would you know about fine minds, Sergeant Trendy?'

A wave of compassion hit Milton. In a gentle voice, he

addressed the heavily breathing philosopher. 'Professor, I wonder could you kindly tell us more about why you and your colleagues so much disliked Lambie Crump?'

Webber stopped glaring at Tewkesbury. As he looked at Milton, the mad look went out of his eyes. 'Like Henry Potbury, we had all come to abominate Lambie Crump because he was such a self-seeking little shit. What made us feel murderous was knowing that he was a double-dyed hypocrite who had paid lip service to the *The Wrangler*'s historic position when it suited him and then shifted his position to support what passes for thinking in New Labour. That's not to do with ideology, Sergeant Numbskull,' he observed, turning to glare again at Tewkesbury. 'It's to do with principle. One had the urge to stand on him as one would on a poisonous toad.'

'Whatever you call it,' said Tewkesbury gamely, 'it's a motive for murder.'

'Good God, have you not even a vestige of a brain? One thing you have to understand about the Right is that it has a sense of history. The English Right, that is – I'm not talking about European fascists or American fundamentalists and, of course, Celts are too obsessed by nationalism to have any real understanding of Left and Right. The English Right know that our time will come around again: our enemies will be routed in due course.'

He turned to Milton. 'I was contemplating resigning from *The Wrangler* because Lambie Crump was using me less and less. I would have hawked myself elsewhere. I would be surprised if my colleagues hadn't been thinking the same way.'

He turned on Tewkesbury again. 'Dwight, Amaryllis, Phoebe and Robert are pragmatists. They would have stayed or gone as it suited them.'

'So you cannot see any of them actually standing on the poisonous toad?' asked Milton.

'I could imagine any one of us having the impulse to assault Willie by breaking over his head the portrait of our founder, but I couldn't see any of us acting against him in cold blood.

And from what I understand, the method of murdering him was cold-blooded.'

'How did you feel about Sharon McGregor's interest in buying *The Wrangler*?'

'Obviously, I hoped it wouldn't happen, but if it had, I could have lived with it. As I was trying to get through to your absurd sergeant, people of my political persuasion are better at accepting that one can't win all the time than are the sort of people he surely supports. *The Wrangler* was going to pot and that maddened me. If McGregor buys it and ruins it, I'll be madder. But it won't blight my life. And besides, McGregor won't necessarily ruin it. Some colonials respect our traditions.'

'But you know that there was some bad blood over the proposals to modify the terms to the trust, don't you?'

'All I knew was what Henry told me at the party and I've heard nothing new since then.' The mad look came back into his eyes. 'For Christ's sake, whatever-your-name-is, can't you understand that I'm busy. I teach, I write, I sit on stupid committees with stupid people. Journalism is an extra and I don't give a fuck about office politics.'

The door opened and a small, harassed-looking woman arrived carrying a tray with a pot of coffee, a milk jug and a mug. 'Oh, I'm sorry, Clement,' she said. 'I hadn't realized you had people with you.'

She turned to the policemen. 'Would you like some coffee?'

'No, they wouldn't,' said Webber. 'They're just going.'

Milton kept his temper and stood up. 'Thank you, Mrs Webber, but we're fine. Professor Webber, we will not go until we have checked out your alibi for the twenty-four hours before Lambie Crump died.'

'I've already given it to one of your stupid people.'

Milton looked him straight in his little lizard eyes. 'Professor Webber. I suggest you cooperate.'

Webber glared. Then his eyes dropped. 'I went to a dinner, came home and didn't leave Oxford that night or the following day.'

'You gave my colleagues details of engagements during that day which proved that you were tied to Oxford, but in theory you have no alibi after eleven p.m.' He bowed to Mrs Webber. 'I know you told the police that your husband was at home all night, but were you not asleep for much of that time?'

'Not for much of it,' she said, in an unexpectedly tart tone.

'You're a bad sleeper?'

'Only when I'm obliged to be. But on this occasion I can certainly give Clement an alibi.'

'Oh, for God's sake,' said Webber. 'Stop pussy-footing and give them the full story.'

'Clement came home from the senior philosophers' dinner assisted by two friends. At my request, they deposited him upstairs on our bed, where he remained until perhaps eight o'clock the following morning, snoring loudly. That's why I didn't sleep and he has an alibi. And in any case, he couldn't have got down our stairs without falling, let alone have driven to London and climbed up Lambie Crump's.'

For the first time, Webber smiled. 'And I can't remember a thing. But I can give you the names of the people who took me home.'

Milton saw the expression on Tewkesbury's face and sympathized with his disappointment.

21

Dwight Winterton's 'The Triumph of Humbug', which savagely attacked the new and cynical debasement of language on both sides of the Atlantic, amused Amiss greatly. Men had followed women in adopting meaningless rhetoric of the 'outreaching', 'inclusive', and 'feeling-and-sharing-each-other's-pain' variety and using it shamelessly to cover shallowness, arrogance and vainglorious ambition. The major casualty was truth.

Amiss had been rather perturbed to find that the male minister whom Winterton had singled out as – if anything – worse than the Prime Minister, was the junior Foreign Office minister for whom Rachel worked. 'Does it absolutely have to be Eric Sinclair that you produce as the prime example of bullshit?' he asked Winterton.

'Why shouldn't it be? He's the worst.'

'It's just slightly difficult for personal reasons into which I cannot go.'

'But, Robert, you can't ask me to find a stand-in for a man who talks of the importance of the peoples of all nations sharing in joy the tapestry of their multicultural experience, can you? Especially when he's trying to cover up the fact that they're carrying out the policy of the previous government when it comes to arms sales.'

'Um,' said Amiss.

Winterton seized the typescript from him. 'Come on, Robert. What about, "We offer a vision where all will give and none will take and Britain's moral leadership as an ethical touchstone will be hailed as a star in a black sky?" You can't ask me to leave that out, can you?' His face crumpled suddenly into dejection. 'But of course you can. You're the editor.'

'Oh, never mind,' sighed Amiss. 'OK, Dwight. I promise I won't change a word. I'll deal with my personal problem as best I can.'

He evaded the issue all evening, pleased that Rachel was in good form, bubbling with excitement about her forthcoming trip to South-East Asia where her minister would be speaking at a conference on International Law about New Britain's approach to human rights. Normally Amiss would have queried whether the best way to win over the representatives of ancient civilizations with problems and priorities different from our own was to send them political neophytes to lecture them on how to run their countries, but tonight he was treading carefully.

'Just one thing, Rach,' he said at the end of the conversation.

'Yes?'

He wriggled back into his chair. 'There's something I have to warn you about.'

'Yes?'

'There's going to be an article in *The Wrangler* this week that I'm afraid you won't like. I'm really sorry if it upsets you, but I'm afraid there was nothing I could do about it.'

'I don't like *The Wrangler* – period.'

'Yes, I know that. But this is something specific that you might really hate.'

She sat upright and looked at him suspiciously. 'Stop procrastinating and tell me.'

'It's just that by sheer chance Dwight is making fun of your minister.'

'What do you mean, "by sheer chance"?'

'I mean he doesn't like him, but he knows nothing of the link with me. He knows my girlfriend is in the Foreign Office, but he's got no idea what you do.'

'And you did nothing about it?'

171

'I can't censor him for personal reasons, Rachel. You know that. It just wouldn't be – if you'll excuse the word – ethical.'

'Have you a copy?'

He gave her a proof and watched lugubriously as she read through and her face darkened. 'This is horrible. What's happened to you? You seem to have come to hate decency and compassion since you went to work for that dreadful Tory rag.'

'It's not a dreadful Tory rag, Rachel. It's a journal of ideas from a standpoint which happens not to be too popular at present.'

'It's a Tory rag and you've made it worse. This is cheap and cruel and abusive of a good minister whose only crime is to use language which old fogeys wilfully misunderstand.' She slammed it down on the table. 'I don't remember any such mockery of William Hague's beastly baseball cap or his bonding sessions with colleagues in silly jumpers. Or the ghastly Portillo's Pauline conversion to caring and sharing.'

'We did run a few jokes about all that.'

'Nothing on this scale.'

Amiss looked at her pleadingly. 'Don't you think it's just a bit funny?'

'I don't, Robert.' She stood up. 'Good night. I'm going to bed now. In the spare room.'

'Jolly good issue,' said Papworth. 'Good and robust. I've had abuse and praise in equal shares today. Congratulations.'

'I'm glad you liked it, Charlie. I feared it was rather over the top myself. I didn't agree with much of it.'

Papworth chortled. 'It's the ultimate irony for you, isn't it? A person who thinks he's a liberal but we think is a conservative is out of sheer fair-mindedness producing a journal that makes many conservatives wince at its right-wingery and rampant libertarianism. You see it as your duty to disagree with yourself, as it were.'

'I was a civil servant, Charlie. I wrote many speeches and drafted many papers I didn't agree with. It comes easier than you might think.'

'Well, keep it coming. If you go on like this, we might even begin to sell some copies and make a profit.'

'Steady on, Charlie. Let's stick in the realms of the possible.'

'Christ, Webber is some looney,' observed Milton, when he dropped in on Amiss that Friday evening for a drink. 'I don't think I've ever come across someone so choleric. Still, it was worth it to see Tewkesbury so abused. And I think he was grateful to me for not rubbing it in. He has rallied since and suggested that that Jack Troutbeck was mad enough to murder for reasons of principle, but fortunately on the relevant night she had been up till one a.m. at a dinner in St Martha's, where, incidentally, she gave a rousing rendition of "The Road to Mandalay". And the following morning she was seen at seven-thirty setting off for London, where she spent the entire day chairing a conference.'

'Doesn't sound like Jack.'

'Oh yes, it does. It was a sort of rally for those in favour of elitism in education. They call themselves the Anti-dilutions because they're against dilution of standards . . .'

'And are making a play on antediluvian. Yes. Very Jack. So where is Tewkesbury turning his attentions now?'

'Still clinging on to you, I think. But afraid to say it at present, in case I bite him.'

'Does he dislike me?'

'Yes, probably because he's jealous as well as disapproving because you've led the journal back from the path of righteousness down which Lambie Crump was leading it.'

'He's not alone. I think I've made more enemies in the last couple of weeks than I have in my whole life. Even the people who are most thrilled that I'm doing a serious job are shocked at the journal's line. God help me, like Rachel, my parents think this government is wonderful and can't understand why I'm being negative. They rang up this morning to tut-tut over several parts of this week's and to ask me why I'm allowing these awful people to attack poor Mr Blair.'

'Did you manage to calm them down?'

'My dad's always calm. And my mother will put up with it. Anyway, the good sign was they'd read nearly the whole thing – apart from the literary pages – and had opinions on several articles and even disagreed with each other about two. And Dwight's attack on New Labour rhetoric was so controversial that he was on the BBC at lunchtime, which gives me hope that we might be able to flog the vastly increased number of copies I ordered this week.'

'You're enjoying yourself, aren't you?'

'Some of the time. Now, what about you?'

Milton spread his hands wide. 'Getting nowhere slowly. I still have no idea how Potbury died and not the faintest idea who did for Lambie Crump and why, unless it was in connection with selling *The Wrangler*. I agree with Webber that ideology had nothing to do with it.'

'Me too,' said Amiss.

'But that would mean the most likely murderer has to be someone who desperately wanted to stop the trustees agreeing to alter the trust.'

'Henry Potbury,' said Amiss.

'Thanks, Robert. That's a big help. What do you think about Papworth?'

'Piers Papworth was all for it.'

'Yes, but his father wasn't. And I've still got a question mark over him. He seems too good to be true.'

He dug around in his briefcase and pulled out a plastic wallet. 'I quote from Tewkesbury's notes, where he records Papworth as saying: "I should be sad to see the journal fall into the wrong hands, but it's not something I'd fight Piers to the death over. I don't know how long I'll go on trying to block him. After all, at my age, what's the point? As my heir, he'll have the last laugh anyway."'

'That's typical Charlie Papworth, Jim.'

'It may be, but it makes him look a bit more resigned to losing than is suggested by a man who replaced Henry Potbury with Jack Troutbeck, the doughtiest of doughty fighters for the soul of *The Wrangler*. Piers can't have been too thrilled with that.'

'Have you asked him about it?'

'I haven't even interviewed him yet. He's been out of the country for three weeks.'

'Definitely out of the country.'

'Yes. He's attending to some family business in Australia. I've had it checked. He's been there all the time.'

'So whatever he did, he didn't kill Lambie Crump.'

'No. But why would he want to kill his main ally?'

'I don't know,' sighed Amiss. 'But in the middle of these shifting sands, doesn't it help to be able to rule people out completely?'

'I suppose so. Though when the field is as broad as this, it's a small consolation. Incidentally, like most of the other obvious suspects, Papworth senior doesn't have a complete alibi. He was at a drinks party that evening, followed by a light supper at his club with a couple of friends. He was back at his pied-à-terre around nine-thirty, he said, and straight to bed.'

'No corroboration?'

'The friends at the club and his wife. But since he went to bed immediately and they occupy separate bedrooms, her usefulness is limited.'

'If I understand it all correctly,' said Amiss, 'we're in the interesting position that Lambie Crump was definitely murdered but there was no apparent motive for anyone doing so, while Piers Papworth or even Sharon McGregor had excellent reasons to get rid of Henry Potbury, who probably died accidentally.'

'That's about it.'

'So what will you do next?'

'What can I do except go on burrowing? I'm focusing at the moment on the trust-busting business and the money involved.'

'Have you met the trustees yet?'

'I had an entirely useless conversation with Lord Hogwood and Sir Augustus Adderly, both of whom are next to gaga and both of whom were busily bewailing the loss of Saint Willie. But I'm glad to report that they think you're doing well.'

'I should hope they do. I've been assiduously following in Willie's footsteps by buttering them up at every opportunity. What did they say about the possible reduction in the powers of trustees?'

'Just that they're there but to serve, that they had always been guided by Crump and that when he had said it was necessary to move with the times they had been happy to go along with him since one must always be on the side of progress.'

'Did they mention Henry?'

'Just said he was a nice fellow who got rather hot under the collar about things and they had hoped he'd come round.'

'Anything about the change in *The Wrangler*'s politics?'

'Adderly said that Potbury had exaggerated the scale of it and it didn't matter anyway since "we are all Blairites now". And Hogwood kept bleating on about the necessity to bend to the call of modernity.'

'God, they really are an awful pair of old idiots. Absolutely classic examples of gutless Great and Good Tories – the kind that would have wanted to make friends with Hitler because he couldn't really be such a bad chap and might be cross if you argued with him. Anyway, whatever they are, they're a fat lot of use to me or to *The Wrangler* and I wait impatiently to hear how Jack gets on on Monday at her first formal trustees' meeting.'

'See if she can do dinner afterwards,' said Milton, as he got up to leave. 'By then I should have talked to the solicitor in charge who's just back from his holidays. It'll be on me. Just agree a restaurant with Jack and let me know.'

As he opened the door, he turned back. 'Will Rachel come?'

'I'll ask, but I should think she'd rather stay late at work. She's pretty pissed off with *The Wrangler*.'

'But she's pleased about you being editor, isn't she?'

'She was, and in a way she still is. But she is, as she put it recently, "disappointed that I've taken it backwards". And enraged that I allowed Dwight to attack one of her ministers.'

'That's not reasonable.'

'It is from her perspective. I hate to admit it, Jim, and I can't understand it, because Rachel always disliked bullshit, but she seems to have bought the rhetoric of this fucking government. She talks about vision and leadership and people power and all the rest of those awful words they use to cover up their complete absence of any genuine philosophy, principle or policy. "Compassion with a hard edge," for Christ's sake. All that means is that you do Tory things but claim you're doing it because you're good, while they did it because they were bad.' He sighed. 'I'm afraid the abandonment of intellectual rigour and scepticism is now afflicting even the public service.'

'Not me so far,' said Milton. 'But perhaps Tewkesbury will yet convert me.'

22

'It was doubly unfortunate,' wailed Amiss. 'Vexed is not exactly the word. Try incandescent. We could have done without all this outside provocation to make things worse than they already are. I didn't realize that taking this job was liable to require such sacrifices.'

The baroness leant across the table and patted his hand. 'I'm proud of you, my boy. You have put principle before comfort. Under you, *The Wrangler* is, as the Prime Minister no doubt would put it if he weren't on the other side, "a beacon of hope in a world of darkness".'

'That's not the way Rachel's looking at it. She thinks I've put Dwight Winterton before Rachel Simon because I'm thoughtless, uncaring, cowardly, bigoted and a lot of other adjectives I'd rather not repeat.'

'She's a silly-billy,' said the baroness.

'I always thought she was very easy-going,' said Milton.

'So did I,' said Amiss.

'It's New Labour,' said the baroness. 'She's been infected. It's like a cult. She needs to be kidnapped and taken to one of those places where they re-educate the brainwashed. Would you like me to seize her and incarcerate her in St Martha's? I could always put her in a padded cell with Plutarch. Speaking of whom . . .'

'Not tonight, Jack, please. I'm worn down by personal problems.'

'I'll let you off tonight, but we'll have to talk about it tomorrow. The anti-Plutarch camp is mutinying, and what she did yesterday didn't help.'

'Oh God, what did she do?'

'You're not up to hearing tonight.' She turned to Milton. 'Right, Jim. Get on with it. What gives from the solicitors?'

'The trust would be very expensive – though conceivably possible – to break if all three trustees stood resolute. If one trustee backed change, the case would be slightly strengthened; two make a big difference. Three and it's a piece of cake.'

'Well, they're not going to get three,' said the baroness grimly. 'That's for sure.'

'So the solicitor said. In fact, he allowed a wintry smile to crease his wintry face and said that the recalcitrant trustee was even more recalcitrant than her predecessor. "I thought her," he said, "a rather odd choice of Lord Papworth's. But that was before I discovered he and his son did not see eye-to-eye on the matter."'

'Any figures put on the price of recalcitrance?'

'He thinks your very existence could add two hundred thousand to the costs and two years to the timescale.'

'How interesting,' said the baroness. 'So that's why Sharon McGregor offered me a hundred-thousand-pound bribe.'

'A real bribe?'

'Not in so many words. Sharon is a direct woman, but even she is not that brash.'

'So how did she put it?'

'She said she would like to make a hundred-thousand-pound donation to St Martha's, but might not have the readies because of legal expenses. A likely tale.

'I asked artlessly what expenses were these, and she said she was funding Piers Papworth's assault on the trust. Then she smiled at me and said that not being a dumb Sheila I would understand her position. It seemed, she went on sweetly, a pity to waste money because some fuddy-duddies opposed making changes to a mag that could only benefit from modernization.' The baroness took a thoughtful swig of Chablis. 'I've rather gone off Sharon McGregor.'

'I thought you liked tough and amoral broads,' said Amiss.

'I do, I do, but they should recognize that Jack Troutbeck is not a purchasable commodity.'

'So it's the end of your brief friendship?'

'Let's say she's gone off me too, though only for the moment, I hope. I retain some optimism that we'll get back together after this battle is over and make beautiful music again. After all, if she wants to climb socially, she could do worse than rope me in. She'd have a good time.'

'Do you think she or Piers Papworth tried to bribe Henry?' asked Milton.

'That would have been more difficult,' said Amiss, 'in that it would have been personal, whereas with Jack, because of St Martha's, it's not so blatant.'

'I'll tell you what I think,' said Milton. 'I think someone had a very good reason to murder Henry Potbury. I'm looking forward to a useful conversation with Miss McGregor and with young Papworth when he returns. Just one question, Jack.'

'What?'

'If I think it necessary with McGregor, can I mention the bribe?'

There was a silence. 'Oh, fuck it,' she said, when she came out of her reverie. 'Yes, I suppose so. If it was only to do with finding fucking Lambie Crump's murderer, I wouldn't. But I don't mind queering my pitch as far as the McGregor millions are concerned if it'll help with the Henry business. We old lags must stick together. Dead or alive.'

'Listen, Mr Milton, I've companies to buy and investments to make and nothing to do with the murder of some obscure bastards on a piddling rag.'

'As I understand it, Miss McGregor, this is a "piddling rag" that you wish to buy.'

'Oh sure. And when I buy it, it won't be a piddling rag for long. It'll be a journal of international significance.' A faraway look came into her eye. 'Of course, it'll have to change. Its gotta have zap and wham and pizazz. Maybe the name'll have to go too. *The Wrangler* isn't a name would mean much in LA or Sydney or downtown Singapore. Thing'd be to keep the spirit of *The Wrangler* but find another word – something like argument, combat, conflict, challenge, discord, dissent. Do you get the idea?'

'Yes, indeed. Clearly you are serious about this, Miss McGregor. In fact, I understand that some time ago you had a management consultant in to look it over to assess the prospects for rationalization.'

'Sure, sure. I called in Walter Bett – guy I used to sort out some bus companies. Stupid bastard came a cropper. Frightened the Abos by talking about firing everyone and replacing them with robots. Headbanger. Fired him. Robots are OK doing robots' jobs. Different in magazines.' She snorted. 'Bastard just didn't understand and he didn't help me one bit by getting them all in such a stew.'

'I gather that though you want *The Wrangler*, you're not happy with its present legal status.'

'That's right. I'm not taking on a company where three old bastards well beyond their sell-by date can tell me who to hire and fire.'

She smiled dazzlingly at Milton. The crimson lipstick was as threatening as it was brilliant and matched the stunningly simple silk suit that screamed money, even to someone sartorially blind.

'So you wanted the trust scrapped.'

'Sure did. Scrapped or castrated – its balls broken. Don't care if it's there or not as long as I can do as I like.'

Out of the corner of his eye, Milton observed that Tewkesbury was gaping at Sharon McGregor like a child looking in awe at a ringmaster in a circus. He sympathized with him. It was all he could do himself to stay calm and on course. Her energy was curiously enervating.

'I'd be grateful for your help,' he said gently. 'I appreciate that your interest in *The Wrangler* is commercial, but my job is to find out who murdered Mr Lambie Crump and possibly Mr Potbury, and I need all the help I can get. You may be able to shed some light on tensions within the paper.'

'OK. What do you want?'

'Perhaps you could begin at the beginning and tell me how

you got to know of *The Wrangler*, when you thought about acquiring it, something about your relationships with people connected with the paper and how things stand now.'

She shot back her left cuff and scrutinized her diamond-encrusted Rolex. 'OK. It's the seventh today. Makes just four months since I went to my first dinner party in London and met Piers Papworth. We kidded about. He asked me what it was like to own half Australia. I asked him about the joys of being a belted earl. He said by the time he got to be one he wouldn't have two pennies to rub together.

'So I say maybe we should get married. You know, like the old tradition of rich foreign heiresses marrying English upper-class poms, though I'm better than an heiress because I have the stuff already. He says sorry, he's married already. Points across the room to some Sheila with a face like a horse. I say why hadn't he married money? He said he'd married some, but if he was doing it again he'd need much more to compensate for all the estate had lost through his pa being so bloody high-minded.

'That sounds really interesting to me. It's not often you hear about people like that. Usually people are complaining about being screwed by greedy bastards. So I ask him what he's going on about and he tells me about *The Wrangler* and how his old man has spent a fortune on it because he thinks it's his duty.'

She looked squarely at Milton. 'Now I'll tell you something about myself. I want to make more money, but I want to enjoy myself as well. Seems to me that a daft magazine associated with nobs might be just the right way into society here. Of course, being rich I'll get lots of invitations, but they'll mostly be from people who want you just for your money. You know the kind. They're either on the fund-raising circuit or they're after you to invest in their business. I wouldn't mind meeting journalists and intellectuals and all those as well.

'So next day I send for a heap of back copies of the mag, tell my lawyer to find out all about it, get a researcher on to the background and by evening I've decided to buy it if the business can be done with the trust. I call in Piers and tell him to get to work and he tells me he's got no influence with the trustees. I say what about his pa and he says pa doesn't either, and even if he did, he wouldn't. He's a nobleman of the old school, apparently, generally full of old-fashioned crap. But then he says if I really want to pursue it I should try going through *The Wrangler*'s editor, Willie Lambie Crump. "Willie," says Piers with a wink, "might be persuadable."

'So Piers brings Lambie Crump along to drinks at my hotel and then bows out tactfully after half an hour. I've got the measure of Lambie Crump by then. He's a sponger and he's a dickhead, but I need him. The only question is what's his price, and I know it can't be used fivers: he's too dishonestly corrupt for that. We've got to do it the English way and be subtle. Then he can keep feeling superior even though he's taking the money to sell out his own paper.

'So I talk to him about my big plans to build up a media empire. I talk about being inspired by Aussies like Kerry Packer and Rupert Murdoch, but say too that I know that since I'm so inexperienced in Britain I'll need wise counsel. In fact, I say, what I really need is someone I can trust who will help me to get started and who can then be chairman of the board of this big, ambitious, expansionist company. And where better to start than *The Wrangler* and Lambie Crump.

'He's purring by now, especially when I get across the idea that this is all going to be big and money's no object. This chairman will be my guru. He'll be non-executive, of course: won't have to spend much time on the job except for advising me and helping me network. I'm painting a picture of a guy who has big influence, big income, big status and big perks, and Lambie Crump's getting orgasmic.

''Course along with all this he's got to keep his shabby little conscience quiet by admiring my vision and smarming that with my sensitivity and intelligence I'd be different from those other foreign proprietors from hell. "I say, my dear," he says, "together we could be a winning team." Kisses my hand and talks about how we're beauty and the beast. How we'll shake up the British press and then move in overseas. And nowhere better to start than *The Wrangler*, though I'll appreciate how difficult it will be to bring the trustees on board.

'So it's all understood. As far as he's concerned, he's going to be rich and powerful if he delivers. Doesn't have the balls to demand a written agreement, more fool him. Doesn't realize that I'd shit on him the moment I could, because I despise people who are that easily bought, especially if they've got no loyalty. What sort of a drongo would I be to trust someone who rats?

'Off he goes to work on the trustees and delivers two proudly within forty-eight hours. But try as he might, he can't get anywhere with that fat, drunken bastard Potbury. Piers tries too but there's nothing doing. I put a private eye on to him and he reports we've hit a real roadblock here. Bugger's got brains and principles and he's honest. No sign he's greedy for anything. Already got plenty of money to get pissed with every day, no higher ambitions: even has all the women he wants.

'Seems we're stymied. I tell the lawyers to get on with it as fast as possible without him. Then it gets worse, 'cos Piers tells me Potbury and old man Papworth are now in cahoots and Papworth's lawyers are going to fight me all the way on what they describe as the high moral ground.'

She paused for breath and Milton nipped into the aural void. 'What I don't quite understand, Miss McGregor, is what is the point in going ahead, since presumably whatever happened with the trust Lord Papworth wouldn't sell to you anyway.'

'But he's very old and Piers says we should be ready for when he goes for the high jump. Might be now, might be next year, might be in ten years' time. But Piers reckons, considering the family history, he won't be around that much longer. And he wants to sell up the day his pa is buried.'

'But you're investing a lot on a gamble, aren't you, if you're fighting a law case?'

'Sure. It could cost a lot. And the old man might hang around for years and I can't afford to wait that long. But that's business. Gotta gamble.'

'What I also don't understand is how anyone can be meddling in the terms of the trust without the consent of the owner.'

'Only through the heir. It's one of the safeguards that either the proprietor or the heir can challenge the trust if they can show sufficient reason. Kind of insurance in case one of them's a fruitcake.'

'How complicated. But I think I understand. Now back to Mr Potbury. There's no denying that it was good news for you and Piers Papworth that Potbury died.'

'Yes, sure, but don't waste your time on me, Mr Milton. If you're worth close on a billion bucks you're not going to go murdering people over a small business hiccup like this.'

'How much were you offering Piers Papworth for an unencumbered *Wrangler*?'

'Five million.'

'Five million pounds?'

'Yeah, sure. I know it's a lot, but I kinda want it. Like some people want a yacht. It's a fun investment and could be good. It's got the name – until I change it – it's got the age, it's got the kudos and it gives me a great jumping-off ground here. And anyway, it'll be a handy tax loss. Besides, Piers drove a hard bargain. Pointed out the grief it'd be causing in the family. And it sure has. His pa's mad. His ma's mad. And though they're being kinda English and civilized, it's a big strain. Piers said, and I agreed, that he deserved a big bonus for fucking up his relationship with his parents.'

'You're not going to renege on him the way you would have on Lambie Crump?'

'Renege on the Honourable Piers Papworth? Fat chance. He got it in writing that if the journal's available and free of the trust within two years, I'll buy it for five mill.' She grinned happily. 'Anyway, the other bonus is that with money like that at stake Piers'll really try.'

'Do you think he might have gone so far as to murder Potbury?'

She shrugged. 'Never thought about it. Thought the guy just fell into the punch. Gave me a good laugh.'

185

'Do you think Mr Papworth would be capable of murder?'

'How do I know? I hardly know the guy. Hard bastard, I'd say, but wouldn't have thought he was as hard as that. And I wouldn't approve of it either. You don't want to bring murder into legit business. I'm not running a fucking Mafia operation.'

'What about Lambie Crump as a possible murderer?'

'Jeez, I wouldn't expect that guy to know how to kill a kitten. But what do I know? Sometimes that kind's the worst.' She glanced at the Rolex again. 'Is that it?'

'Almost, Miss McGregor. But I'd like to know what happened after Potbury's death.'

'Oh, that was pretty pissy. Thought it was going to be OK then, but the old man pulls a fast one and puts on that Troutbeck broad instead of him. I wasn't bothered at first. I'd met her and thought she was OK. Sure, I knew she was tough. But she was on the make as well. Wanted big bucks for that college of hers. So I thought I had her.' She snorted. 'Canyabelieve I offered her one hundred K just like that to buy the land she wanted and when I make it clear there's a string attached, she turns me down flat?'

'Do you mean you tried to bribe her?'

'I don't bribe, Mr Milton. You can get into trouble bribing. I pay people for their help and I pay them well. That's why I get so much help.'

'But not from Lady Troutbeck.'

'No. Who'd have thought it? She's just as soft in the head as the Potbury bastard when it comes to funny old notions: *noblesse oblige* and all that, Piers says it's called. And now Lambie Crump's dead so I'm worse off than before. I'll bet old Jack Troutbeck'll be beating up those gaga trustees even as we speak. Well, may the best woman win. Now, is that OK? Have you got all you want?'

'That's fine for now, Miss McGregor. We're grateful to you for being such an admirably frank witness.'

'Frankness saves time: bullshit costs money.' And with a nod she got up and strode from the room.

23

'Can you believe it, Jack? Sales were up by forty per cent last week.'

'Not bad. How much is because of publicity arising from Crump's murder?'

'Only a little. Circulation went up by just a few thousand in the first week, but because I got going immediately with the advertising campaign, we've gone up another twelve thousand. Now we're going hell for leather devising various kinds of circulation-boosters and subscription-bribes and all the rest of it. In other words, at last we're going to be doing what all our competitors do.'

'I saw one of those ads. Thought it was pretty revolting.'

'Which one?'

'We *Wrangle*. Do You?'

'Stop being so bloody critical, Jack. I had to think it up pretty rapidly, since name-recognition is all the rage these days and I wanted to capitalize on the wider fame that poor Willie's death has brought us.'

The baroness had lost interest. 'I've found you some talent.'

'Go on.'

'I've always fancied myself as one of those influential behind-the-scenes dons who select the perfect recruits for higher academia or sexy media jobs or MI5 or whatever, and I think I've found just the one for you: young, female, sexy and iconoclastic.'

'But we've got one of those, Jack. We've got Amaryllis.'

'No, no, no. Amaryllis is precocious. Her stuff could be written by someone twenty-five years her senior. This one is fresh, lively and irritating but demonstrably young. She's still an undergraduate, for God's sake.'

'What are her politics?'

'Rabid libertarian, of course.'

'You mean she's a clone of yours?'

'No. I'm an old libertarian: she's a young libertarian. Basically she'll be writing about what a crowd of dumbed-down tosspots the younger generation are. I told her to try something out for you and I'm faxing it now: it's mostly a savaging of all those ill-fated attempts of universities to bring themselves up to date by providing courses in subjects they shouldn't touch – like business studies, computer technology and – God help us – even writing and publishing. Pretoria Rooke's a great one for rigour.'

Amiss could not deny the article was entertaining: the Troutbeck protégée had wit, ruthlessness and originality. With amendments amounting to no more than two commas and – as a gesture to the lawyers – the removal of the names of two particularly excoriated vice chancellors, Amiss approved the article for that week. He added to the list of articles on the cover, 'Letter From an Undergraduette' – a title he hoped that by annoying everyone, including the author, would start up an enraged correspondence.

A week later, the Honourable Piers Papworth opened his front door, looking red-eyed and irritable. 'Who the hell are you?'

'Chief Superintendent James Milton and Sergeant Tewkesbury, Mr Papworth. I arranged with your wife that I would catch you here now.'

'I don't know what possessed her to agree to that,' said Papworth. 'I've had a twenty-four-hour flight and I'm tired and want to go to bed. I certainly don't want to be crossexamined. You've got a cheek waylaying me at home like this.'

'Too bad,' said Milton in a steely voice. 'A conversation

with you, Mr Papworth, is long overdue. We've waited three weeks and can't wait any longer.'

'Oh, fuck,' said Papworth. 'I suppose I'd better get it over with. Come in.'

He led them through the hall and into a pleasant drawing room. 'Sit down, then,' he said, as he threw himself into an armchair. 'What do you want to know?'

'The nature of your involvement with Miss McGregor and what exactly you've been up to with regards to *The Wrangler*.'

'You must know all that already. I don't want the bloody thing. That's been pretty strikingly obvious, hasn't it? All sorts of people must have been snooping to you about that, not excluding my dear old pa.'

'And you didn't want it because . . . ?'

'Because it's a fucking drain on the family finances, that's why. A piece of out-of-date sentiment. The Papworths can't afford that kind of expensive nostalgia. Pa should have got rid of it years ago or at least stopped it taking every spare penny we had.'

'Though I gather the losses have been stemmed pretty dramatically over the past few months.'

'Yes, that's true. It's bad now but it was much worse then. But he wouldn't even have done something about that if I hadn't nagged and nagged.' He looked at Milton crossly. 'The days are long gone when people like us should be proprietors of anything except the public conveniences we call home. And I'll do my bit there when Pa dies to try to keep Papworth Castle going. That's been haemorrhaging money as well, but I know what has to be done to keep it going. If I have to turn it into a fucking theme park I'll turn it into a fucking theme park.

'My family and I will live in the warmer bits. We'll take fivers off the proletariat and in exchange they'll be allowed to overrun our property, peer at our belongings, ride on our roundabouts or whatever we install for their diversion. We'll have vulgarities like Papworth potpourri and teatowels, and if we do all those things we might save the place, despite the bloody death duties. But there's no chance of doing that until we can raise money for investment from selling *The Wrangler*.'

'You expect a sizeable sum of money, sir, I gather.'

'Yes, but as you'll have heard, that depends on doing the business with the trust, and up to now we've been buggered by the high-minded intelligentsia. How sodding easy it was for Henry Potbury to emerge from his stupor to lecture about principle and tradition and what we owe the great intellects of the past. He's had a fat salary for years out of the Papworth estate – the same as Lambie Crump and the rest of the wankers. And now there's this old bitch of a baroness, who's even more of a menace.'

'Yet your father was on Potbury's side, Mr Papworth.'

'Sodding easy for him too. He's a great man for the *pro bono publico* shit. Spent most of his life slogging away in the Lords defending tradition and decency in public life. And where does that get him and the others like him? Despised and mocked and threatened with extinction by these miserable gits that we've got ruling us now. And meanwhile he let *The Wrangler* bleed him dry and obstinately refuses to face what's going to happen when he dies. He just can't accept that the whole Papworth heritage will crumble because I simply won't be able to pay the death duties. Unless I can get that money from Sharon McGregor.'

'What do you do for a living, Mr Papworth?'

'I've been a moderately successful banker, I'm a moderately successful farmer and I keep a moderately successful eye on our Australian property, which, of course, has been yielding too small a profit because my pa naturally took a high-minded view of our duties to sitting tenants. I wish he'd take a similarly high-minded view of his duties to his son and heir. I've just been spending three weeks trying to sort out a dispute between two tenants and the net result is another great loss for the Papworths, since Pa decreed that neither of them must suffer financially.'

'So clearly it mattered hugely to you to break this trust.'

'Yes, it did. And it does.'

'And Mr Potbury was in the way.'

'Indeed he was. And so is Baroness Troutbeck. And so, above all, is my father. But murdering people for money is not the Papworth way.' He smiled quite pleasantly. 'Our motto is "endure or perish" and we're good at enduring. If it comes to it, my wife and I will endure whatever hardship and humiliation is necessary to save Papworth Castle.'

He sat up and looked straight at Milton. 'Listen, do you really think I'm prepared to put the whole family fortune in jeopardy by knocking off old Potbury – richly though he deserved to be knocked off. For God's sake, if I did and was caught, my wife would have to cope alone with the castle and two useless teenage children who'd burn the whole place down if the insurance was good enough.'

'And you've no idea who else might have wanted to kill him?'

'No. Like me, Sharon would have liked him out of the way. Like me, murdering him wasn't an option.'

'And Lambie Crump?'

'Good God, what can I say about Lambie Crump? He was on our side. He'd have lied and cheated for us when it came to the crunch if he was going to make enough out of it.'

'But would he have murdered Potbury?'

'I never believed Willie Lambie Crump had the balls of a gnat, though I suppose you never know. Sorry, I can't help you. I don't believe Potbury was murdered. If I were you, I'd write that off and just concentrate on Willie. I'll lay you ten to one he was done by some pansy he picked up, patronized and under-paid.'

'I give up,' said Milton to Amiss.

'What do you mean, "give up"?'

'I mean there's nowhere to go on this. I can find motives and opportunity for the murder of Potbury but no evidence. I can find no motives and lots of opportunity for the murder of Crump and again no evidence. It makes no sense whatsoever to view them both as murders.'

191

'I admit it's hard to see why the same person would have done for them both.'

'It's bloody impossible. But neither can I think of any hypothesis that explains two murders and two murderers. Can you?'

'Oh, bugger it,' said Amiss. 'I can't. I admit that the more I think about it the more I begin to think that Henry wasn't murdered at all. After all, why has nobody tried to murder Jack, who's filling precisely the same role as Henry, but even more effectively?'

'One reason is simply that we're about. It would take a brave man to try to kill her when we're around the place: the Cambridge police have been keeping an ostentatious eye on St Martha's. What's more, if anyone got her, it would be virtual proof that Henry was murdered too and would therefore narrow down the suspects. It'd be madness.'

'So what are you going to do now?'

'Quit if I can. For the moment at least. Even Tewkesbury agrees. He still believes in his heart that Lambie Crump was rubbed out by some mad right-winger, and I still think it was because of greed. But we see no option but to write a report recommending that the case lie fallow.'

'Which leaves us in a very difficult position here, still not knowing if there is a killer on the staff.'

'I think you can assure Lord Papworth that it is highly unlikely that either Winterton or Phoebe Somerfield murdered Crump, while it's quite definite that neither Webber nor Amaryllis Vercoe did. Anyway, he'd be mad not to keep you on as editor. That last issue was terrific.'

Amiss beamed. 'Things are certainly going extraordinarily well. I think the literary section's going to be wonderful since I replaced that boring pillock Wilfred Parry with someone who actually loves books. Circulation's doubled and we're almost breaking even. Costs are down too. I finally managed to boot Naggiar off to early retirement at Chateau Hypochondria on medical grounds and Ricketts actually asked if he could go part time. I've brought in an assistant for Jason, who's now gradually taking over as administrator, which he'll do fine if

I'm there to take strategic decisions and do the tactful things. All is going beautifully.'

'So if Lord Papworth offers you the job permanently, will you take it?'

'I'm trying not to think of it. I've still got a question mark over the politics and I'm still not sure that the world of the media is for me. And as well as that, I'd hate to decide I wanted it and then be disappointed.'

'But you will.'

'I might.'

'And if you did, would it make Rachel happy?'

'I don't know if anything will make Rachel happy, so I'm not taking that into account. She wants me to be successful, yet all my better coups drive her frantic. She froths at the mouth over the advent of Pretoria, for instance.'

'But Pretoria's fun.'

'You're not supposed to be or have fun these days. Who was it who said that the trouble with the new young Labour MPs was that they thought "fun" was an acronym?'

'Well, I hope Papworth has the sense to beg you to stay on and that you've the sense to agree. I'm delighted how it's worked out for you, Robert. If anyone deserved a break, you did.'

He stood up. 'I'll be in touch. But formally I wish you a future at *The Wrangler* uncomplicated by deaths and detection.' He wondered as he left the room if he'd been right to conclude that the expression that flittered across Amiss's face as he spoke was slightly wistful.

'About time you met,' said the baroness.

Amiss eyed her companion rather apprehensively. Pretoria Rooke was thin and sexy. She wore a short, tight-fitting ribbed sweater that showed off her navel-ring to advantage. Her jeans were skintight, her dyed blonde hair spiky with gel. She had four rings in one ear and two in the other, but mercifully – for Amiss was squeamish – her nose was innocent of metal.

As they began dinner in the mistress's private dining room,

Amiss felt like a grandfather, but Pretoria's precociousness, her mischievous sense of humour and the surprising extent of her intellectual capital shrank the years. And since she and the baroness were so familiar with each other in a jolly, female-anarchist kind of way, all barriers of age disintegrated. Even Plutarch, prowling around and demanding food and attention, added to the general gaiety.

Amiss realized that – like the baroness – Pretoria had in abundance a quality he had always lacked. She knew whom she hated, she knew why, she wished to hound them to their death, she loved the thrill of the chase and she most enjoyed the kill. She was a star, and one with the brains, breadth, originality and verve to keep *Wrangler* readers – particularly the young – happy for a long time to come. He felt very relieved that as a result of guessing the competition must be after her, he had written to her after her second article thanking her and quadrupling her fee. He hoped that this evening would help to bind her to *The Wrangler* with bonds of loyalty and affection.

It was after the second brandy and a conversation raucously uncharitable at the expense of great stars of the written and broadcast media, that the baroness jumped up, said abruptly: 'I'm off. Early start,' and disappeared.

'That's not like her,' said Amiss.

'Never mind,' said Pretoria. She stood up, walked around the table and kissed him. After a couple of minutes, Amiss pulled himself away. 'I'm sorry, I'm sorry,' he said as they disengaged. 'This is unethical. You're a contributor, I'm an editor and I don't approve of casting couches.'

She put her hands on her hips. 'You're an idiot, Robert,' she said. 'I've already been cast. Now, let's get back to business.'

Amiss lay agonizing as Pretoria breathed gently beside him. He thought guiltily of Rachel and then even more guiltily about taking advantage of someone so young. At the thought of all the hideous complications that could ensue, he shuddered. Had he even told her the night before that he was to all intents and purposes married – even if going through a rocky marital patch? How could he tell her that this could be only a one-night stand? Would she be hurt or would she be furious? Might she abandon *The Wrangler* forthwith out of pique? And anyway did he want it to be a one-night stand? Did he truly still want to be with Rachel despite all the angst? Wouldn't it be hugely invigorating to have a passionate romance with a creature like this. And besides, maybe Rachel would be glad to be rid of him.

As he fretted at his inability to know what he wanted, Pretoria opened her eyes and fell upon him enthusiastically. When an hour later they disentangled, Amiss looked at the clock and saw that it was just after eight and he had fifty minutes to catch his train. He gave Pretoria another hug. 'I'm going to have to get up now,' he said. 'I have to go.'

'Before you do,' said Pretoria, 'there's something I have to say to you, Robert.'

He felt panic washing over him. Would she declare herself as having fallen in love? What would he say in return? What did he feel anyway? What did he want?

She settled snugly into his left shoulder. 'Look,' she said, 'I don't want to hurt your feelings in any way, but you do understand, don't you, that this is just a one-off?'

He felt much more indignation than relief. 'How's that? What do you mean?'

'A) you're shacked up with someone else and I don't break up relationships, b) you're my editor and to continue would be unprofessional, and c) I'm young and I want to play the field. It's been great fun, but we need to stop it here. No hard feelings.'

Amiss looked at as much of her as he could see. He looked at the earrings, he looked at the navel-ring, he looked at the tattoo on her right breast, he looked at the spiky hair and he felt his age. 'You're a new breed, you lot,' he said and laughed. 'Don't worry, Pretoria. No hard feelings.'

24

'Lord Papworth can see you early evening at his flat.'

'Fine. Tell him I'll be there at six.'

Amiss spent the day putting together the best issue yet. Unencumbered by Lambie Crump and given more time to develop her interests, Phoebe Somerfield had produced a classic *Wrangler* leader on integrity in public life, as well as a three-page essay under her own name on the arrogance and dumbing-down of the BBC; Winterton had been let rip on sanctimonious and purposeless paternalism in the Home Office; and the baroness – with special reference to Napoleon and Bill Clinton (hated particularly for his anti-smoking crusade) – was arguing that liberalism always led to malevolent despotism, as Britain was beginning to find out. He was modestly pleased too with his own much more moderate leader on the dangers of futher politicizing the civil service – a subject on which he had unambiguous views.

'So that's that, Charlie. There's just nothing to go on. The Met extends its apologies but there's bugger-all it can do without evidence. It's Milton's considered view that neither Dwight nor Phoebe had anything to do with it, but he can't formally give them a clean bill of health any more than he can give one to me or Jason or Josiah Ricketts. It's not great for the journal and it remains tricky for you if you want to make either of them editor.'

'But I don't,' said Papworth. 'I'm very happy with you.'

'I've got a problem, Charlie.'

Papworth looked at him wearily. 'What sort of a problem?'

'Do you remember the conversation we had the night before Willie died?'

'What conversation?'

'On the telephone. About my plan to move to a new printers. You were very pleased because it was bringing in a five-figure saving.'

'Was that really the night before Willie died? But I was out.'

'You were back at ten-twenty-five when I rang.'

'Can you be sure?'

'I'm afraid so. I checked it this morning when my telephone bill arrived.'

Papworth looked straight at him. 'Fair enough. If you say so. I couldn't place it myself.'

'I know too that your wife says Willie had rung ten minutes earlier and been told you were in bed.'

'You don't want to read too much into this, Robert. I got up to get a nightcap.'

'That might have convinced me, Charlie. But unfortunately I remember you telling me that Imogen was out and you were waiting up for her because she'd left a message on the answering machine saying she'd forgotten her keys.'

'Bugger.' Papworth snuggled into his chair and said nothing for a minute or two. 'I've been worrying a bit about this,' he said at last. 'But I thought I was in the clear since there was no reason for you to know about Lambie Crump's call. But I suppose you got chummy with that policeman.'

'It came up in conversation, yes.'

'So you told him?'

Amiss looked squarely at Papworth. 'Not yet.'

'And why not?'

'Because I couldn't bring myself to without telling you first.'

Papworth leaned over and patted Amiss on the knee. 'I appreciate that,' he said. 'And don't be afraid. I shan't take advantage of your kindness by slipping a little-known South American poison into your drink.'

'And I shan't take advantage of your situation by asking

you for half your kingdom. You know I've got to tell Milton the truth, however much I hate to do it.'

'Will you have another whisky with me and give me the chance to get the story off my chest before you go to the police. It would make things easier for me.'

'Of course.'

'And can what I tell you remain in confidence? I mean, will you just tell the police what you know now?'

Amiss thought for a moment. 'Yes,' he said.

Papworth poured them both another large measure, added as much water again to his own drink and then pushed the jug over to Amiss, who followed suit. Then Papworth took a sip and began.

'Crump came up to me at that drinks party at the Ritz and said he needed to talk to me urgently. "Something of profound importance for the future of *The Wrangler*," he said. Would I come to his flat later that evening? I demurred. I'm getting on a bit for evenings as packed with appointments as this would have involved, but he was very insistent, so reluctantly I agreed.

'I arrived on the dot at nine-fifteen. He was waiting for me in reception – which I thought was unusually thoughtful for him. We went up in the lift, he waved me to an armchair and poured me a drink. "I really want you to stop fighting Piers over the trust," he said.

'I told him I knew he did and that while I respected his position . . .' He caught Amiss's eye. 'Yes, I know, but one has to say something. While I respected his position I wouldn't give in. I knew what my duty was and I would persist. He looked at me insolently and said, "Charlie. One has to make it clear that this would be an unwise course of action." Unwise for whom, I asked. "Unwise for you and Piers, but particularly for Piers."

'At which stage, my dear Robert, as you can imagine, my head was beginning to spin. "Piers and I are on opposite sides, don't you remember, Willie?" I said. "What the devil are you talking about?"

'"The murder of Henry Potbury," said he.

'So we stared each other down a bit. I'm quite good at that, as a matter of fact. And after a minute or two he dropped his eyes and said crossly, "Didn't Piers tell you he murdered Henry?" No, I said. "How remiss of him," he drawled.

'"Clearly," I said, in my most pompous voice, "you are privy to information to which I am not." "Not information," he said. "Observation. It was for Piers an unfortunate happenstance that I had popped up to my flat to collect my coat and thoughtfully returned to the dining room just to check that all the guests were gone, only to see Piers emerging from the playroom. It was what these frightful critics these days call a defining moment, although that was not apparent until he spoke. 'Ah, Willie,' he said. 'This is a little unfortunate.' 'In what way?' I asked. 'There's been a sad accident,' he said. 'I'd better show you.' And then he showed me. 'Shouldn't we pull him out?' one suggested, admittedly without much enthusiasm. 'Too late, Willie. Too late,' said Piers. 'Besides, even if it were not, it would defeat the purpose. I suggest we leave.'"

'That didn't prove that Piers drowned Henry, I pointed out to Willie. "Even if you are telling the truth, he might simply have discovered him and realized he was dead." "In which case," said Willie, "he would have called the police." "You didn't," I said. "That was because – as Piers said as we left together – it was much better to muddy the waters and leave as much time as possible before Henry was discovered, so as to make it harder to pinpoint the time of death. 'After all, Willie,' he said, 'we would be the prime suspects, and it would therefore be very unfortunate that we were on the spot."'

'At this stage Willie looked at me and said, "And the waters would have been well and truly muddied, had it not been for that"' – Papworth stopped and looked apologetically at Amiss – '"that busybody and tiresome do-gooder Robert Amiss rushing back like some fussy nanny to look for Henry."

'He stopped then and I said, "Willie, for all I know you're making this up." "You were bound to say that," he said. "And you can of course check with Piers. It may very well be that he'll say it was the other way around and he discovered me. But he would still be implicated."

'At that moment he put his head on one side and smirked at me. "You know this has to be the truth. Willie Lambie Crump is an improbable man of action, whereas Piers is a daredevil and well known for his impulsiveness."

'"Why are you telling me this, Willie?" I asked. "Do you wish to blackmail me?" "Of course," he said blandly. I was still foxed: "But why should I believe you would tell anybody about this. Surely it's not to your advantage to have your ally denounced in this way – especially if he counter-accuses you?" "Oh, don't worry about that," the shit said. "One took a small precaution." And he switched on a tape recording of a brief telephone conversation in which he could be heard saying something along the lines of, "One is trying to play the white man, Piers, but one does have the occasional qualm of conscience. Still, you can rely on me. I shan't tell anyone about Henry." To which Piers unfortunately remarked, "Thanks, Willie. I appreciate it."'

'That's not exactly definitive in a court of law,' said Amiss.

'No, but it would help with a motive as strong as Piers's.'

'But surely . . .' said Amiss.

'Yes, I think I know what you're going to say, Robert. And I said it. "Why would you get yourself into trouble and face possible prosecution for having suppressed this information?" I asked, and he looked at me blandly and said contemptuously that I should not worry. He would plead that he was a coward who was frightened that Piers might be violent with him too.

'I still didn't believe that this was anything but an empty threat and I said so. Then he looked at me and said, "Charlie, I don't think you quite understand. One has had it up to here with this little tin-pot journal. There's only one way out and Sharon McGregor's offered it to me if I can sort out the trust business once and for all. You are standing in my way."

'He laughed then. "Were one a violent man, one would kill you somehow or other," he said. "But one is not so minded. Or to put it more frankly, one doesn't have the nerve. But one certainly has it in one to take revenge if one doesn't get one's way."

'He smiled offensively and said, "Come now, Charlie. You know I've got a nasty streak. Surely you realize you can't afford to take the risk that your son and heir gets locked up for life. Awful blot on the family escutcheon, for one thing."

'Then he leered again. "Sorry, Charlie. But one does like to get one's own way." And I thought of all those occasions over the years when Willie had wanted his way and I've given in because if I didn't he whinged to the trustees, and I thought how the little excrescence was more than capable of shopping Piers through spite just to get at me. So I got up and said, "I'm an old man, Willie. I need time to think. Now perhaps you'll be kind enough to advise me where's the best place to get a taxi this time of night."

'He got up too, and advised me to go out the back if I could face the fire escape, and with exquisite politeness steered me to the back, switched on the light at the gate and waved me off. I wasn't back at home five minutes before he rang and said, "Charlie, you must understand I mean it, and if I don't have the right answer within forty-eight hours, that's it."'

'What a bastard,' said Amiss.

'Indeed. But I feared he was probably telling the truth. Piers is not capable of cold-blooded murder, but I can all too easily see him having an altercation with Henry, getting a rush of blood to the head and slamming his head into the bowl. There were a couple of worrying incidents in his youth. No fatalities, you understand. But indications that his temper could suddenly turn uncontrollable and vicious.'

'So then?'

'Well, I couldn't talk to Piers: this wasn't the sort of thing one wishes to chat about over twelve thousand miles of telephone lines. But I knew in my bones that Henry had died at his hands, that Willie had colluded and that from my point of view there was only one way out, for I would never give in to blackmail of that kind.

'So I decided. To kill Willie, I reasoned, was a bit like culling a diseased stag. Willie was rotten to the core. He was happy to destroy a great journal that had made his life interesting and comfortable for reasons of pure greed. Because I wanted to stop him, he was quite prepared to destroy my son, who had done nothing Willie disapproved of, and who – for all that I believe him to be a murderer – is not a bad man. Anyway, he's my son.

'So when my wife had returned and gone to bed I found the wire and tiptoed out of the house. I don't need to tell you the rest.'

'How did you get back through the garden gate?'

'I'd left that open so my options would be too.'

'What did you do in the war, Charlie?'

Papworth grinned. 'Good question. Young people forget we did things. And some of the time I was a commando. I often think that having been in a war sometimes gives us the edge over the young. Certainly, had I not seen action, I doubt if I would have embarked on a new career as a murderer at the age of seventy-six. Apart from anything else, I wouldn't have known what to do.'

'What a pity . . .' said Amiss, and stopped. Papworth raised an eyebrow.

'The telephone call from Willie. If only . . .'

'Ah yes, that fateful telephone call. If only I had admitted to receiving it, I wouldn't be in the pickle I'm in. But you see I didn't want to draw attention to myself, and in my innocence I didn't know that the wretched telephone company now can snoop on who rings whom. Then I thought I had covered it up all right, or rather I thought Imogen had covered it up all right, but unfortunately I had forgotten until now that it was that night you phoned about the printers.'

'How much does Imogen know?'

'Just that I told a stupid lie and that it could be incriminating. Naturally she didn't ask anything more. One of her great merits is that she never seeks to know that which people don't want to tell her. But though she is an honest woman, she would lie to anyone for my sake and do it well too.'

Amiss looked at Papworth. 'Charlie, I know you are calm by

disposition. But really you seem extraordinarily unperturbed by the prospect of ending up in court and in jail.'

'I am really, but I thought it all through before I actually went back to the *Wrangler* building and set the ambush for Willie, and I was prepared to take the consequences of my actions. Having said that, I'll wriggle out of this if I can, though I suppose there's a fair chance that they'll find some cab driver who remembers me or something else incriminating. If I have to, I'll confess to having murdered Willie because he was trying to destroy *The Wrangler*. Obviously, I'll say nothing about Piers. And I suspect that prison won't be too bad since they'll be kind to me for the few months I've got.'

'The what?'

'Of course, I haven't told you this, have I? Piers knows I'm not in the most robust of health, but only Imogen knows I'm dying. Leukaemia. Indeed, one of the things that made it easier for me to embark on this crime was being terminally ill. It's the best time to choose to do the sort of thing that gets you a life sentence.'

He cradled his glass in his wizened old hands. 'Robert, I can't pretend that I wouldn't be grateful if you could keep this to yourself, but I understand that you probably can't. You're an honest man and a supporter of law and order. You know too that since I made you the offer of permanent editorship before you told me about your phone call, I'm not trying to bribe you. If you go to the police, as far as I'm concerned, you can still stay editor and I'm sure I can rely on you to send me copies of the journal when I'm in jail. But I know too that I can rely on you not to tell what I've told you in confidence.'

'Yes,' said Amiss. 'You can rely on me for that.' They both sat in silence for a few minutes. Then Amiss spoke. 'I'm going to forget about that phone call, Charlie. I wouldn't have if you hadn't been ill, because I am a puritan when it comes to murder. But on humanitarian grounds I simply could not bear to be the cause of you being put away. However, this does mean that I can't stay editor.'

Papworth sat bolt upright. 'My dear boy, I am, of course,

extremely grateful to you for this decision. But in God's name, why do you feel you must turn down the editorship?'

'I'd be compromised. It's as simple as that. At least I'd feel I was. And besides, I was in two minds about it anyway. You know I think that really it would be better to have the journal run by someone with right-wing fire in his belly rather than by an open-minded facilitator. So that'll be the official reason I'll give.'

'But, Robert, don't you think you take high-mindedness to a level of lunacy?'

'That's what my girlfriend will say when I give her the official reason. I'd hate to think what she'd say if I gave her the unofficial reason. But it's no good, Charlie. I know you were giving me the job anyway. I know you wouldn't feel you were being blackmailed if I stayed on. But don't you see that I'd be inhibited from arguing with you. I wouldn't be able to look for more money for the kind of investments I want to make, without feeling that you couldn't say no.'

'I could, you know, Robert. We trust each other that much.'

'No one,' said Amiss, 'even you, could be under that much of an obligation to anyone else without chafing sometimes. I'll stay on for the moment and together we'll search for the right editor and when you find him, you can give me a good party.'

'But you're a good editor, dammit. I don't want to lose you.'

'No, I'm not really, Charlie. Sometimes I worry because already I'm beginning to feel the urge to argue in my own leaders against the line being taken by the journal. I don't really believe that Tony Blair and Bill Clinton are the anti-Christ. I'm wishy-washy, always a man for on the one hand and on the other. I don't see how I could go on with a journal that doesn't suffer from doubt. Anyway, that's the story I'll tell everyone.' He got up. 'Now I'd better go home and break the news to Rachel.'

'There's just one thing,' said Papworth. 'And I've been feeling bad about it ever since . . .'

Amiss laughed. 'Ever since you heard that I nearly went the same way as Willie.'

'It honestly didn't occur to me that anyone else could have any reason to come down those stairs until he'd been found. I have to tell you that if you had been seriously hurt or killed, I'd have given myself up. I have no guilt about Willie, but had you died, I'd have been in sackcloth and ashes.'

'What a scrupulous pair we are,' said Amiss. They laughed and shook hands and Papworth showed him to the front door.

'I've got something to tell you,' said Amiss and Rachel virtually in unison.

'You tell me first,' she said, her voice tense.

'Charlie Papworth offered me the editorship.'

'Oh, Robert, that's wonderful. Despite all my criticism, that is wonderful news.'

'And I turned it down.'

She shut her eyes and compressed her lips. When she regained her composure, she looked at him again. 'And what quixotic reason determined that?'

Amiss laughed. 'You should be pleased, really. It was because I couldn't be wholehearted about the journal's politics.'

'And is that a good enough reason to wreck what had suddenly become a really promising career?'

'I think so.'

'Knowing you're prepared to argue all shades of opinion without help from anyone else,' she said, 'I shan't even bother. But I'm sorry. Apart from anything else, I'd rather have left you when you were on a high than when you were once again heading off into limbo.'

'Left me?'

'Yes, Robert. That's what I have to tell you. And don't look so shocked. You can't really be that surprised, can you? It's a long time since we've been enjoying each other much.' He said nothing. 'Isn't it?'

205

There was a pause. 'Yes,' he said. He paused again. 'You're not inclined to give it another chance?'

'No, I'm not. There's no future for us. All we do these days is that I snap at you and you feel aggrieved and misunderstood. Besides, there's someone else and I'm going to live with him.' She stopped and looked embarrassed for a moment. 'Or to be more precise . . .'

'It's all right,' said Amiss. 'I'm with you. You mean he's going to come and live with you. To be precise, when you say you're leaving me you mean you want me to leave you. Don't worry. I'll be obliging.'

She went over and sat beside him. 'I knew you would be.'

'So who is he?'

'Can't you guess?'

'Rachel, how can I guess? I only know a few of your colleagues. At least you might spare me having to guess who's been screwing you.'

'I'm sorry,' she said. 'It's Eric.'

'Oh, Christ. Not your minister. Isn't he married? Not to speak of being twenty years your senior?'

'Yes.'

'Kids?'

'In their mid-teens.'

'Don't you mind breaking up his marriage?'

She sounded defensive. 'They've grown apart. Only saw each other when he got up to the north at the weekends and then, of course, he was busy with constituency business and the rest of it.'

'It's a bit hard on her, isn't it? How could any woman lumbered with looking after the kids hundreds of miles away from her husband compete with the dishy clever private secretary who's by his right hand by day and – of course, as I now realize – quite frequently night? But, Rachel, isn't this going to screw up your career? You surely can't stay in the Foreign Office if you're publicly known to be living with one of its ministers.'

'I'm going to be his political researcher.'

'But isn't that a great comedown? You had everything going for you in the Foreign Office.'

'Eric and I are a partnership.'

'I just can't see you as a political wife, Rach. Chatting up constituents and smarming up to senior ministers and charming the Prime Minister surely isn't for you.'

'You'd be surprised,' she said. 'You don't really know me any more, Robert. We were apart for too long. And I'm not as high-minded as you.' She grinned. 'But then no one is.'

He grinned back. 'More feeble-minded than high-minded. And you don't even know the half of it.'

There was a pause. She looked worried. 'What do you think you'll do next?'

'On the job front I've no idea, but I needn't worry for a few weeks. On the home front, I don't see why I shouldn't move into the flat at the top of the *Wrangler* building for the moment.'

Her face cleared. 'That's a great idea. It'll give you time to look around.'

There was another pause. She got up, went over to him and gave him a hug. 'I'm still very fond of you. You know that, don't you?'

'Yes. And me of you.'

'But it's better this way.'

'I suppose so.'

'I've got a suggestion, if you don't think it in poor taste.'

'When do I ever think anything's in poor taste?'

'Let's go out and have a bottle of champagne and drink to both our futures.'

'Yes, please. But don't tell Eric. He'd recommend sparkling water.'

'So she's thrown you out.'

'Why do you always have to put such a brutal interpretation on everything, Jack? Rachel and I have agreed in a civilized fashion to separate and since it's her flat and she wishes her new chap to move in, the least I could do was to move out as fast as possible. So this evening I'll be transferring my belongings to Willie's old pad. Thank heaven I hadn't had time to get round to arranging to let it.'

'Good. This solves my problem too. Plutarch is packing as we speak. I'll deliver her to you tomorrow.'

A feeling of dull dread swept over Amiss. 'Do you know what you're saying, Jack? That although I'm suffering a broken heart after being ditched by my long-term inamorata for a hypocritical wanker, you intend to rub salt in the wound by replacing Rachel with Plutarch.'

'Simple choice. You can have her alive in Percy Square or dead in Cambridge. I sense here that a lynch mob is gathering. I would not wish to tell a lad of your tender years of the murderous light I glimpsed yesterday in the eyes of the Fellow of Comparative Religions. Take her tomorrow, or her blood is on your hands.'

'Oh, God, I suppose I've no choice. Anyway, compared to my other problems this is truly a mere bagatelle.'

'What do you mean by other problems? You're not making a fuss about moving, are you?'

'No, that's minor. But I can't tell you about what's major over the phone.'

'Oh goody,' she said. 'Sounds promising. Tell you what. I'll deliver you Plutarch in the morning and come back around six to visit her and find out with what trivial issues you are bothering yourself.'

'It's a deal.'

'So that's an account of my trivial worries,' said Amiss.

The baroness stopped vigorously stroking an appreciative Plutarch. 'Well, my boy, I withdraw the word trivial. I think you have had enough human and moral problems in the last couple of days to justify the use of the word "weighty".'

'What do you think, Jack?'

'I think that you must deal with what you can deal with, and what you can't deal with there's no point in worrying about. You're fine really. Rachel may have expelled you, but you've got somewhere even better to live. There's nothing more to be said except that she's a foolish girl who will live to regret it when she gets fed up with that sanctimonious jerk. And if I were you I would be off in search of plenty of jolly women to cheer you up.

'Plutarch is back with you, which I accept is not an unmixed blessing, but the circumstances could hardly be better. She has no Rachel around moaning about her, she's got a fine apartment, the fire escape, the garden, and the rest of the inhabitants at Percy Square to torment. And since they're your subordinates – at least for the moment – I suppose they'll put up with that. So two problems you had two days ago – viz, keeping Rachel happy and finding some way of reconciling her needs with Plutarch's – have miraculously disappeared at a stroke.'

Amiss nodded reluctantly.

'However, we now proceed to the bigger issues. First of all, I think you were an idiot to turn down the editorship because of what Charlie Papworth told you, but you're that kind of an idiot, it's the way you are, and there's no point in my bleating about that: it's one of your attractions. One certainly never worries about you becoming corrupt. Ending up in the gutter, yes. Being burnt at the stake, yes. Being hauled off in chains for fiddling the books, no.

'Which leads us to the two issues you need to address at the moment. First, have you any second thoughts about covering up for Charlie Papworth?'

'I gave my word,' said Amiss wearily.

'Indeed you did. And in your place I expect I'd have done the same. But there's the corollary that you're also covering up for Piers. And how do you feel about that?'

'I don't like it, but I can't do anything about it. The only evidence against him is what Charlie told me in confidence. And that would be hearsay, anyway.'

'Precisely, so it's not really an issue.'

Plutarch emitted a resentful yowl of deprivation, and the baroness absent-mindedly recommenced the stroking. 'There's such a huge moral difference between the two murders. Piers knocked off Henry: bad. Charlie knocked off Willie: good.'

'Oh, really, Jack. You don't actually mean good.'

'I don't mean I'd do it. I don't mean I want anyone else to do it. But at least Charlie's motives were honourable.'

'Yes, but I would point out that Piers did in Henry in hot blood and Charlie did for Willie in cold.'

'We're splitting hairs and it's pointless. We've two murderers and you can't sneak on either of them.'

'And even at that, we're making an assumption that Piers did the murder, when there was only Willie's word for it.'

'Quite right. And we'll never know otherwise, because of course Piers, if asked, would say he didn't do it whether he did or not. So let's make things easy for you by adopting the benign interpretation, which is that Willie lied either because he did it himself or because it was an accident, and proceed on the assumption that Piers Papworth is innocent. That makes the road ahead and the choices clearer.'

Amiss lay back on the sofa and passed a hand wearily over his forehead. 'I'm punch drunk, Jack. Clarify my mind. Please.'

'Your job is quite straightforward. You must safeguard the future of *The Wrangler* by sorting out this trust business once and for all and by finding the right editor.'

'You know as well as I do, Jack, that there's bugger-all I can do about the trustees. That's in your bailiwick.'

'You can carry on smarming up to them while I beat them up. But point taken. It's mostly a matter for me. The problem of the editorship, I'll leave with you.'

With total disregard for Plutarch, she jumped to her feet. The cat, who had landed on the rug with a thump, set off a piercing yell. 'Shut up, Plutarch,' said the baroness: instantly the yells diminished in intensity and, shortly afterwards, ceased.

'Talk to you soon, Robert,' she said. 'But before I go, pay attention. Your duties to *The Wrangler* are twofold and both require you to hang on for a bit. First, you need to make sure that the editorial line is solid before you hand her over to a new captain. Second, you have to find the right successor, so you should be vetting talent at leisure. So whatever you do, don't tell anyone you're going. I can see it would appeal to you to walk out now in a haze of moral rectitude, but that would be sheer self-indulgence.'

'But . . .'

'Bugger the buts.' And after enfolding him in a bear hug, she picked up her cloak from an armchair. 'Are you going to tell Jim about this?'

'Probably, but obviously only off the record.'

'Make sure you've got him to sign the confidentiality clause in blood. He's a nice bloke, but he's a cop.'

Throwing her cloak over her shoulder, she demanded, 'Lead me to the fire escape.'

EPILOGUE

'It was a good funeral.'

'Charlie deserved it,' said the baroness. 'Murderer or not, he was one of the best of men.'

Ellis Pooley stiffened slightly. 'I'm afraid that professionally, at least, quite apart from personally and morally, Jack, I have to take a rather dim view of that pronouncement. I understand why Robert decided not to provide Jim officially with the information that could have nailed Papworth, but you can't expect me to approve. Murderers shouldn't get away with it.'

'Oh, bugger off, Ellis. You didn't know Charlie, and, for that matter, you didn't know Lambie Crump and you should remember that blackmail . . . I mean serious blackmail – not the sort of thing I go in for – is the most loathsome of crimes and deserves the most condign punishment.'

'Piers Papworth seemed very cut up when he read the lesson,' observed Milton.

'He was,' said Amiss. 'I spent a fair bit of time with him over the last few days and there's no doubt that he mourns Charlie deeply. One thing that came through in conversations with both of them throughout the family row was that it never appeared to affect in any way their mutual devotion.'

'Any repercussions at the Yard?' the baroness asked Milton. 'About your having failed to nab the murderer, that is.'

'That's not the sort of thing that gets you into trouble. I'm having more difficulty with an internal policy row than I ever will about an unfinished case.'

'What's Tewkesbury's position?'

'His mind isn't on *The Wrangler*, or the sins of the Right, these days. In fact, he's having such a horrible time working on a gangland murder in Soho that he seems to be developing some sense of perspective. We met in a corridor last Friday, and he greeted me with respect. I have some hopes for him: he might be just young enough to allow reality to penetrate that sanctimonious carapace and stop being such an asshole.'

'OK,' said the baroness. 'Now for the hard news. I've got some and Robert's got some. I'll start. I've done a deal with Sharon McGregor.'

'What kind of a deal?' asked Amiss. 'And why is this the first I've heard of it?'

'Because I only fixed it up last night, you blockhead. It's taken a while.'

'Well, go on. Tell us.'

'You remember that a couple of weeks ago I told you to let me have the run of the building undisturbed one Saturday.'

'Yes.'

'I spent the morning taking her round every nook and cranny of *The Wrangler*, telling her about the founder, his successors and the great journalists along the way. I told her of the Papworth involvement down the ages, and then I took her to lunch and told her about Ricketts, and about Ben and Marcia and about loyalty and tradition and continuity and the little *Wrangler* corner of New Britain that is forever the best of England. And having put all that in her head I brought her straight down to St Martha's again and introduced her to the two most eloquent traditionalists in Cambridge – apart from myself, that is. Then last night I took her out to dinner, put the proposition to her and she accepted.'

'Accepted what?'

'That she's rich enough to do what she likes, rich enough to indulge herself and rich enough to be a great benefactor by becoming the custodian of something worthwhile that might otherwise become extinct. She's taken onboard the notion that *The Wrangler* is a metaphor for an English Conservative tradition that is at present as close to extinction as the white rhinoceros. The woman has a sense of humour and the idea that she could become a great hostess and mentor of the Right tickled her no end. A powerful weapon in my arsenal was that she hates meaningless rhetoric so the present British and American governments piss her off seriously.

'Forget the idea of internationalizing *The Wrangler*, I said. Just make it the most effective anti-crap guerrilla organ in Britain.'

'Do you think she'll do it?' asked Amiss.

'We shook hands on it; we agreed to be allies; and we will be. By the time we've finished, *The Wrangler*'s going to be the biggest thorn in the flesh of the complacent Left that there's ever been in this country.'

'That's all very well,' said Pooley. 'But you're not editing it. I didn't like to say anything earlier, but I have to say I was surprised to discover today that Papworth had appointed that dull woman Phoebe Somerfield to the job just before he died. She's hardly colourful or young or hungry, is she?'

'It was on my recommendation,' said Amiss.

'And mine,' said the baroness.

'Because . . . ?' asked Milton.

'Because of the kind of editor that's needed. There are journals that need to be shaken up, restructured, relaunched and all the rest of it. And maybe they need thirty-year-olds with vision and energy to turn them upside down. That's what Robert did,' said the baroness.

Amiss was so stunned at having had a compliment of this magnitude from such a source, that he could hardly speak. 'Thanks, Jack. But you're exaggerating my contribution.'

'Balls. What you did was to rediscover the journal's soul and set it on the path of righteousness.'

'Are you two saying,' asked Milton, 'that what's now required is a safe pair of hands?'

'Yes and no,' said Amiss. 'Phoebe's safe, in that she understands what *The Wrangler*'s about and will not go in for any mad gambles. But there's much more to it than that; given scope, she's shown a genuine instinct for quality and an enthusiasm for young talent, at a time when I believe what's required is someone low on ego and high on appreciation of others.

'I made up my mind after a dazzling lunch at the office when Dwight, Amaryllis, Pretoria and Clement Webber jockeyed for position as top intellectual dog, traded ideas and fought each other brilliantly to a standstill. Phoebe contributed little, except occasionally to destroy an illogical argument with a well-timed arrow.

'Mostly she listened, and afterwards she gave me an assessment of their respective strengths and weaknesses which to my mind was spot on. I think she just could be one of the great discoverers and nurturers of talent. And as she put it herself when I asked if she might be interested in the job: "Why not? I've got nothing to lose."'

'Let's go back to Sharon McGregor,' said Milton. 'You're saying that she's agreed to buy *The Wrangler* even though the trust remains intact. But for how much, now that she won't be going global?'

'It's just edged into profit and there's no reason why it couldn't be a modest money-spinner, so it might be possible to get about a million on the open market. She's offering three.'

'Will Piers Papworth take that?'

'He's jumped at it. It won't solve all his problems, but he seems to think it enough to save the Papworth estate from disintegration. Apparently the good news is the state of things is slightly less disastrous than was expected, although the bad news is that Charlie was more generous with bequests than Piers would have wished.'

She stopped and looked at Milton and Pooley. 'Which leads me to Robert.' She turned to him. 'Come on. Talk.'

Amiss looked unhappy. 'It's very difficult. I was told yesterday that Charlie Papworth left me a hundred thousand pounds in gratitude for what I'd done for *The Wrangler*.'

'That's marvellous,' said Milton. 'And well deserved. Materially it slightly makes up for the lunacy of your decision about the editorship.'

'But I don't think I can take it.'

'Sweet suffering Jesus,' said the baroness. 'Let me guess. Today's scruple is that he might be rewarding you for not splitting on him. Is that it?'

'I suppose so.'

'Listen, you cretin, how much money have you saved Charlie since you took over this job? Now come on, don't give me a conservative guess. I want a realistic one, which includes what you saved him through the cost-cutting and what you earned him through the increase in circulation.'

'It's very hard to put a figure on it,' said Amiss, 'but maybe in the region of half a million.'

'And did you ever hear of such a thing as a bonus?'

'Yes, but . . .'

'Oh, shut up,' she said. 'Even if you can't grasp that you're entitled to a generous bonus for doing so much better than expected, you might view it as some compensation for not having the job you would have had if you hadn't been such a high-minded idiot as to sack yourself when Charlie spilt the beans.'

Amiss looked doubtfully at Milton. 'She's right, Robert. This is not a moral issue. Take the money, which you richly deserve; it'll help tide you over until you get the next decent job. Whenever that is likely to be.'

'Ellis?'

'You'd be mad and ungrateful not to. And I'm the official puritan of this group.'

'Besides,' said the baroness, 'you have to find a decent home for you and Plutarch.'

'Phoebe suggested I should keep the *Wrangler* flat indefinitely. But I said I'd be out within a month.'

'Why?' asked all of them in unison.

'Because I think a clean break would be better for the staff.'

'Oh, God,' said the baroness. 'You really do have a genius for making things difficult for yourself, don't you?'

The others nodded.

Amiss looked at them in dejection. 'You all think I screw up, don't you?'

'You do and you don't,' said the baroness. 'It's a peculiar gift you have. You drift into situations unwillingly and by the time you've drifted out things are better. That's why we're all so pleased, you halfwit, that for once you've had some recognition.'

'So what now?' asked Milton. 'What sort of job are you looking for?'

'God knows. I'm open to offers.'

'Don't worry,' said the baroness. 'I have the very thing.'

Murder in a Cathedral

Ruth Dudley Edwards

For many years Westonbury Cathedral has been dominated by a clique of High-Church gays, so when Norm Cooper, an austere, intolerant, happy-clappy evangelist, is appointed dean, there is shock, outrage and fear.

David Elworthy, the gentle and politically innocent new bishop, is distraught at the prospect of warfare between the factions; contentious issues include the camp lady chapel and the gay memorial under construction in the deanery garden. Desperate for help, Elworthy cries on the shoulder of his old friend, the redoubtable Baroness Troutbeck, who forces her unofficial troubleshooter, Robert Amiss, to move into the bishop's palace.

Amiss, Troutbeck and the cat Plutarch address themselves in their various ways to the bishop's problems, which very soon include a clerical corpse in the cathedral. Is it suicide? Or is it murder? And who is likely to be next?

The latest in Ruth Dudley Edwards's wickedly funny series taking an irreverent look at the British Establishment.

'This blithe series puts itself on the side of the angels by merrily, and staunchly, subverting every tenet of political correctness'   PATRICIA CRAIG, *Independent*

'A wise and witty read'   MICHAEL PAINTER, *Irish Times*

'Lovely stuff'   MIKE RIPLEY, *Daily Telegraph*

ISBN: 0 00 649864 7